Sir Gawain and the Green Knight AD499

ISBN 978-0-6480789-6-8

Aenghus Chisholme

Connect with Aenghus Chisholme:
www.aenghuschisholme.com

Cover by Andjela Vujic (Varvara11 on guru.com)

Also by Aenghus Chisholme

Merlin the Sorcerer AD491

Guinevere the Queen AD494

Sir Gawain and the Green Knight AD499

Arthur the King AD517

Murder on the Mary Celeste

Jack the Ripper: The Murder of Madam Athalia

The Best Things in Life Begin with the Letter B

This book is dedicated to all readers that enjoy Arthurian tales.

Contents

Chapter 1: AD 499 - Shore of the River Usk; Moonrise

It rose from the murky depths of the river Usk. A Knight, long since dead, slowly made his way to the muddy shore. The animated corpse had the stench of death oozing from every limb. Its flesh was half rotted away and the chainmail covering its decayed body was filled with moss and lichens, giving it a green appearance. The lifeless eyes, unable to focus upon the surrounding woodlands, didn't stop the Green Knight from making its inexorable way towards its destination – Caerleon Castle.

***

Night was falling, the Knight on guard duty supervising the soldiers on the battlements was feeling a little left out. It was the feast of Beltane in the month of Equos; the celebration to mark the coming of summer. Sir Lamorak wanted to be in the Great Hall enjoying the entertainment and the feasting with the other Knights of the Round Table, however his duties were keeping him here. With a sigh, he gazed over the rear wall of Caerleon castle. The hill was quite steep and it lead down to the river, tactically, it would be inadvisable for anyone to attack from that direction. Besides, there was no talk of any immediate threats. Nothing to watch out for; yet here he was on the battlements instead of filling his belly with wine and meat.

If only he had gazed more carefully at the surrounding landscape he may have noticed the green figure in the distance walking slowly toward the castle. The green covering the body of the dead-man gave him a naturally-grown disguise. He blended into the landscape quite well. Nevertheless, if Sir Lamorak had not been so preoccupied with his self-pity there was a chance that he would have seen the forthcoming danger.

It took some time for the Knight to reach the wall. In all of that time, two of the soldiers, bored of making their rounds, also failed to notice the creature. Instead they gave a cursory glance to the ground, overlooking the supernatural being and watched the sky's disappearing light and the full disc of Gaelach shining brightly above them. They exchanged some words about finishing their duty and looked forward to joining the Beltane feast, even if it was just the tail-end of it.

The Green Knight had reached the wall by this time. It had taken the most direct route from the river to the castle and therefore it faced the rear of Caerleon. The road would have taken it through the village and to the front gates of the mighty fortress, but this was not human and didn't think like a living being. It had one purpose, and in order to carry out that purpose it needed to gain access to the castle. It 'looked' at the wall with its cold, dead eyes. The scale of the vertical wall would have normally been a barrier to an invading Knight, but not in this case. Skeletal-like fingers reached out and grasped the wall with an inhuman connection. With what appeared to be the greatest of ease the Knight began to climb the wall as though it were a snail or insect.

Soon its feet too were adhering to the stonework of the castle wall. With all four limbs now working in unison the Knight scaled the wall with eerie and methodical speed. Reaching the battlements was not a part of the plan. There was no need to climb to the very top of the castle. High up there was a window; the wooden shutter open to allow the evening air to fill the room. Clambering through the opening the Knight stood for a moment and surveyed the room. Whether it knew it or not, the Knight was in Morgan Le Fay's chamber. It was empty. Morgan, like almost everyone else in the castle, was enjoying the feast in the Great Hall below. The merriment could be heard even from this distance. It attracted the Green Knight.

Walking up to the door its putrefying hand lifted the latch and opened the door. The noise of many people having a merry time could be heard more clearly. Like a moth to a flame it drew the decomposing corpse forward.

Chapter 2: Caerleon Castle, the Great Hall

It was Merlin who noticed the feeling first. There was something seriously wrong, that was clear. He stopped in mid-conversation with Sir Degore; the subject and content of his spirited argument with the Knight forgotten in an instant. Although he couldn't see it, he could feel that there was a fog surrounding him. If he had to describe it he would have said that it was cold, frightening and somehow smothering. And there was another thing too, but exactly what it was he couldn't quite define. The sum total of this feeling of fog had done something to him. He felt that he had lost something very dear.

"Merlin!" insisted Sir Degore for the fourth time. "What ails ye?" Merlin looked up at the Knight. He could see the concern written all over Sir Degore's face. Merlin tried to answer the query but could not seem to find the words. Instead he looked over to the last place that he saw Morgan. He became aware of the noise all around him again. People were having a wonderful time; laughing and enjoying the wandering entertainment that had been brought in to the Great Hall for this years' Beltane feast.

Morgan had moved from where she'd been but when Merlin finally located her in the throng of people he could see that she too was bothered. She looked up, either sensing that Merlin was seeking her attention, or feeling too that she needed some magical help, just as Merlin did. They could see from the expression of each of them that something was wrong.

"Forgive me Sir Degore," Merlin managed to say. Then without another word he began to make his way through the crowd to Morgan.

Morgan for her part had felt like she was drowning in the thickest fog that she had ever seen. Yet she could not see any fog. And it would have been unusual for this time of year to see fog anyway. But this 'invisible' fog, although it defied definition, felt very real.

***

Walking down the great staircase the Green Knight thus far hadn't encountered any of the castle's many servants. They were either engaged in their own Beltane feast in the castle's kitchen or serving in the Great Hall. However, there were two carrying yet another carefully prepared beast on a large intricately carved wooden platter from the kitchen to the main hall. They were passing the bottom of the stairs when one looked up and saw the Green Knight at the landing. It was hideous, mouldy and crumbling – the very sight of it sent the male servant into a convulsion of fear. Dropping his side of the platter he screamed and ran back in the direction he had come.

Taken completely unaware, his companion was reeling from the sudden abandonment of his friend. The roasted pig fell onto the flagstone floor with a thud. The heaviness of the wooden platter was too much for him to bear alone and it too fell to the floor with a clatter. He looked with utter dismay at his hysterical and hastily retreating compatriot. What could have caused such an outburst of calamity from him, he wondered.

There was a feeling at the back of his neck that caused the hairs on the back of his neck to stand on end. Suddenly the room felt cold. He was at the base of the stairs with his back to them. He heard the thud of boot on the stone. There was a familiar sound of chainmail creaking as well. The man turned around expecting to see one of Arthur's knights. Instead, only a few steps away, was the deteriorating body of a corpse that was descending the staircase toward him. The servant lost bowel control and with a stifled shriek ran in the opposite direction faster than he'd ever run before. He ran straight out the main doors and into the main courtyard. It wasn't far or fast enough for the man though, and in an instant he vowed to not stop running until he had reached his parents hut in Caerleon village below the castle.

Up on the battlements Sir Lamorak watched the man running out of the castle grounds and down the hill toward the village. He looked at the two closest soldiers. "What….." he began and trailed off.

***

Inside the Great Hall Merlin had just about reached Morgan when a scream interrupted his passage through the crowd. Everyone in the room instinctively turned to see who was causing such a fracas and almost in unison saw the Green Knight standing at the entrance to the hall. There was the briefest pause whilst the reality of what they were looking at struck them. The man was clearly dead. Parts of his bones could be seen through his hands and the part of his face that was not covered with a lichen encrusted metal helmet was so decayed that the jaw-bone could be seen through the weeping skin. What was left of his clothing and chainmail had become so soaked with the decomposing skin that they were for the most part indistinguishable from each other.

Those closest to the Green Knight could smell the putrid stench of decomposing flesh. Women screamed at the sight of the revolting creature. Its gruesome presence sent shockwaves of terror throughout the room. The closest Knights, rather than instinctively drawing their swords, were so taken aback with trepidation at the sight of the shocking creature that they too joined the women in retreating from it.

It was King Arthur that took matters into his own hands. He drew Excalibur from its sheath; but immediately he knew that something wasn't right. The sword felt heavy. It was normally so unbelievably light that it felt as though it was made from air. This was enough of a shock for Arthur to hesitate before advancing on the Knight. But advance he did.

"Hold Sir Knight!" he said to the nauseating corpse. "What brings ye to Caerleon Castle? Be ye friend or foe?" Arthur stopped some way from the Knight and pointed Excalibur at him to emphasise his words.

The Green Knight seemed to be uncertain of what to do and where to go. He could be seen facing left and right as if he were making up his mind about something. Then without warning the repulsive creature drew his sword and with an inhuman screech ran forward to engage Arthur in battle.

Chapter 3: The First Apparition

Sir Guaen was between Arthur and the Green Knight and he drew his sword immediately after the Green Knight had unsheathed his. The scream from the Green Knight sent a shiver all the way up Guaen's back. But he moved to intercept the vile creature nevertheless. It was Knightly instinct and training that took over Guaen's movements now. Doing his best to push aside his revulsion for the loathsome corpse, Sir Guaen neatly intercepted the pointed sword of the Green Knight.

With a clang, he knocked the sword's point away from Arthur. The Green Knight stopped and immediately lost all interest in the king and now focussed his attention on the man that had parried his charge. Using both hands the creature adjusted his grip upon his sword. It made Guaen shudder. The movements were that of a well-trained Knight, but done by this repellent corpse. They engaged in a spirited battle. A circle formed around the two warring parties. Guaen took the initiative and thrust, then had his thrust countered by the knight. Swords clashed and clanged loudly echoing around the Great Hall. The speed at which the two Knights fought was amazing.

Guaen was fuelled by a hearty meal. He had many years of swordsmanship from which to draw upon. And he did. Again, and again the two Knights dodged and fended off sword swipes, thrusts and jabs. Guaen and the Green Knight seemed to take turns in either being the aggressor or the defender. The Green Knight fought with a vitriol that was palpable. It grunted and growled throughout the exchanges. Guaen huffed and puffed as he sought to find a way to get through the Green Knight's defences.

It was becoming obvious to the other well-trained Knights that Guaen was evenly matched by this antagonistic intruder. The clash of metal upon metal rang over and over again. It was Sir Garethe that was the first to see the sweat beads on Guaen's head. Nothing out of the ordinary for a Knight engaged in battle, but Garethe knew his brother. He could see that Guaen was worried about how the exchange was progressing.

Drawing his sword, he approached the Green Knight from behind. With a loud voice, he challenged the abominable man.

"Come this way, hideous creature! See if ye can fight two of the Knights of the Round Table at once." It was enough of a distraction for Guaen to take the initiative. In the instant that the Green Knight was distracted by Garethe's words, Guaen managed to get one clear swing of his sword. He skilfully aimed it at the neck of the corpse, just below the helmet. Guaen's sword neatly sliced-off the head of the Green Knight.

He watched it fall to the floor. Various women in the room screamed at the sight of the decapitation. The body however did not slump to the ground as Guaen would have expected. Instead it stood motionless, unnerving the already frightened people in the Great Hall.

Merlin pushed his way through the onlookers to better inspect the scene. Guaen looked at Merlin in the hope that he may be able to offer some insight as to the origins of the Knight.

"Merlin," he began, “the Knight was clearly dead to begin with. How…" he never got a chance to finish his sentence. A brilliant light emitted from the severed neck of the Knight. It brought any conversation to a complete halt. The light bent itself over to form a column that stretched between the body and the fallen head of the Knight.

In a timeframe that was shorter than a single heart-beat, the head had travelled along the column of light and reattached itself to the body of the Green Knight. The same women who had screamed at the sight of the decapitation now screamed all the more loudly at the sight of the animated corpse once more becoming whole. Everyone was shocked almost beyond their capacity to endure.

Arthur looked desperately at Merlin for answers.

“Merlin, put a hex on the creature – quickly!" he demanded of his chief Sorcerer.

Merlin for his part was both perplexed at the happening as well as the instruction from the King. *What, by the gods names, did he mean by a hex?* There was no time for the old man to question his King's orders – the Green Knight had once more engaged in battle with Guaen.

"Assistance!" was all that Guaen managed to shout before once more the clash of swords being thrust and swung filled the hall. Two of Arthur's Knights that were behind the Green Knight drew their swords. They hesitated briefly; it would not be the chivalrous thing to attack the aggressor from behind. But Arthur motioned to the both of them to attack with a definitive point of his hand.

They closed in on the Knight and in turn thrust their swords into the body of the Green Knight. There was no acknowledgement from the Green Knight that anything had happened. Arthur's Knights looked at each other in the hope that some other idea would come from the exchange.

"Cut off its arms and legs!" shouted Arthur.

Dutifully the Knights advanced once more. They motioned to each other that one would take the left arm and the other the right. With swooping violent swings of their swords, they did just that and the arms of the Green Knight fell to the ground. More screams. Just as before the torso did not seem to follow the felled limbs to the floor; it remained standing.

"Now the legs!" demanded the king. Again, signalling to each other they stepped forward to complete their orders. But now two columns of light erupted from the points of severance. They found the fallen arms and were reattached before Arthur's knights could complete their task. More screams. The Green Knight again engaged Guaen. It seemed to have no interest in the other Knights of the Round Table.

Arthur was flabbergasted. The corpse could mend itself faster than they could slice it up. He wracked his brain for another solution to the supernatural problem. Unable to find one he once more turned to Merlin.

"Merlin," he commanded, "Do something!"

Merlin looked helplessly at the situation before him. Sir Guaen was clearly tiring. Two other Knights had stepped forward in an effort to engage the Green Knight. Now it was three to one. Yet the Green Knight seemed to only marginally acknowledge Sir's Galahallt and Garethe, preferring to attack Guaen.

Merlin tried to levitate the Green Knight upwards. If it was not on the ground it could not fight Sir Guaen. Nothing happened. He tried a simple banishment spell that would have worked on any faerie; once more nothing happened. Morgan had joined him by this time and she blurted out her words to Merlin as softly as she could under the circumstances; her heart was racing. "Merlin, I cannot perform any magic, any magic at all!"

She looked left and right suddenly, sensing that she may have confessed her condition too loudly.

Merlin grabbed her forearms.

"Together then," he said. "Concentrate on the spell of fire – we shall burn the Green Knight to a cinder!”

They worked in unison. This was easy for them as they were so accustomed to and trusting of each other. Yet even unified, they could not make a simple spell like the creation of fire.

Arthur burst in on their efforts. "What ails ye? Destroy that thing, quickly before it kills Sir Guaen!"

Merlin and Morgan looked at Arthur. The silence of their reply instead of their immediate compliance said everything to Arthur that he needed to know.

"Ye have tried and failed," the King surmised. Both Merlin and Morgan nodded.

"Aye," they said simultaneously.

"How is this possible" he queried the magical twosome. It was Morgan who began the answer and Merlin who completed it.

"There is a force that surrounds the Green Knight."

"That prevents magic from being worked."

This was not what Arthur wanted to hear. They were facing a supernatural enemy and he should be able to avail himself of a supernatural solution. The King looked over to the three battling brothers. There were now four of the Knights engaging the Green Knight. He watched as Sir Galahallt made the most of an opportunity to once more slice the head off the intruder. The powerful slice should have been more than ample to once more decapitate the aggressor. But instead Galahallt's sword became lodged in the neck of the Knight. It felt like he had hit a petrified tree and the shock of the hardened rotting flesh was so great that the sword striking almost knocked Sir Galahallt off his feet.

The Green Knight was distracted enough for Sir Ectorde Maris to raise his sword and try to strike-off the Green Knight's left arm. Just as with Sir Galahallt, Sir Ectorde Maris' sword hit an unbelievably hard body joint. His sword too was now confiscated; stuck in the shoulder of the Green Knight.

Seeing the horrifying situation that was unfolding before them, Arthur, Merlin and Morgan plotted briefly.

"What now?" said Arthur, bereft of a strategy to implement. and Morgan simply shook her head. She had nothing to offer. Merlin was scratching and pulling at his newly trimmed beard.

"I want to try something," he said. This offered a glimmer of hope to both Arthur and Morgan. He pushed his way through the crowd to get closer to the ongoing battle. "Knights of the Round Table!" he shouted above the din of battle. "Cut off its legs."

The Knights were only too happy to receive some sort of directive in the current situation. Whilst Sirs Guaen and Garethe continued to engage the Knight Sirs Alynore and Pellus moved behind the demon and motioned to each other silently on who would sever which limb they attacked in unison. Sir Alynore sliced his sword from right to left, Sir Pellus sliced his from left to right; both aimed at the knees of the Green Knight. There was a 'clang' as both swords ripped through the rotting flesh of the Knight and clashed with each other.

The Green Knight fell over face-first onto the flagstone floor. Without delay it propped itself up and using its arms to scurry forward, still clutching its own sword, and made toward a horrified Sir Guaen. The macabre sight of the corpse trying desperately to reach him put the Knight into a state of shock. He couldn't hear Merlin screaming orders to him.

"Quickly Sir Guaen!" yelled Merlin. "Run to mine chamber."

Sir Guaen backed away from the terrifying apparition. His brother goaded him into action.

"Guaen!' shouted Garethe, "to Merlin's chamber, quickly."

This snapped the knight out of his stupor. He looked over to Merlin and then almost numbed with fatigue began to stumble through the crowd toward the main doors to the Great Hall. Everyone stood aside to give him clear passage.

Merlin too went to exit the Great Hall. He looked around him. Time seemed to stand still. Queen Gwenhwyvar was nowhere to be seen. She was with the young Prince Amhar and Mordrede when the Green Knight had entered the hall. He guessed that she must have retreated with the children when the fighting broke out. Sensible he thought. She was an astute woman. The other children that had been in attendance were similarly missing, Wigaloith and Akhera along with their mothers Lady Florie and Lady Elamite. Merlin instantly guessed that Queen Gwenhwyvar would have been behind that too. Her first thought would have been to get the children and their mothers to safety.

He didn't have any further time to speculate on what else had happened as a result of the incursion of the Green Knight. Out of the corner of his eye he saw the now familiar flashes of light. The legs of the Green Knight were once more attached. It had begun its relentless stalking of Sir Guaen once more.

Chapter 4: The Great Staircase

When Merlin entered the room that contained the Great Staircase Sir Guaen was already at the middle landing. He was breathing so loudly that Merlin could hear him even from this distance.

"To mine chamber, Sir Guaen, and do not open the door to any but me!" bellowed Merlin at the Knight.

Sir Guaen, too out of breath to respond verbally, nodded and continued to ascend the staircase.

Merlin glanced behind him. Some of the Knights had engaged the Green Knight in an attempt to delay its progress. He made his way as quickly as his many years would allow and followed Guaen up the staircase.

Meanwhile in the Great Hall Arthur had taken it upon himself to begin battling with the Green Knight using Excalibur. The swords of Sir Galahallt and Sir Ectorde Maris were still wedged in the neck and shoulder of the monstrosity. In spite of efforts by both Knights to recover their swords, they remained firmly stuck in the flesh of the Green Knight.

Arthur tried to dislodge them himself to no avail. With Sir Dagonet to one side and Sir Brumean to the other he instead positioned himself to prevent the Green Knight from leaving the Great Hall. The corpse raised his sword ready to engage the obstacles.

Swords could not pierce the flesh at the points where they had previously. Only new incisions could be made where the body had not healed itself with the other-worldly power. It was apparent that wherever the Green Knight had healed itself, it had become stronger in the healing. The hardest of wood was more giving than the repaired flesh of the Green Knight.

Arthur thought quickly. "Sever the torso at the stomach!" he commanded the Knights.

This would not be easy for the Knights. Although this part of the thing's body had not been wounded before it was covered in chainmail, and would prove more difficult than the exposed arms and legs.

"Surely, Sire, Excalibur could do that with one blow," ventured Sir Brumean.

Neither Sir Brumean nor Sir Dagonet could see the worried look that he gave in response.

"Advance!" Arthur commanded his right and left wings.

The Knights engaged the Green Knight. When they were through with the initial assault Arthur set himself up to give a single almighty blow that would he hoped cut the knight in two. When he felt he was in position he ordered them away.

"Move!" he shouted.

They dutifully got out of Arthur's way allowing him to deliver the enormous blow.

Excalibur sliced into the flank of the Green Knight just as any other iron sword would do. There was no magic to assist the immense force that he had used. He managed to sever the chainmail and only cut a little way into the gut of the creature. Arthur ordered the knights to do something that under normal circumstances they would never have done, as it was so unchivalrous.

"Hold him down!" shouted the King. The Knights nearest to the action needed no further cajoling. A small clutch of them surged forward and piled upon the supernatural being, toppling him to the hard flagstones once more.

The Green Knight struggled with inhuman strength. His legs thrashed about at first and then he began to kick the Knights that were restraining him.

"More!" the single order from Arthur motivated some nearby Knights to come to the aide of the three that were trying their best to contain the Green Knight. In the end, it took one Knight to hold down the head of the intruder, two Knights each on the right and left arm and two Knights on each leg.

Then Arthur had to position himself so that he could get a decent swing at the beast and complete the incision that he'd begun. He briefly saw the look upon two of the Knights' faces. He knew exactly what they were thinking. How could Excalibur fail to slice this daemon in two with a single blow? Arthur did not have the time or the inclination to explain the sudden magical short-comings of his fabled sword. He needed to concentrate on the task at hand.

He finished summarising his plan to all of the participating Knights.

"When I hath severed the torso from the waste, carry the lower half out into the courtyard, and the top half to the fireplace. Make sure it is well stoked!"

He did not bother to look up to ensure that his directions were being carried out. Servants ran to the largest of the fireplaces that warmed the Great Hall and began poking and prodding the flames to ensure that it was as full as was possible.

Arthur had meantime lined up the next swing and with all of the finesse of a woodsman felling a tree, began to chop at the mid-rift of the Green Knight. Over and over again he swung and cut the creature in half, the sound of breaking chainmail mixing with the unmistakable sound of tearing flesh, muscle and sinew. The gathered crowd were as horrified as they were mesmerised with the proceedings. A palpable feeling of hope entered the air. Surely this would end the maniacal rampage of the otherworldly being? How could it not?

The Knights holding down the top half of the creature waited for just long enough until they could see Arthur was almost through, then as one they began to pull the torso away from the lower section.

Their compatriot Knights, seeing what was happening, similarly pulled the lower section away stretching the final bits of rotted flesh that held the two halves together.

With a final tug from both directions combined with the concluding cut from Arthur the Green Knight was cut in two.

"Quickly!" screamed Arthur. "Top half to the fire, bottom half to the courtyard."

Even has he spoke, the Knights scurried to fulfil his command. Arthur swung around to shout a further order after the Knights carrying the bottom half of the Green Knight.

"When outside, close the main doors."

Arthur hoped to not only destroy the top half by fire, but ensure that the bottom could not again enter the main section of the castle. After all, even if these disembodied legs could walk on their own, and he assumed they could, how could they open the doors to once more gain entry to the Castle?

But the expected column of light was too quick to form. The combined efforts of the king and his Knights would not be rewarded. The Knights carrying the top half had by this time reached the main fireplace in the Great Hall. With a loud grunt, they hurled the top half of the Green Knight into the roaring fire. The column of light erupted from the severed torso and snaked toward the front doors to the castle. The second set of Knights entrusted with separating the two haves had barely reached the door when the column of light found its mark.

The legs almost jolted out of the hands of the Knights carrying them. They strained and groaned to hold their ground. It rapidly became a case of simply trying to not have the bottom half of the Green Knight drag them backwards. Suddenly getting their prize out of the castle as ordered was no longer an option. The force that the legs and mid-section exuded was uncanny.

Meanwhile in the fireplace the top section was well alight. It erupted out of the fireplace and with the hideous smell of burning flesh, scraped its way across the floor toward its dismembered section. People ran to get out of the way of the burning mass of flesh and bone. Arthur watched with horror as his plan unravelled. With the top part alight nobody could touch it or hope to hold it apart from the bottom section. He only had moments to reconsider his strategy. Unable to come up with a solution he concentrated on simply getting the lower half as far away from the top part as possible.

"Knights, get the lower half outside and shut the doors, help them!" He ordered the others who had not yet become engaged in his plan. Arthur too ran forward to assist the knights with the bottom section of the beast.

None of their efforts were fruitful. The speed at which the inflamed torso was travelling was incredible. The Green Knight was now hurling itself along the floor using its arms in unison to grotesquely propel itself. Even with the combined force of the extra bodies trying to keep separate the two sections they failed.

Knights jumped backwards out of the way of the torso as it threw itself toward its formerly decapitated section. The top and bottom halves somehow twisted themselves into alignment and became whole once more.

The fire diminished on the surface of the creature. It sprang to its feet with uncanny speed and agility. The flames now disappeared leaving the bubbled and charred remains of the face and torso on show for all to see. The disgusting mess that made up the top half of the Green Knight was sickening. The helmet however was intact, which was a small mercy given how much damage the fire must have done to the distorted face of the beast.

Getting its bearings, the creature made toward the great staircase. Arthur was out of ideas. His sole thought was to delay the Green Knight so that he could give the old Sorcerer time to do whatever it was he was doing?

"Two in front and two behind; attack!" bellowed the king.

Without hesitation, the Knights divided themselves into attack forces. Two running up past the Green Knight now slowly ascending the staircase, to position themselves in front of the enemy, two approaching from behind.

With the now familiar sound of clashing metal the Knights engaged the creature once more in sword-battle. The Green Knight seemed to becoming more skilled with swordsmanship with each new engagement. It parried away what should have been deathly blows from the two Knights engaging it head-on. The two Knights behind contented themselves with simply jabbing the beast in any area that a sword would penetrate.

Arthur watched with mounting concern. There were fewer and fewer blows actually piercing the body of the Green Knight. It was apparent to him that the parts of the Green Knight's body that were injured and had healed themselves were somehow much stronger than they were before.

"Sire; its fire wounds are gone!" shouted Sire Bedwere who was fighting with the Green Knight, now at the landing mid-point of the staircase ascension.

Arthur ran to get a better vantage point to oversee the fight. Sir Bedwere was correct; the charred skin was now simply the horrible rotting flesh that it was when it first appeared. The clothing, such as it was, had renewed itself. A further observation from the landing interrupted Arthur's assessment of the relative-appearance of the Green Knight.

"Sire, it can no longer be….*injured*," Sir Alynore who had been busy trying to engage the Green Knight from behind, faltered at little with his report to the King. The tone of his voice made it plain that they'd not managed to further injure the Green Knight.

With skilful flicks of his sword the Green Knight deprived Sir Brumean of his sword and pushed past him, turning his attentions on Sir Pellus. With a similar sleight-of-hand sword-play the Green Knight managed to gash Sir Pellus's forearm. Blood spurted from the deep cut. Distracted by the pain he was caught off-guard when the Green Knight grabbed him and hurled the injured Knight at the two other Knights behind him. The three went tumbling down the stairs together some distance before coming to a halt. The Green Knight, no longer opposed, finished climbing the staircase and headed in the direction of Merlin's chamber.

Chapter 5: Merlin's Chamber

Guaen could not believe his ears. That was Merlin's plan? He must be playing a joke upon him? Surely there was a more mystical reason that he had ordered him to the Sorcerer's chamber than simply putting a heavy wooden door between the Green Knight and himself?

Merlin was well aware of the feeling of incredulousness that Guaen was experiencing in stunned silence. He too was surprised at his lack of imagination under the circumstances. The old man briefly wondered if it had something to do with the magic-suppressing and invisible fog that surrounded the Green Knight. Maybe that same force was inhibiting his ability to come up with complex strategies as well. He didn't have time, however, to dwell upon such things.

Instead he began to rummage through his scrolls for some kind of inspiration for how to combat this deceased Knight. He pulled out scroll after scroll and gave each a cursory look before harrumphing in disappointment and pushing it back into its untidy place. This went on for some time. Eventually Merlin could feel the eyes of Sir Guaen upon him. He felt duty bound to offer some sort of solace, if not explanation.

"Sir Guaen, we do not know the full strength or the abilities of this otherworldly being. Maybe a seasoned oak door is enough to defeat it? Besides 'twill give me time to think." Merlin scratched at his beard. *What to do?* he thought.

Sir Guaen was exhausted. He slumped-down and sat on the edge of Merlin's bed. It was comfortable, soft. He paused to gather his thoughts. The Green Knight seemed not to tire at all. What caused the creature to target him? How could this hideous thing be combatted successfully? Surely magic can stop a magical being?

"Can ye crush it beneath a floating rock?" enquired Guaen.

Merlin knew that the Knight had been witness to many such floating rocks in the past and now more recently. Sir Guaen had been present at the building of Caerleon Castle and had seen first-hand how Merlin was able to float large slabs of rocks carved by the stonemasons into place to form the huge walls and structures. Sir Guaen had also been present at the building of Arthur's newest castle to the west of Caerleon. Mynyw Castle was constructed close to the western most point of Wales to better watch for sea-going threats.

"Magic does not seem to work in the presence of the Green Knight."

Merlin's one sentence answer filled Sir Guaen with dread. The Knight then recalled only a short time ago that King Arthur had ordered the Sorcerer to "Hex" the intruder. If Merlin was able to use his magic, surely, he would have done so long before now, wouldn't he? Sir Guaen felt sick.

"What manner of beast is this? How can it affect ye magic? How can it be defeated Merlin?" Sir Guaen's barrage of questions were understandable and expected.

Merlin looked at him and answered with an even voice. "I do not know."

Just as he finished answering there was a violent push on the latch of the door from the outside. It didn't budge as Merlin had inserted a beam in place to ensure that nobody could enter. Then there was an almighty thump on the door. Without doubt it was a sword impacting the timber. The Green Knight had reached Merlin's Chamber and was trying to break-through. Sir Guaen jumped up from his position on Merlin's bed. His heart began to thump hard in his chest. His breathing became strained and rapid.

Again, and again the resounding crash of metal on the door was heard. The sound of wood splitting pushed Sir Guaen's heart down into his stomach. It would only be a matter of time before the Green Knight gained entrance to the chamber. Both Merlin and Sir Guaen were thinking along parallel lines. It was Merlin who put their thoughts into words.

"Should it gain entry, Sir Guaen, there is a plan to escape." He announced quite mysteriously.

Sir Guaen for his part was both relieved and confused. He had put all of his trust in Merlin when he followed the Sorcerer's command to retreat to his chamber. Sir Guaen had assumed that there would be a good reason that he should take refuge in a room with only one entrance. The window was high above the courtyard. There was no way to navigate to the ground below safely.

A huge crack appeared on the inside of the door. "It is unbelievably strong for a dead man" observed the Knight. Merlin nodded and tried to guess how much longer the door would hold. Even a skilled woods-man would take some time to break down the heavy wooden door, but the Green Knight seemed to be making short work of it.

Merlin decided that it would be best not to wait around and find out how quickly the creature could gain entry. He hurried to the wall opposite the door. The only adornment was a tapestry that had been skilfully created by the women of the court shortly after the completion of the castle. It was a scene of Merlin laying one of the stones on the battlements. Merlin pushed it aside. Behind it, unsurprisingly, was a blank wall. Sir Guaen watched with mounting awe as Merlin pushed on the wall. It gave way and a section just large enough for a man to crouch down and exit through silently swung open.

It was dark in the passage that was now presented to them. Merlin reached over to the shelves that contained his scrolls and retrieved a candle. Thankfully the fire in his room still had some hot embers from which he lit the candle. There would be no using the spell of fire, he thought.

"Where does it lead to?" inquired the Knight.

A loud crack of wood behind them made Sir Guaen forget his question and obediently follow Merlin into the passageway; the tapestry that had been covering the secret door fell back into place; once more obscuring the doorway.

"Shut the door behind ye!" ordered Merlin turning around to ensure that Sir Guaen did just that. "This way," whispered the old man.

The passageway was narrow, it was impossible to walk side-by-side. Sir Guaen contented himself with following the flickering silhouette of Merlin. He was relieved to be heading in any direction that was away from the Green Knight. The passageway seemed to be very long; or maybe progress was just slow given the cramped proportions. Eventually merlin stopped and pulled at something that Sir Guaen could not see. Another door swung silently open.

"Quickly!" he ordered the Knight. But with the doorway open, Sir Guaen had to squeeze around it before he could follow the old man.

Merlin was holding aside a tapestry that must have covered the secret door. He walked into a room and was a bit disorientated at first. Then it came to him. This was the King and Queen's chamber! There was a secret passage that connected it to Merlin's chamber.

"How did I not know of this before?" asked Sir Guaen rather stupidly.

"If ye knew of the passage," rebuffed the sorcerer rather irately, "it wouldn't be a *secret* passage, now would it?"

Sir Guaen shook his head. He realised that what he had said was rather silly and not what he had meant to say.

"No Merlin," he stumbled, "what I mean is that I saw ye building Caerleon castle, along with all of the tradesmen and soldiers and Knights and villagers that assisted. I was here every day during construction. How did this remain a secret?" Sir Guaen was genuinely flummoxed. Surely, he thought, somebody or a group of people must have come across it during the building of the Castle.

"Some of the stonemasons and ironmongers knew of the passage and worked on it with me," admitted Merlin. "But I swore them to secrecy during the building of it and then when it was done – I took the memory of it from them," he admitted.

Sir Guaen almost rolled his eyes. "Of course" he said "Ye used magic to ensure that what is secret remains so."

Merlin acknowledged the Knight's correct summary of the events with a wry smile. "There is no more time for such frivolous discussions Guaen. Come outside quickly."

Chapter 6: Outside the King and Queen's Chamber

The Sorcerer and Knight emerged from the Royal chamber much to the surprise of a passing foot soldier. Merlin barked a query at him.

"Where is the Green Knight?" he said rather tersely. The soldier looked startled. "I do not know, Merlin," he said.

"Find out and report back to me!" barked Merlin. The now anxious soldier managed a muffled "Aye" before hurrying away in the direction of the great staircase.

"What now?" asked Sir Guaen.

"We find Morgan," answered Merlin.

He led the way after the foot soldier, Morgan's chamber was in the same direction, but more importantly, so was Mordrede's chamber. He had to find where Queen Guinevere had taken the ladies and children of the court. Of course, he was only assuming that Morgan had managed to join them. *She was not to be underestimated*, he thought, *perhaps she has remained near the Green Knight observing and trying to find a weakness. Alternatively, she may be consulting her own magical texts that she has in her chamber.*

Best to start there and then figure out his next move later. He quickened his pace with Sir Guaen in tow.

They hurried through the passageways past tapestries and flaming torches. Eventually they rounded a corner and came to Morgan's chamber door. Without knocking he barged straight in. Merlin was correct. Huddled over her own scrolls Morgan was indeed looking for a magical solution to their current problem. She looked up in alarm at the sudden intrusion to her private quarters. Concern turned to relief when she saw who it was that had so unceremoniously burst into her chamber.

"Merlin, Sir Guaen, thank the gods ye are safe," she began, but Merlin had no time for niceties.

"Hath ye found anything that may be of assistance Morgan?" he asked, urgency in his voice. She disappointedly shook her head.

"No Merlin, nothing" she responded.

It was a vague hope at best thought Merlin. He altered his question slightly, hoping for a different outcome.

"Hath ye observed any weakness in the Green Knight that we may exploit?" His eyes widened in anticipation of the answer. He knew Morgan to be an astute observer of everything that happened around her.

"Arthur has tried to burn it, and cut it in half and keep the two halves separate; all to no avail." She announced. "Whenever it is wounded and heals itself it becomes stronger than before. Now there are no swords that can penetrate its flesh, not even Excalibur."

The looks upon both Merlin's and Sir Guaen's faces at hearing this news made Morgan immediately regret telling them. Merlin's mind raced. If only he could use his magic he could battle this monstrous apparition.

"Where does it come from?" he said aloud. "Why hath it focussed its wickedness upon Sir Guaen?" again the old man spoke his thoughts aloud. "How does it prevent us from using our magic?" This was a spoken thought from Merlin that Morgan wanted to explore more fully.

"Merlin" she asked "this…magical inhibition that surrounds the Green Knight; do ye think that it has a size, or limit to its range; like a bow and arrow?"

Morgan finished her query by standing up from her wooden stool. She could see that Merlin had seized upon her words and was mulling them over carefully in his head.

"Aye Morgan; an interesting and intriguing thought; one that we should put to the test," answered the sorcerer rather mysteriously.

He looked as though he were about to expand upon his thinking when the soldier that had previously been sent upon an errand by Merlin similarly burst into Morgan's chamber unannounced. Merlin only had a brief moment to wonder how the man had figured out where he was.

"The Green Knight!" shouted the soldier, pointing behind him.

It appeared that Merlin's efforts to elude the creature had now expired. It had somehow either gained entry to Merlin's chamber and upon not finding its prize once more picked up the scent of Sir Guaen like a fox hunting for chickens. Or maybe it had found the secret passage and followed them here. Whatever the cause, it did not bear thinking about at the moment. Merlin grabbed the forearm of Sir Guaen and pulled him outside. The Green Knight was just rounding the corner of the hallway that led to Morgan and Mordrede's rooms. Following behind it, there was a group of Round Table Knights with defeat written all over their faces. Even with a fleeting glimpse Merlin could tell that they were out of their depth trying to engage this supernatural being.

The only way back to the great staircase was now blocked by the Green Knight. Merlin finished formulating a plan in an instant that would both confront the intruder and test the limits of the Green Knight's influence.

"Sir Guaen" he said urgently. "Run to the battlements; the section overlooking the main courtyard and await my signal."

Sir Guaen needed no encouragement, he ran in the opposite direction, eyes bulging and heart thumping. This passageway eventually lead to a small staircase that would take him up to the battlements. Pushing Morgan into her chamber Merlin followed and slammed her door shut with a loud thud. It was a simple precaution. He was sure that the Green Knight would not bother engaging him in battle. Nevertheless, it was prudent to be cautious of this powerful being.

The sorcerer, sorceress and soldier stood holding their weight against the door. The sound of the repulsive Green Knight could be heard coming closer. At the point where it was just outside Morgan's door it stopped. The three hearts inside Morgan's chamber skipped a beat. After what felt like an eternity the dreadful sound of footsteps could be heard to resume. Relieved, the three of them sighed in unison. Merlin grabbed the bicep of the soldier.

"I hath further orders" he said.

The soldier nodded quickly. "Aye Merlin, anything," he offered in response.

Chapter 7: Caerleon Battlements.

The night was not particularly cold, nor was it dark, thanks to the bright disc of Gaelach hovering in the sky above Caerleon castle. Her soft yellow light bathed everything around. Sir Guaen hurriedly slammed the door that led to the battlements behind him and searched to the left and right for the wooden beam that would lock the door. In his hurry he overlooked it and panicked. It was not there! He hurriedly checked again and found the wooden beam this time. Quickly snatching it up and putting it into place he felt some small amount of relief that another locked door was between him and the seemingly unstoppable Green Knight.

There were soldiers nearby and they came running to see what was happening. Like everyone in the Castle they had heard about the supernatural happenings in the Great Hall and were both horrified and intrigued at the same time. They tried to engage Guaen in conversation about

"What happened?" but he waved their questions away.

"How many guards are there on duty tonight along the battlements?" he countered.

One of the soldiers answered that there was the usual amount of four guards and Sir Lamorak supervising them. However, the Knight had gone to see what was happening in the Great Hall upon first hearing about the disturbance.

Sir Guaen went over in his mind Merlin's instructions. *What is the old Sorcerer planning now?* he thought. Without any further word to the foot soldiers he made his way to the section of the battlements that overlooked the central courtyard. Looking down he could see nothing out of the ordinary. There was no sign of Merlin.

There was the sound of a huge bang on the access door. The Green Knight was on the other side. All four guards gathered in the general vicinity of the door and looked at each other and then over to Guaen for confirmation of what they were thinking. One of them voiced their question.

"Is that…the…daemon?" he asked wide-eyed.

Even from the distance the four of them could see Sir Guaen's almost imperceptible nod in affirmation. Another bang on the door and the soldiers jumped with fright. They backed away keeping a close eye on the door.

Sir Guaen looked once again over the side of the battlements to the courtyard below. Apart from one of the guards preparing three horses he could see nothing that was out of the ordinary. Again and again with monotonous and upsetting regularity the beating upon the door came. The sound seemed to get louder with each fear-provoking thump. Sir Guaen found that it was hard to breathe. It was as though his throat had contracted to a fraction of its normal size and would no longer allow enough air to get into his lungs.

He had never before known fear like this. Even as a youngster, his first battle, which he had thought would be the most terrified that he would ever be in his life, did not compare to this absolute horror. He felt sick. When the Green Knight came through that door he knew that there was no way to kill it. No hope that he could win this battle. It seemed to be unstoppable. It did not show any sign of fatigue. He could continue to run, but eventually the creature would catch-up with him and then it would all be over.

The soldiers had formed a small barrier between him and the door. It gave Sir Guaen little comfort. Even if he'd had derived some small solace by having four soldiers between him and the 'daemon' as one of them had called it, then it would have been short-lived. In a moment of unspoken communication, clearer than any order he had ever given or received, the four soldiers looked at each other, then at the door which had begun to splinter, then at Guaen, the known target for the monster. They moved around Sir Guaen as though he were a diseased animal and moved further away from the door. Sir Guaen was aghast. The soldiers that he had helped train were abandoning him.

"Sir Guaen," Merlin's voice broke into the Knights consciousness.

It broke his concentration and he looked down to the courtyard. Merlin was there with Arthur and Morgan and a sizeable number of the Knights. They were busy unfurling a huge tapestry. Sir Guaen looked in bewilderment at the scene. *Now was not the time to weave a tapestry!*

Merlin interrupted his confounded musings. "Jump down onto the tapestry but land flat on ye back," instructed the old man. "Throw down thine sword first," further ordered the old man, but this time pointing at the ground that was not yet covered by the tapestry.

All of the Knights present were holding the border of the tapestry. Guaen could see now that it was not a tapestry that was still to be woven with various images; this was one from near the main staircase. Still completely confounded he shook his head in puzzlement.

"Throw ye sword first!" yelled Merlin, clearly annoyed that Sir Guaen had not done as he was instructed the first time.

It took every bit of concentration that he was capable of in the circumstances but he capitulated. Tossing his sword down to a part of the courtyard that was devoid of people he suddenly felt naked before his enemy. More vulnerable than when he first engaged the creature. Although he was wearing his finery it did not include chainmail. It was not called for to attend a festive banquet.

An almighty crash brought Guaen right back to the present situation. He looked at the door. It had given way at the Green Knight was kicking and pushing his way onto the battlements.

"Now Sir Guaen!" ordered Merlin.

The hesitant knight mounted the small part of the wall between two of the stone-shields. He looked down at the expectant faces of his fellow Knights holding up the tapestry. The Green Knight was not advancing as it had done so up till now. Instead it was running toward him sword raised and with a low growl emanating from its dead and decomposing mouth.

In fright Sir Guaen tripped over what must have been a rough part of the wall and went tumbling head over heels off the battlements. As luck would have it, he somersaulted and landed perfectly flat on his back on the tapestry. There was a loud "*Ooof*" from Sir Guaen that was echoed by some of the Knights that had helped to break his fall. Sir Guaen looked up at the Green Knight. With a blood-chilling howl of tormented anger it bellowed across the courtyard.

The Knights of the Round-Table lowered the tapestry to the grown and a few of them rushed forward to help Sir Guaen to his feet. He looked around for Merlin. He and Morgan were on horseback.

"Quickly Guaen!" ordered Merlin, indicating the third horse.

He needed no further encouragement. Running forward he found the stirrup and took his mount.

"Look!" pointed and screamed Morgan.

Guaen finished mounting his horse. There was a shared gasp of horror from everyone witnessing the event as the Green Knight hurled himself off the battlement walls and landed with a stomach-churning thud on the ground near the now-grounded tapestry.

The Knights nearest to the creature instinctively backed away, fearing the worst. They were wise. The Green Knight was making to stand up.

"Ride Sir Guaen!" shouted Merlin. He looked up, Merlin and Morgan had already begun their exit through the main gates. Fearful of being left behind with the object of his terror, Guaen spurred his horse into action. The fear pumping through his body made him dig his heals into his horse too hard and the steed reared up and threw Guaen off its back.

Sir Guaen tried his best to break his fall with his left arm. He could hear a bone crack when he hit the ground. Amazingly, he was too scared to immediately register the agonising pain of breaking his arm.

The Green Knight had by this time regained his feet and was running toward his fallen victim.

"Knights!" ordered King Arthur and the entire group of them hurled themselves upon the Green Knight to try and restrain him. Arthur hurried forward and helped Sir Guaen to his feet.

"Are ye injured?" he asked. Sir Guaen nodded but couldn't manage any words.

"Retrieve his mount" bellowed King Arthur. Some servants ran after the horse who had only galloped off a short distance before calming down. Merlin and Morgan had ceased their flight through the exit and were watching the scene in alarm.

"Arthur, get Sir Guaen back onto his horse without delay!" ordered Merlin.

Arthur was already complying with the yelled order. Two of the servants had recovered Sir Guaen's mount and had led it back to him.

The pain of his broken arm made itself known to Guaen. He doubled over in agony and cried out.

"It is his arm," Arthur shouted over to Merlin.

"We can fix it but we must get away from the Green Knight," replied the Sorcerer. Behind them the Green Knight again bellowed a hideous shrill. Knights were hurled off of him in a display of superhuman strength.

Arthur guided Sir Guaen's foot into the stirrup. Fate came to the aide of the hapless Knight for a second time. It was his left arm that was broken, but he always used his right to mount a horse. With a great effort and a huge push from the king, Sir Guaen once more positioned himself upon the horse. Not wanting to repeat his mistake he gave the horse a gentle jab, which may still have been too much of a jab because the horse took off. Sir Guaen didn't see that the Green Knight had freed itself from the Round Table knights and was running up to him just at the moment that he goaded his horse into motion. The Green Knight lashed out with his sword and barely touched the end of the tail hairs of the horse.

Merlin and Morgan had by this time vacated the exit to the castle and were already heading down the hill to Caerleon village.

Guaen bolted after them. It was only after he’d cleared the main gates that he chanced a look behind him. The Green Knight was running in pursuit. It made Guaen's heart once more skip a beat.

"Hahhh!" he shouted to the horse in order to gain more momentum from the beast.

Chapter 8: Caerleon Village

The sound of galloping horses filled the night. If it weren't for the fullness of Gaelach they wouldn’t have been able to see the ground around them. But her light was bright tonight, more so than usual. The three riders could see the candle and firelights of the village ahead of them. The villagers too would have been celebrating the feast of Beltane. The sound of revelry could now be heard above the din of the horse hooves.

As they approached the outermost dwellings of the village they could see that a large number of people were still out on the streets. Fires had been lit here and there and people were roasting pigs and chickens over some of them. The smell of freshly cooked meat mixed with the dust that the horses were kicking up.

Merlin, Morgan and Guaen raced into the village causing people to look up in fright. Some had to scramble to get out of the way of the three riders. Pushing their horses, they pounded their way through the main section and through to the other side of the pretty setting. Guaen became aware that Morgan and Merlin were shouting something to each other. He strained to hear what was being said.

"Anything?" asked Merlin.

There came what Sir Guaen thought was "Nothing" from Morgan, but he couldn't be sure over the din of the horses. He tried to position his mount closer to the two riding in parallel in front of him.

"We go as far as the horses will take us..." said Merlin. Sir Guaen did not catch the end of the instruction. There came a short scream from Morgan. Both he and Merlin looked over to her. She was holding a ball of fire in her outstretched palm – fire created by magic.

Both Merlin and Morgan knew the significance of the event, but at first it was lost on Guaen. He had seen both of them create fire many times before. Wait; he thought to himself. They couldn't use magic in Caerleon Castle but now for some reason Morgan could once more create fire!

By this time, they were most of the way through the village of Caerleon and only a few scattered huts were left. Merlin shouted out an order.

"We ride as hard and fast as we can until the horses' tire, then we will stop and combine our magic to go for help."

Go for help? The thought crossed Guaen and Morgan's mind at the same time, but neither of them sought clarification at this point. Spurring on their horses they galloped into the night.

***

It was a short time later that the horses began to show signs of wearying. Although they were accustomed to carrying knights wearing heavy chainmail, and their current riders were much lighter by comparison, they'd been ridden hard since leaving the castle. The area they were in was slightly wooded. Gaelach was so bright that the trees cast moon shadows onto the ground. Merlin signalled that the party should stop.

They pulled up their mounts who were now audibly panting, but they did not dismount. Instead they formed a three in-line troupe with Merlin on one side, Guaen in the middle and Morgan on the other. Merlin spoke first.

"Morgan, I want ye to use the power of travel."

Morgan was reticent. "Merlin, I hath not felt that there was much of the power that I," she looked at Guaen before carefully choosing her words and continuing, "acquired in Gaul, to assist us now."

She looked apologetic, but Merlin was hearing none of it.

"I shall assist ye Morgan, together we will form a bridge to our destination," he said.

Sir Guaen was confused; what help would a bridge be over such even ground? There were no rivers or gorges ahead that needed crossing. He wanted to intervene with his questioning of their strategy but thought the better of it. Instead he contented himself to simply listen to the exchange between the two magical beings.

Morgan questioned Merlin's offer. "Merlin, I did not know that ye were able to cast the travel spell?"

The old man waved away the query. "I had used that spell long before ye were born Morgan. However, as ye know, it takes a great deal of effort. But together, combining our magic we can do it; I know we can."

He smiled at Morgan. This together with the intriguing offer to combine their magical abilities convinced Morgan to give it a try.

"Where shall we travel?" Morgan asked. "To Gaul or Magna Frisia to elude the Green Knight?"

The Sorceress had forgotten Merlin's earlier affirmation to travel for help.

"To Llyn Callyfyrth to consult with the Lady of the Lake," he said.

The words seemed to hit Morgan like an arrow, she was visibly shocked. Looking at Guaen then at Merlin she questioned Merlin's plan.

"The Lady of the Lake? Are matters *that* desperate Merlin? And what of Sir Guaen?" she said assuming that he would not be accompanying them to meet with the reverential magical being.

Merlin answered flatly, "He is coming with us."

Sir Guaen was relieved to hear that he was not being abandoned, but was still confused as to their destination. Llyn Callyfyrth was two and a half days' ride away from Caerleon. Surely that inhuman untiring creature would catch up with them before they got anywhere near Dumnonii?

"Give me ye hand" instructed Merlin to Morgan. She stretched out and reached over past Guaen to Merlin. He took her hand into his. Instantly she could hear his thoughts. "Excalibur was useless against the Green Knight. And I know of no more powerful magician than the Lady. If she cannot help us Morgan I fear that I have no other solution to offer. Do not be concerned about Sir Guaen knowing the location of the Lady, I shall take the memory of it from him after we have found a solution to this other-worldly problem. Now concentrate upon the magic that ye took from the Minotaur. Feel the shape of it and the strength of it, and when ye are ready look into mine magical powers and see the same capability. Use the touch that we share to combine the two and think of our destination. Llyn Callyfyrth."

Somehow everything that he had communicated to her was ringed with other sentences that she could perceive but somehow not quite understand. She thought that maybe each sentence was repeated in another language spoken more softly in the background thoughts of the old magician. But she did not dwell upon the thought; instead she followed Merlin's instructions and found the power that she had taken from the Minotaur. Looking across at Merlin she could see a shimmering outline surrounding Merlin's head. Morgan knew that it was the same power that she was now accessing.

Focussing her thoughts, she pushed the magic through her body and into her arm, Merlin was doing the same, she knew without a shadow of a doubt that he was. At the point where they touched, together they pushed out the magic it in front of them. A rectangular shimmering image of the lake solidified. In an instant, it was done. The moment was triumphant but silently shared between the two magicians.

"Now Sir Guaen" whispered Morgan "forward!"

Guaen was amazed, to say the very least. A tapestry of unbelievably detailed colour and beauty had appeared before them. It was a lake similarly bathed the moonlight that washed over them. He was too stunned to react to Morgan's instruction. Seeing this, Morgan took hold of the reins of his horse and gently nudged it forward along with her own. The three of them rode up to and into the image of the lake shore, moving effortlessly from North Wales and into Dumnonii in an instant of time.

When they had passed through the doorway all three turned to look behind them at the landscape that they had just left a moment before. The image briefly shimmered and vanished without a trace. They were at Llyn Callyfyrth.

Chapter 9: Llyn Callyfyrth

Sir Guaen looked like a doe startled and unsure of what to do next. Before him lay a beautiful moon-lit lake; he could feel a breeze coming across the water and gently caressing his face and hands. He barely noticed that Morgan and Merlin had dismounted until Merlin tapped the Knight on the leg and motioned for him to join them on the ground.

There were so many questions in Guaen's mind he scarcely knew where to begin. He was about to launch into a tirade of questions when Merlin held up his hand to stop him before he began.

"We are in Dumnonii near Cellewig castle. We are safely out of the reach of the Green Knight. If he ran all night and day he would not be able to travel this distance that we have traversed in a moment of time. A magic spell ye had not witnessed before aided us here. Now if that is enough information to keep ye satisfied for the time-being, Morgan and I hath work to do."

Nodding dumbly, Guaen indicated that he would not ask for any further clarification of what had happened and where they were.

Guaen felt the fear and anxiety that had threatened to consume him ebb from his body; it felt good. He had no reason to doubt Merlin, and this could easily be the lake near Cellewig. It did somehow look familiar. Moreover, this meant that the Green Knight was hundreds of mille-passum away. He had been spirited away from it by Morgan and Merlin. The sense of relief fell upon Guaen like the dawn light of a summer's day. He sat down on the ground and looked over at Morgan and Merlin. It was then that his broken arm began to hurt again. Guaen groaned and clutched it. From where he stood, Merlin looked through Sir Guaen's skin and to the bone beneath; he could see it was broken. He waked up to the Knight and placed both of his hands over the break. The touching of his arm should have caused Sir Guaen even more agony but instead it dulled the pain considerably. Merlin concentrated and knitted the bone back together, mending the break. The pain was infinitesimal now, just a mere dull ache.

This was not the first time that Merlin had used his magical abilities to heal the Knight.

Sir Guaen looked up at him and said "Mine thanks Merlin."

Merlin did not acknowledge the gratitude but instead re-joined Morgan. They walked together up to the shore of the lake with their feet almost within it.

Merlin was breathing hard. It had been an effort to quell Guaen's unspoken questions. Using the ability of instantaneous travel was something that he had not done since before Arthur was born. He looked at Morgan and once more offered her his hand. They conversed in thoughts.

Morgan first: "Merlin it was so much easier to use that travel spell than the last time all of those years ago, but I feel that it is even more depleted than before."

Merlin responded; "Aye. The spell hath been known to me for many years and as a young man in the service of Uther I found cause to use it on more than one occasion. But the body is weak and this one of mine powers is fragile. Its light does not shine within me as it once did."

Morgan: "Do ye think that we are safely out of reach of the Green Knight?"

Merlin: "No. I think that it is pursuing Sir Guaen even now. But we have purchased time; time to re-group and more importantly time to seek help from the Lady."

Morgan: "Queen Gwenhwyvar simply called out for an audience with the Lady the last time that we were here. Shall ye do the same?"

Merlin: "Aye"

With their secret conversation over Merlin let go of Morgan's hand and raised it in greeting to the moon-lit lake.

"Lady, it is I Merlin. Please speak with me for there is an evil that threatens us."

He waited for a sign, a ripple upon the serene surface of the lake. Nothing happened. Again, he beseeched the Lady to appear.

"Lady, I beg thee, appear to me, thine counsel is needed now more than ever before."

The moments of absolute silence that passed after Merlin's second plea were slow. There was no response. No sudden appearance of the beautiful and powerful creator of Excalibur. Merlin was looking exasperated. He shouted one more impassioned plea across the lake. Now bolder because of the lack of response, he called out the mysterious Lady's name.

"Matrona! Please help us. Please help me!"

Nothing; the night was still, the surface of the lake unbroken. Dejected Merlin slumped to the ground. Morgan took up the mantle of trying to summon the magical being.

"Hear us oh great magician. A daemon afflicts Caerleon and we are powerless to help those who need us the most." Morgan's words went unanswered. Desperate she tried once more, "Lady Matrona, I beg thee, help us, our need is great!" Silence.

Morgan looked at the lake – nothing. Now, feeling as disconsolate as Merlin, she joined him and slumped to the ground. They both looked at the unbroken surface of the lake unable to grasp why Matrona had not responded to them. For what felt like an age they sat together and pondered their situation. The occasional night bird calling or fish breaking the surface of the water gave them both hopes that were just as quickly dashed.

"What are we to do?" Morgan asked after a long silence. She looked up at Merlin hoping to see in his face a glimmer of hope. A plan that the crafty old Sorcerer had in reserve to implement in case this plan failed. She saw nothing there. He looked crestfallen.

They sat in silence for a long time, neither able to think of a way to overcome their situation. Eventually the sound of footsteps from behind, reminded them that Sir Guaen was still with them. He sat down with Morgan and Merlin. The next words he spoke felt as though a decision had been made for all of them.

"We should rest at Celliwig Castle." It seemed to be the perfect solution for their tiredness. Without acknowledging that it was indeed a good plan they stood up and made their way back to the horses.

Chapter 10: Cellewig Castle in Dumnonii

When the three riders had reached Cellewig castle it was close to midnight. The caretaker was taken completely unawares and was at first annoyed to be roused from his slumber and then amazed to find the two Caerleon magicians with one of the Knights of the Round Table knocking at the front entrance. He hurriedly opened the gate and ushered them inside, taking their horses whilst the party made their way to the main hall. Sir Guaen stoked the fire back to life whilst Merlin and Morgan prepared some food from the nearby scullery.

They were eating in front of the now roaring fire when the caretaker came to report that the horses were fed watered and safely stabled for the night. He saw that they had helped themselves to the food supplies so asked for leave to return to his bed which was granted by Merlin. None of them noticed that apart from their brief interaction with the caretaker and some small amount of words spoken between Merlin and Morgan whilst getting the food ready, they had not really spoken since leaving the lake.

Morgan was the first to break the long silence with her idea for how to handle the situation in an ongoing manner.

"We can send Guaen as far away as the travel spell can take him. The Green Knight is fixated upon him. If we send Guaen to the farthest reaches of the Roman Empire, or what is left of it, then it could be enough to save his life."

Guaen was a little enthusiastic about the idea but wanted to know about his wife Florie and son Wigaloith. "What life would I hath without them?" his rhetorical question seemed to put an end to the idea of sending Guaen out of reach of the Green Knight.

Merlin too was unconvinced. "How long before it found its way to Sir Guaen?" he said. "We know that it does not tire. It could conceivably travel day and night without rest in order to acquire Sir Guaen as his victim," he further stated. The very thought sent a shiver through Guaen.

"Bury it under stone," suggested the Knight.

"Ye are forgetting we cannot use our magic when in the immediate area of the Green Knight," Merlin rebutted.

Guaen took the idea a little further. "It does not have to be done by magic Merlin, we dig a hole and set a trap, just as we would for a wild animal. When it hath fallen in, the combined strength of the Knights and Soldiers can throw heavy stones and dirt into the hole burying it, where it belongs, under the ground!" he practically shouted the final part of the sentence, so convinced was he that it would work. Merlin and Morgan both contemplated the idea once more. Maybe he was right, perhaps they were too eager to find a magical solution to the supernatural problem when a simple trap-strategy would suffice?

Merlin offered to give the idea some more thought but did not want to settle upon a single solution. He was invigorated with the discussion about how to remedy this problem and wanted to explore more options. Together they came up with a number of back-up plans such as training wolf-hounds to attack the Green Knight; binding it in iron-chains and sinking it in the deepest part of the sea and a variation of the burying scheme which involved carving a huge rock with a cavity to barely fit the Knight and encasing him within it.

It took some hours to explore the merits of each of the back-up plans and discussion on the finer points of how each of the plans would be executed to their maximum possible effectiveness. Eventually though, they felt the weariness of sleep making itself known to them. Merlin agreed that they should rest for the night safe in the knowledge that even if the Green Knight ran the entire way from Caerleon to Cellewig without stopping he could still not reach them before the next night.

They retired to the beds that they would normally use when in residence of Cellewig. Each of them barely had their heads on their respective pillows and a blanket covering them before they were fast asleep.

Chapter 11: Gaul AD494

Morgan's vision was at first confusing. She had seen this place before. Then it struck her, she was in the Minotaur's labyrinth in Gaul. But how did she get here? The last thing that she remembered was going to bed in Cellewig Castle in Dumnonii. She did not use the instantaneous travel spell, did she? Maybe she was spirited here by some other magical being. It was disconcerting being in this place. Merlin's hand touched her shoulder and she spun around in fright.

Merlin and Sir Guaen were standing behind her looking similarly confused.

"Merlin? Sir Guaen? What are ye doing here?" she asked the obvious question.

"I thought that I was asleep in the Castle" responded Guaen. "I too" said Merlin.

"Where is this place?" asked the Knight.

Merlin shrugged and shook his head.

"I know this place," said Morgan. The other two begged her to tell them with their expressions. "It is the labyrinth of the creature that held Excalibur hostage all of those years ago. We are in Gaul." The announcement only heightened the men's befuddlement.

Both Merlin and Sir Guaen were about to ask 'how?' when the would-be question was interrupted by a scream in the distance. They all looked with dread in the direction of the cry.

"Someone is in distress" stated Sir Guaen his chivalrous Knightly nature taking hold.

"Let us see who" said Merlin indicating that they should follow the sound.

It came again. None of them remembered running the distance toward the scream, but suddenly they were at the archway leading to the centre chamber in the labyrinth. Without thinking Sir Guaen and Merlin rushed through the archway. Morgan hesitated. There was something wrong, but she didn't quite know what.

Following the men inside, the scene that greeted them answered her suspicion. There over at the stone altar was Queen Gwenhwyvar approaching the Minotaur from behind, who had in turn lifted Morgan onto the huge carved stone and was preparing to rape her. The two men looked astounded. Morgan was in two places at once.

"We are having a vision of the past" stated Morgan. "This is what happened to me in Gaul in the Minotaur's labyrinth."

Merlin was still a little perplexed. "At first, I thought this to be a shared vision Morgan, but the presence of Sir Guaen made me think otherwise. And even so, why a vision of the past?"

They watched as Queen Gwenhwyvar approached the giant beast with Excalibur raised and cleanly and evenly thrust it into the back of the creature. It hollered in agony, its burst heart still managing to pump copious amounts of blood out of its body.

Gwenhwyvar pulled the sword out of the creature's body and the Minotaur fell to the ground motionless.

"Queen Gwenhwyvar and Excalibur saved mine life," said Morgan to Guaen and Merlin.

As she spoke the images of Gwenhwyvar Morgan and the Minotaur faded away. They were left alone in the chamber. Merlin was curious about the events that immediately followed the slaying of the beast because he knew that it was then Morgan managed to appropriate some of the Minotaur's magical power. It was something that he had discussed with her at length, interested because he had never before encountered such an ability. But he thought better than to question Morgan whilst they were sharing a vision with Sir Guaen. The less that he knew about these magical matters the better. Instead it was this that he concentrated on.

"I hath never before shared a vision with a non-magical person," he said, looking at Guaen and stroking his beard, contemplating the occurrence.

Morgan was sanguine about Merlin's musings and more interested in the fact that she was forced to relive an episode from her past.

"The vision seems to be complete, but what message hath it delivered to us?" she pondered aloud. There was nothing else in the chamber, it was empty. Apparently, the vision had run its course and now being here seemed superfluous. "I know the way out of the labyrinth. Let us leave this place." She suggested.

As one they turned around to exit the chamber. Standing immediately behind them was Garlon, the man who had stolen Excalibur five years ago and given it to the Minotaur to use as bait to lure Merlin to the labyrinth. He did not register that the three dreamers were there. Instead he cautiously entered the chamber. Morgan, Merlin and Guaen instinctively parted to allow him past. They needn't have bothered. He would have collided with Sir Guaen who was not as quick to make way for the man but instead found the Garlon was able to pass right through him as though he were made of smoke.

Guaen quickly felt himself.

"But I feel solid?" he said to his magical companions.

"Ye are having a dream Guaen; a vision of the past that were not a part of; we cannot interact with the people we see here" explained Merlin.

Intrigued to see what was happening they watched as Garlon approached the Minotaur. He walked around to the far side of the fallen beast. He poked the creature with his drawn sword; there was no sign of life. Gently lowering himself to one knee he inspected the

Minotaur at closer range. Quicker than was humanly possible the Minotaur's arm shot out and his giant hand gripped Garlon's throat. He spluttered and choked beneath the grip of the beast.

Morgan was horrified. "It did not die!?" she screamed.

Lightening shot from the mouth of Garlon and into the Minotaur. Bit by bit it drained the life from the thief and traitor. The entire process was over in a matter of seconds. What was left oozed out of the creature's hand and fell as a viscous liquid to the chamber floor. The observers were shocked at the ferocity and speed of the attack, as well as the result.

"A fitting end to Garlon, traitor to King Arthur and Briton," observed Merlin.

Morgan was more concerned with the fact that the creature from which she stole a substantial amount of magic, was not dead as she had thought all of these years. "This is the answer Merlin, to why we are having a vision of the past. The Minotaur is not dead. Perhaps it has something to do with the appearance of the Green Knight?"

"That may be Morgan, but it does not explain why the Green Knight is so fixated with Sir Guaen and why he is sharing a vision with us?"

Morgan kept her eyes on the Minotaur. Even though it had fed on the life-force of a human, it lay motionless upon the ground. It appeared to still be dead but now Morgan knew better.

"How long would that infusion of life keep the beast alive?" she asked, not expecting an answer from either of them. "Is it still alive today or did it eventually die of its injuries?" another question from the Sorceress that none of them could hope to answer. "What if some of the villagers from Avyze came to the Minotaur's labyrinth? Gwenhwyvar and I assured them that it had been slain!" the mounting questions from Morgan were raising her state of alarm.

"There must be more to this vision," she said. She was almost posing the question to the vision itself, pleading with it to yield more information that it had done already. "There are too many unanswered questions; what else should we know from this vision!? What does any of this have to do with the Green Knight?" she was almost frantic now.

"The Green Knight is mine revenge for interfering with mine monarchy!" bellowed a voice from behind them. The three spun around surprised at the intrusion. Standing behind them was a very handsome man with dark hair wearing black shiny clothing. He wore a look of anger. No, more than that, it was a look of absolute malice.

Merlin, eyes wide addressed the man.

"King Hellekin of the faerie people?"

Chapter 12: Hellekin's Curse

Somehow the former King of the faerie people in Briton had entered their collective vision of the past. Maybe he was controlling this vision somehow thought both Morgan and Merlin. They did not have time for further speculation. Hellekin stepped forward and, raising his hand, he pointed accusingly and directly at Morgan's face.

"Ye turned Nimue against her King! Against me!" he growled. "Now I am forced to live away from mine country forsaken by mine people."

Hellekin was livid. It was apparent that he intended to continue venting his frustrations at being deposed by his people but Merlin for one was having none of it.

The wise old Sorcerer was not about to let a mere faerie rant at him or anybody else for that matter.

"Hellekin, ye are a murderer and a failure as a ruler!" shouted back Merlin at the enraged faerie.

Whether or not Hellekin had heard the rebuttal was not clear as the infuriated Hellekin continued his spiteful tale of woe. "But know this Sorceress, I am more powerful than ye, and mine revenge will be brutal and absolute!"

Morgan was so affected by the malevolence in Hellekin's voice she actually took a step backwards. He was pleased that his words were having the desired effect upon her.

"All of the Caerleon Knight's will be forfeit, followed by thine King, Queen and ye former lover!" He moved his accusatory finger, now directing it at Merlin.

That was more than Merlin could take. He took a deep breath and began the faerie expulsion spell in the old tongue. Realising what Merlin was trying to do, Hellekin practically spat his mocking laughter in Merlin's face.

"Haaaaa ha haaaaa haa haaaa ! What do ye think that a failing old Wizard can do to me here? Ye are foolish and weak old man. This is mine vision Merlin, ye hath no power here at all; none! I look forward to depriving ye of ye precious King Arthur and his Knights of the Round Table. I will see everything taken from ye, just as everything has been taken from me!"

Chapter 13: Cellewig Castle; First Light

The shared dream came to an abrupt end. Unknowingly Merlin, Morgan and Guaen sat bolt-upright in their beds at the same time. It was a jarring experience suddenly leaving a vision that seemed so completely real and finding themselves back in their comfortable and familiar beds once more. Merlin was the first to throw off the blanket and race out of his small bedroom. Morgan's room was at the far end of a short corridor. Her door opened before he'd managed to take three steps toward her room. She emerged and their eyes locked.

"Hellekin?" she said asking in one word for confirmation that the dream had indeed been shared.

"Aye," came the reply from behind Merlin. He turned around to find Sir Guaen standing behind him. His room was around the corner from both Merlin and Morgan's.

"That evil faerie has set the Green Knight upon us. Why did his people not execute him when they found out the truth of his deception?" asked Merlin, not expecting an answer from either of them. Sir Guaen was the most in-the-dark of the trio, not having the insight to Hellekin's treachery as Morgan and Merlin did. Nevertheless he was smart enough to realise that this 'Hellekin' as he was called was somehow at the centre of their current predicament. Guaen picked up on Merlin's open question about Hellekin's life. Thinking like a typical Knight he offered a strategy to overcome the enemy.

"Merlin, if we can find Hellekin and slay him, will that end his magic and stop the Green Knight?"

There was hope on Guaen's face. Merlin and Morgan could see it plainly in the dim light of the corridor. Some light was filtering through the open shutters that led to the main courtyard. There were the sounds of birds awakening with the coming of the light of day. Merlin looked over to Morgan who had by this time joined them. Neither of them answered him.

Sir Guaen was impatient to have his solution to the problem validated by the two magical counsels of Caerleon.

"Surely….." he was about to repeat his plan but Merlin held up his hand to stop Guaen.

"Sir Guaen, there is so much we do not know about the faerie people and the strength and longevity of their magic. It would be premature to assume that killing Hellekin will see the Green Knight stop its attack." Morgan wanted to explore the rest of Hellekin's threat rather than dwell simply upon the immediate reaction to assassinate their enemy.

"Merlin; Hellekin said that *all* of the Knights are threatened by him as well as the King and Queen. Perhaps now that we have removed Sir Guaen from the immediate threat of the Knight it hath turned its carnage toward others in Caerleon?"

Even as she finished the thought it turned her cold. Merlin and Guaen were both clearly shuddering at the thought as well. What if after they had made good their escape the Green Knight had continued to wreak havoc at Caerleon?

"Let us not jump to conclusions Morgan," offered Merlin by way of comfort, as little as it was. "We need to know the facts. We need to know everything that there is to know about the spell that animates the Green Knight. I agree – the situation at Caerleon needs to be taken into account. But what if the Green Knight is still on his way here? Unrelentingly making its way toward Guaen even as we speak?" Merlin paused, Morgan made to speak again but he cut her off. "Morgan ye shall accompany Guaen to Pen Rhionydd in Galloway. I shall return to Caerleon. We can still communicate in our dreams and inform each other of matters."

Morgan immediately saw the value in Merlin's plan.

"The Christians in Galloway; if our magic does not work around them, perhaps the magic of Green Knight will not either?" she said.

"Exactly," he responded. "Sir Guaen will be safe and we can concentrate on finding out more about this spell and how to defeat it."

Merlin's plan was simple but effective. Sir Guaen had understood little of the exchange, magic not working in Galloway? Communicating with each other by dreaming? Was it something that these magicians took for granted? What did it all mean? But he did understand that Merlin and Morgan believed that he would be safe in the far north of the country. And that Merlin was returning to

Caerleon to answer the main question of King Arthur and Queen Gwenhwyvar's safety as well as that of the other Knights of the Round Table. Somehow in a few sentences the way forward was clear. There was a sense of collective purpose that grew in each of them.

"Merlin, Morgan; if the Green Knight is still on its journey to Cellewig, what is to stop us from coming across it; we must journey back toward Caerleon in order to then travel north to Galloway?" Guaen asked about the only flaw that he saw in the current strategy. Merlin however was confident that his answer would stop any further fretting from the Knight.

"Water" he answered simply. Sir Guaen was none the wiser. However Morgan had figured out exactly what the cunning old man was thinking. She smiled and turned to Guaen to offer him a more complete explanation.

"The village on the coast directly to the north of Cellewig has one of Arthur's longboats and a crew ready to sail it.

"Sail it to where?" he enquired.

Merlin answered. "Seek refuge in Mynyw Castle and gather supplies there before sailing onwards to Galloway. The longboat can sail most of the way up the River Deea to Pen Rhionydd, then it will only be a short walk the rest of the way."

Sir Guaen understood and approved of Merlin's plan. On horseback, they would always be facing the possibility of being overtaken by the relentless corpse. However, on water and if the winds were favourable they could make much faster progress. The only real danger then was coming across the Gael raiders. But that was a chance that Guaen was willing to take. A Gael would die at sword point; there was still no way as yet to stop the Green Knight.

"Prepare to leave as soon as we hath eaten. Wake the caretaker" directed Merlin.

There was something that Merlin had not yet told Morgan and Guaen, but it could wait until they were ready to depart.

***

The morning meal was eaten quickly. The caretaker had already roused himself by the time Sir Guaen had come looking for him. He was keen to ensure that the Caerleon guests were well taken care of beneath his watch. Preparing the trio a hearty first meal of the day, he was surprised at how quickly they scarfed it down and how little conversation they made between them. It appeared to him that they must be on some urgent mission for King Arthur and were now anxious to see that it was done. It was none of his business of course, but he couldn't help wondering about it all.

Observing how quickly the trio were eating their meal and now directed by Merlin to prepare their horses for travel, he hurried away from the kitchen where they had chosen to eat to do as he was bid.

He had barely finished preparing the horses for travel when the three had arrived at the stables ready for departure. Bidding them well he handed over the reins to the trio and scurried to open the front gate to allow them egress. It was now that Merlin revealed his intention to travel back to Caerleon instantly.

"Morgan, I must know that the King and Queen are safe." He said. "Of course Merlin, I imagine that ye shall ride hard to return to Caerleon as quickly as possible." She stated in reply. But he was shaking his head even as she spoke.

"I must know now," he said forcefully. The true meaning of his words became apparent to the Sorceress.

"Ye want to invoke the spell of immediate travel" she said. It was not a question. But her tone had the mark of defeat in it, not lost upon Merlin. He responded sympathetically.

"Aye; the spell hath taken its toll upon mine body and vitality as well."

Morgan was glad to hear that Merlin was just as distressed at using the magic-depleting spell as she was.

They had had many discussions about it when she had first returned to Caerleon from their adventures in Gaul. Morgan had always assumed that he was curious about the magic because he had not encountered it before. However now she knew that it was a part of his magical repertoire from many years ago. His curiosity must have been more around the way that she had come across the ability, rather than the spell itself. That was clear to her now.

"Even though casting the spell together made it easier Merlin, it still drained me of more power than I feel I can afford to lose."

She was about to continue but Merlin's pleading expression and the want to see him return to Caerleon as quickly as possible made her end her objections there and then. She offered a small compromise.

"Together we can open a small doorway, and it will take much less magical power. Leave the horse here. We can send ye straight to the front gate of Caerleon."

His eyes lit up with glee at her acquiescence. Leaning forward mischievously he countered.

"Straight into the Great Hall, where the morning meal will surely be being served."

She laughed at his cheekiness. It appealed to her sense of humour.

"To the Great Hall then" she smiled.

Guaen and the caretaker watched with awe as Morgan and Merlin combined their powers. They stood side-by-side and held hands. The concentration was evident upon their faces. It took longer than the first time that Sir Guaen had seen this. Perhaps it was because of the drained state that Morgan had been referring to. Maybe, thought Guaen, once the magic has been used too many times it cannot be re-invoked. Just as he was pondering this the two magicians raised their clenched hands and pointed at the empty space in front of them. A thin silver streak of light emitted itself from the length of their arms and made a small arched shape just ahead of their reach. The Great Hall could clearly be seen through the shape. Even the noise of the morning meal and the odour of the food being served could be heard and smelt through the passageway.

Breathing a sigh of relief, they released their hold and quickly hugged each other goodbye. Merlin waved to Guaen and stepped through the doorway. It shimmered and was no more.

Trying his best not to laugh at the aghast expression on the Caretakers face, Guaen stepped forward to assist Morgan on to her mount. She had a strange expression on her face. Her fair skin seemed even more pale than usual. Indeed, she looked very poorly. Morgan's eyes rolled upwards into her head, her eyelids closed and she fainted into Guaen's arms.

Guaen instinctively caught her before she fell to the ground.

"Morgan?" he said trying to revive her.

He shouted to the Caretaker. ."Bring something for Lady Morgan to drink."

The Caretaker ran back toward the main entrance to the castle leaving the gateway open. Guaen looked up and suddenly felt exposed. They could not ride to the village and make good their escape in the longboat with Morgan unconscious. The gate was left open. What if the Green Knight had travelled faster than Merlin had anticipated and arrived right now? What would he do?

Chapter 14: The Great Hall in Caerleon Castle

Florie, Elamite and Lyonors were sitting together at the side of the secondary table. Elamite and Lyonors were trying to console Florie about the disposition of her husband.

"With Merlin and Morgan as travelling companions he is sure to be somewhere far away and safe by now," offered Elamite.

Lyonors joined in the comforting thought.

"They hath by now surely cast a spell to destroy that hideous Green Knight," she said.

Florie was grateful for the words of encouragement, but could not reconcile why Merlin and Morgan did not cast a spell to stop the Green Knight when they first encountered it last evening.

Word had spread throughout the servants and soldiers that the magicians of Caerleon were powerless to stop the daemon. It was petty gossip that a lady of the court could not possibly entertain. However, she could not help but worry. All of these things were going around in her mind when she noticed something strange about the tapestry on the far side of the hall to where they were sitting. It seemed to have formed an arched doorway through which she could see what looked to be a man and woman dressed as Morgan and Merlin were when they'd left Caerleon the night before with Guaen.

Just as she was trying to make sense of it all Merlin stepped out of the tapestry and into the Great Hall almost colliding with a servant carrying a dish to the table. The servant let out a loud cry at the sudden appearance of Merlin attracting the attention of everyone on the hall.

"Merlin!" shouted Florie in a most un-lady-like manor. Standing up to project her voice she said, "Is Guaen with ye?"

People did not know which way to look; at Merlin who had seemed to appear through the wall-hanging or at Lady Florie who was making quite an uncharacteristic scene.

A loud murmur of "What is this?," "Merlin?" "Where did he come from?," "Did I just see him walk through a wall?" and similar comments erupted from the diners.

King Arthur took the sudden appearance of his sage in his stride and stood up from his seat beside Gwenhwyvar and Amhar.

"Merlin; 'tis good to see ye. Where is Morgan and Sir Guaen?" he said, looking expectantly at the old man.

Merlin in his typical way did not answer directly.

"More to the point King Arthur, where is the Green Knight?" he began to walk toward Arthur so that he wouldn't have to shout across the hall to have a conversation with him.

Arthur responded. "It followed the three of ye by all accounts from the soldiers on the battlements and the people in the village. We thought that it would still be hunting down Sir Guaen. Did it catch up with ye? Has a way been found to stop it?"

Arthur fired a barrage of questions at his Sorcerer. The silence in the normally raucous hall was awkward. Clearly everyone present wanted to know the situation since they fled the castle last night. Merlin was not inclined to let everybody in on what was happening though.

"It has not caught up with Sir Guaen, and I hath sent him and Morgan on a journey to surely elude the evil thing."

Lady Florie was so relieved that she groaned a sigh of relief and slumped back into her chair.

Now at Arthur's chair he lowered his voice and leant forward, "There is treachery afoot from an old foe Arthur."

He indicated that they should retire to more private surroundings and continue their conversation.

Chapter 15: The King's Study in Caerleon Castle

"Tell us everything!" it was the Queen's command rather than Arthur's that directed the Sorcerer. Merlin was a little put-out that Gwenhwyvar had insisted on handing over Prince Amhar to her servant and accompany Arthur and he to the King's study to discuss the situation.

His annoyance was plain to see but the Queen brushed it aside. She was not content to leave this extraordinary situation to Arthur and Merlin to handle alone. Merlin was wise enough to accede to the Queen's wishes, he began his summation of the events.

"The Green Knight's ability to inhibit magical power has a limited range. Once we were no longer under its influence, Morgan and I used the power of instant travel to take us to Llyn Callyfyrth; I needed to consult with the Lady of the Lake."

Both Arthur and Gwenhwyvar were shocked at both the action that Merlin had taken and the inference that ensued. *The great magician Merlin needed to seek consultation with the Lady of the Lake?* He barely ever spoke of her and how he was presented with the magical sword Excalibur and told to use it to make Uther King of Briton and unite the disparate native factions. And Gwenhwyvar knew from first-hand experience when she dared to do the same thing, Merlin was astounded to say the very least. If Merlin felt it necessary to seek help from the Lady of the Lake, then matters were much worse than either of them had imagined.

He noticed their amazed expressions but continued his story without acknowledging it. "The Lady would not appear. Morgan and I both pleaded to no avail."

The Queen looked as though she were about to interrupt with a thought of her own, but did not. She was too anxious to hear the rest of the story to offer her own musings as to why the mystical being may not have appeared to him.

"We took refuge in Cellewig castle and it was there that we found why this unstoppable creature has been inflicted upon us." He paused briefly to catch his breath. "Morgan, Guaen and I shared a vision of the past; Gaul in 494 the Minotaur's labyrinth."

This made the Queen's eyes widen. "What of it?" she said, a note of iciness in her voice.

"We saw the Minotaur slain at thine hands Gwenhwyvar and thought it dead. In the vision, Garlon came into the cave and was consumed by the beast."

Gwenhwyvar interrupted now quite loudly and violently. Standing from her stool she said, "That foul creature lives?"

Merlin was conciliatory he gestured with both his hands.

"It consumed Garlon, a fitting end for the thief, but did not raise itself from the ground. It is not important." He was about to continue but Gwenhwyvar was too focussed on the knowledge that the beast had not been killed by her and Excalibur.

"If it can consume one person then it may consume more and once more raise itself against us. It was the Minotaur then that set the Green Knight against us as revenge?"

"No" countered Merlin. The topic was being skewed and he did not wish it to be so. He regretted telling the Queen about the Minotaur component of the vision now, but it was too late. But he wanted them to know that Garlon had met a fitting fate for his transgression against the King of Briton by stealing his magical sword.

"If not the Minotaur of Gaul, what then?" pleaded Arthur of his sage.

"Hellekin," said Merlin in a voice dripping with revile. The Queen took her seat again, dumbfounded by this twist to the story. "The King of the Faerie people that conspired with Aelle to defeat ye at Anderidae appeared at the end of the vision and told us that the Green Knight is his revenge for interfering with his monarchy." Merlin finished his abbreviated recounting of the events of the shared vision. Arthur offered his first thoughts about what the implications of this could be.

"Because we gave Nimue all of the evidence that she needed to make witness as to Hellekin's treachery, we are being punished?" it didn't make rational sense. "And how does Guaen fit in with this revenge from Hellekin? He did nothing to assist in the–"

Merlin talked over the top of Arthur.

"Arthur there are still many unanswered questions. But now we know that the deposed King of the faerie people of Briton is involved then I have a starting point to gather more information."

Both Gwenhwyvar and Arthur looked at each other and asked the old man "How?" in unison.

Merlin was disappointed in the both of them, could they not see the obvious link to the recent events? "This must surely be a faerie spell of some description. I can infiltrate the faeries and find out more about it."

The further clarification from the old man did nothing to illuminate the proposed course of action.

This time it was just the Queen that asked, "Infiltrate the faeries Merlin?" There was silence as both the King and Queen expected more information from the Sorcerer.

"Tis time that I paid a visit to the faerie ruler," he said with a wily smile covering his old face. It looked to Arthur that Merlin had made up his mind to seek out the current ruler of the faeries and have words directly with them. Arthur had a more pressing need for Merlin's services however and hastened to remind the old man.

"Not before ye hath healed the injured from last night." It was a statement rather than a request and it brought Merlin's mind back to his duties as magician of Caerleon. "Aye, aye, of course" he said.

Chapter 16: Dumnonii

Progress was slower than Guaen had hoped for. It was mid-morning and Morgan and he were barely back at Llyn Callyfyrth which was on the way to their destination; the village on the coast directly north of Cellewig castle. Morgan could not be revived and Guaen could not leave her at Cellewig. She was an integral part of Merlin's plan. Both of the magical beings could somehow communicate over great distances and he had hoped more than anything to hear from Merlin about the safety of everyone at Caerleon, especially his wife Florie and his son Wigaloith. He tried to put those thoughts to the back of his mind, without much success.

He looked back at the two horses he was leading. Together he and the Caretaker had rigged a make-shift bed that sat between the two horses. The horses were tied together at the reins and the rear mountings. The bed of straw and rope was being carried aptly by the two horses. Tied securely into the bed was Morgan. He imagined that it would have been uncomfortable. But it was preferable to somehow tying the Sorceress to him and riding double on the same horse. At least this way they could continue for longer without the need to give the horses rest.

Guaen had tried to supress his fears that somewhere lurking nearby was the Green Knight. If it appeared, he decided, rather than risk Lady Morgan he would leave her to regain consciousness in her own time and lead the Green Knight away from her. He hoped that his plan did not need to be enacted.

At this rate, it would be nightfall before they reached the village. Again, he looked back at Morgan. There was still no sign of her waking from her unconscious state. He continued their path toward their eventual destination.

Chapter 17: The Faerie Forest North of Caerleon Castle

It was a beautiful day. The sky was clear and blue. The sun was shining and everywhere life was filling the forest. The tree that Merlin believed to be where the presiding ruler lived was easy to spot. Apart from the overpowering sense of feeling a faerie presence there was nothing out of the ordinary. There had been comings and goings all morning of every type of bird. So, unless it contained many nests for many different types of birds that somehow co-existed together, then he was sure that this is the destination that he was searching for.

Faeries in their various guises did not give Merlin a second glance, for he had transformed himself into a wren. Had they been more sensitive to the presence of magical beings as he was, then they would have been alerted. But it suited his mission to be mistaken for an actual bird and not an otherworldly being. By Merlin's estimation an opportunity had arisen. He had been keeping careful track of which types and how many birds had entered the tree, now it seemed that there would only be one other bird/faerie inside. Now was the time to move.

He flew from the branch that he had perched upon all morning over to the hole that was being used as the entrance and exit by the faeries. Peering down he could see that there was a passage that opened up at the point where the bulbous tree was at its widest. This was surely what he was searching for. Flinging himself forward he flew down the short passage and entered the intricately carved and quite large room. Landing neatly on the floor; Nimue was there. She was sitting on a chair, no a throne, carved from the same type of wood that made up the tree. She looked up at him with a bemused expression on her face.

"Surely ye should know to take on thine miniature human form in the presence of the Queen?" she said to the wren.

Merlin was amazed. Nimue had somehow replaced Hellekin as the ruler of the faerie people. She had not sensed that he was not one of them; a credit to his own powers of transformation. What happened next shocked Queen Nimue enough to have her summon her guards.

Instead of the faerie simply assuming a miniature faerie human form, the wren began to gasp. It fell over writhing in apparent pain. Queen Nimue knew immediately that something was dreadfully wrong.

"Guards!" she hollered.

The moths that resided on the wall and ceiling of the hollow descended and took miniature human form surrounding their Queen to protect her. They carried faerie swords ready to battle this bizarre intruder, and raised them appropriately.

By this time the wren had begun to shift its form. Instead of the simple glimmer of light and immediate transformation that any faerie was capable of, this one was experiencing absolute agony changing itself. It was disconcerting for Nimue. Could this be a challenge to her rule? Unlikely as there was a process for presenting such an undertaking. Perhaps it was a sick faerie in need of help? Either way she was glad to be surrounded by her personal guards.

The bird's head contracted into that of a man. Even though the face was a grotesque parody of both bird and man features, Nimue recognised it still. See pushed herself outside of her guard's protective circle.

"Merlin?" she said, amazed at not only who had entered her hollow, but how he had chosen to do so.

Bit by bit the transformation of the bird into the Sorcerer happened until it was done. Laying there on the floor of the hollow was Merlin, naked and in miniature human form.

"Fetch him some faerie silk to wear!" she ordered her guards.

One of them rushed away and through a doorway that lead to a room within a branch of the tree. There were various supplies there including some of the finest faerie silk that had ever been made. The guard grabbed an outfit that used to belong to King Hellekin and raced back into the main chamber.

Nimue was helping Merlin to his feet. He was breathing hard. The transformation back from a bird must have exhausted him she thought. As if in answer to her line of thinking Merlin managed a few broken words between breaths.

"Transforming…into a wren…was difficult but…transforming back and into …a small version of mine body…was more so."

Nimue helped him over to her throne and guided him to a sitting position.

"Sit and rest Merlin, recover ye strength" she said sympathetically. *What could Merlin be doing here?* She thought. She wanted to ask him so much.

"Bring something for Merlin to drink," she commanded another of the guards.

The first had by this time arrived with the faerie silk outfit. In an instant and with what seemed like very little effort the Nimue made the silk robes disappear from the guard's hands and reappear comfortably fitting around Merlin's seated body. He reeled with surprise. This was magic he had not seen before. He touched the robes, they were the softest thing that he had ever felt. He also recognised the shimmering black cut of the outfit. It was the same that he had seen Hellekin wear in the most recent vision of him.

"Hellekin's?" he asked Nimue.

"Aye," she replied. "The faerie craftsmanship that hath gone into making his wardrobe of clothing was so excellent that I thought to hold all of his robes in storage awaiting the next King that saw fit to use them."

"Queen Nimue?" queried Merlin. He had had no contact with Nimue since he last spoke with her at Caerleon castle all those years ago. Gwenhwyvar and Morgan had returned from Gaul safely with Excalibur. Their experience with Matrona, the Lady of the Lake was saved into a thought stone by Morgan and presented to Nimue in the hope that the faerie people would use it to convict him of interference with human affairs. Clearly that had happened. "I came to see the present ruler of the faerie people of Briton. I did not expect it to be ye."

Now the second guard that had been dispatched to fetch a drink for Merlin arrived with a carved wooden cup filled with a very fragrant wine.

"Here drink this, 'twill aid in ye recovery," said Nimue offering the cup to the old man. Merlin took a sip of the wine. It was good, much more viscous inside his mouth than he would have thought. But that could simply be his diminished size. A cup full of the same wine drank by his full-sized body would have probably been of normal consistency. He was still pondering this thought when Nimue brought him back to the point at hand.

"Why hath ye sought out the ruler of the faerie people?" she asked.

He looked up at her and beat his chest with the palm of his hand.

"Hellekin is threatening us" he said.

Nimue was shocked. If anyone had cared to look at the expression on the royal guards faces, they too would have shown the same feeling.

"How? What hath he done? Is he in Briton? He hath been banished from this land Merlin never to return. If he does so he will be put to death!"

This was good news to Merlin's ears. "Hellekin appeared to Morgan and myself in a vision. He said that our current predicament was his revenge for turning the faerie people against him," explained the old Sorcerer.

"Current predicament, Merlin? Which is what?" inquired the Queen.

Merlin finished off the wine; it had indeed helped him recover his strength. "The reason that I am here Nimue; Hellekin hath released a deceased Knight upon Arthur and the Knights of the Round Table. For now, it is obsessed with slaying Sir Guaen, but if Hellekin is to be believed then the remainder of the Knights are the next to be beset upon followed by King Arthur..." he was still speaking when Nimue screamed a curse upon Hellekin.

"That evil coward; I should have put him to death for his crimes but wanted to see him suffer as much as he made me suffer by murdering our unborn daughter!"

The venom in her voice was enough to make Merlin shiver. The murder of the unborn progeny of Merlin and Nimue, Ellergia by Hellekin even though it was eight years ago still invoked the strongest emotions in Nimue.

Merlin thought it best to let Nimue vent her hatred of Hellekin and everything that he had done.

"I swear Merlin; if he has set foot in Briton he will be hunted down and publically humiliated before being executed."

She had almost forgotten the other details of Merlin's rhetoric. Slowly in the pause that followed her threat it began to seep into her thinking. She shook herself out of her musings of killing Hellekin.

"A dead Knight is threatening King Arthur's court?" she asked.

"Aye" responded Merlin "Do ye know of the faerie spell that hath animated the corpse and set it upon us? If I can find the original spell, maybe I can find a way to counter it?"

Merlin's further explanation did not help Nimue's understanding. She tilted her head and shook it slightly before asking.

"Why do ye simply not use thine own magic to stop the creature?" To her it seemed the logical thing to do under the circumstances that he was describing.

"I cannot; and nor can Morgan. Our magic is inhibited somehow by the presence of the Knight. Tell me then Nimue, does this spell sound familiar to ye? How has Hellekin done this?" he leant forward hoping to hear the answer that he sought.

Nimue stood upright and gazed into the distance. "Merlin, I hath spent many years now reading through all of the spells within the faerie library of magic. Give me a few moments to think" she offered.

It was not the resounding 'yes' that Merlin had hoped for but it did give him a glimmer of reassurance that he was at least closer to finding what he came for. A faerie library of magic, he thought. Wondrous; he would love the opportunity to delve into such a repository of knowledge.

"Merlin, I think that I may know of the spell that hath animated a dead human and turned it against ye, but I shall need to consult with our texts. Yet if it is the one that I am recalling, the material used to cast such a spell would be so rare as to make it nearly impossible to use."

Nimue finished her declaration with a wave of her hand. To Merlin's surprise the throne upon which he sat moved backwards revealing a hole in the floor.

Merlin leaned over to peer down the dark opening. With a further spell, the small candles that were placed in the hidden chamber below ignited, lighting up the room. From what Merlin could see it was about one third the circumference of the total area of the throne room, a similarly circular room. The walls were covered with niches that contained what looked to flat pieces of stone and bark.

Merlin's face lit up like a child receiving a gift. Nimue looked up at the old man just in time to catch the expression on his face. She could not help but smile herself.

"This is the library of faerie magic," she said, confirming his speculation on what the room contained.

He practically jumped out of the throne and knelt at the edge of the hole in order to get a better view of the inside of the secret room.

"Everything?" he asked, the hope in his voice apparent.

"Every spell that hath ever been worked by faeries since the beginning of our society here in Briton," she confirmed. Merlin actually clapped his hands together in glee.

"I must see Nimue please allow me to enter," he was bobbing up and down on his knees like an excited infant.

Nimue could see the yearning in his pose. "Come down Merlin, I grant ye access.." she was still talking when the old man threw his legs over the entrance and hurled himself in a most undignified manner down into the room. He landed with a thud surprising Nimue with his lack of finesse. Normally a faerie would change into a moth or something and descend with dignity before taking upon miniature human form again. She had not allowed for the fact that it was difficult for Merlin to transform himself from one form to another.

He sprang to his feet and looked around the entire circumference of the circular room. There were bits of flat bark piled into the niches. He did not know where to begin. He wanted to look at it all. Nimue however had other plans. She had taken up position about where the throne was in the room above. These carved niches seemed to have more intricate carvings surrounding them.

"Here," explained Nimue, "are all of the spells that are concerned with the reanimation of the dead. It is a precarious set of spells that are not usually called for as they are not easy to prove because the ingredients required are so…unusual. " She said her voice tapering off a little toward the end. She was flicking through a particular pile. Merlin joined her and looked over her shoulder.

What he saw was amazing. There were spells written in Latin, Northumbrian, Kentish, some in the runic alphabet and others in languages that he did not recognise. One thing was for sure, these seemed to be elaborate and very wordy spells.

He was still exploring this realisation when Nimue stopped and held up a particularly large piece of bark. She swung around to face him.

"Tell me again about the Knight that cannot be stopped. Ye mentioned something about it becoming fixated upon one person?"

Merlin looked at her eyes; he could tell that she was worried. He answered, "Aye Nimue, it seems obsessed for the time being with Sir Guaen…" he continued to describe the circumstances but Nimue had stopped listening and was once more reading the spell in her hands.

She shook her head.

"What part did ye not understand?" asked Merlin thinking that he had said something that required further explanation.

"What?" she said looking up at him. Realising the mistake she shook her head too. "No, no Merlin, it is the fixation with Sir….Guaen?" she paused for confirmation.

"Aye," he said.

She held up the spell by way of explanation.

"According to this spell a dead warrior reanimated and turned against a King's guard will eliminate them one by one, not hunting another until the first is dispatched."

Merlin froze; that could very well be the situation that they were facing right now.

"What else does it say?" he looked at the writing but it was unfamiliar to him, he would need Nimue to translate it for him.

"When all of the ruler's guards are dead, it will turn its attention to the king and his family. Only then will it stop." She read and re-read some of the passages almost not able to believe what she was discovering. "It is a spell that is meant to bring terror to the intended victim, a King or ruler of some description. Seeing his protection murdered one by one at each full moon."

"What?" interrupted Merlin. "What about the moon?"

Nimue looked over that section of the spell and recounted what she had read.

"The corpse will rise only at the peak of the full-moon and will cause mayhem and murder until the moon is in the sky no longer. It hath only that time in which to carry out its instructions. So, the warrior will only appear on one day in the month; twelve times a year," she said.

Merlin walked away from her scratching his beard fiercely. He turned around "What does it say about decapitating the thing?" Nimue found the relevant passages and told him the news that without a doubt confirmed that they had indeed found the spell that was being used against Arthur.

"Any injury to the corpse will make it stronger and more resistant to future attack. Does this sound like what is happening?" she asked.

"Aye" he replied.

"The warrior becomes stronger the more it is attacked," she continued, "it will kill one by one the King's guards and will only appear upon the peak of the full moon on a single night of the month."

She finished her summary of the situation that was being faced.

"Gaelach shows her face before nightfall and can stay in the sky well into the following morning," Merlin said. He was calculating exactly how much time the Green Knight would be appearing to them.

"It first appeared just before sunset on the day of the full moon just gone by." He said.

Nimue was convinced with the evidence that Merlin was presenting.

"Then this is surely the spell that hath been cast against King Arthur and his Knights; but…."

She again shook her head as though in disbelief.

"But what?' asked Merlin gesturing with both hands in the air.

"Merlin, the primary ingredient of this spell is a still-born child from the bloodline of the King that is to be cursed," answered Nimue. "It is simply too inconceivable to assume that Arthur hath fathered a still-born child and somehow Hellekin hath come across such a thing."

Silence filled the room. Realisation descended upon Merlin like the heaviest tapestry being slowly lowered over him. Nimue could see the darkening of his features. She could actually feel the dread welling up within him. It caused her anxiety. Almost fearfully she took a timid step toward him. His eyes were far away. His thoughts were rooted in the past. After a very long time, he seemed to come back to the present. There was no accusation in his tone; he looked evenly at Nimue.

"Nimue the reason that this spell was able to be cast, lies with ye."

Chapter 18: The Most Evil of Spells

Nimue was shocked. "Me?" she said incredulously. "Merlin, I would never use this evil spell upon anyone."

She was indignant but also surprised to find herself pondering the use of that very spell against Hellekin. She waved her hand dismissively at Merlin.

"I would not use such a spell Merlin because even if I found cause, and I hath found cause with Hellekin, I could never bring myself to use a still born child, a royal child in a spell of such revile and hatred. Even after everything that he hath done to me, I would not, could not use this magic against Hellekin." She finished her self-justification not realising that she had completely misunderstood Merlin's inference.

"No Nimue, listen to what I am saying to ye." He stepped forward to be closer to the faerie ruler so that there would be no further misinterpretation of his words. "Eight years ago, in order to spend a night with me, ye tricked Morgan into sleeping with Arthur. Three baby boys were to be born from that union except that an accident took two of their lives. I drew out the stillborn children and had them disposed of. Somehow Hellekin hath found and used them."

The words cut into Nimue like the sharpest of knives. She wanted to resist what she was hearing, to scream that it was not true but somehow, she knew that Merlin was speaking the absolute truth.

She finished off his recounting of the events that had led to this moment.

"One child was used to murder Ellergia whilst still in mine womb, and the other," she choked off her sentence in a sob of regret. Merlin concluded, "the other hath been used to inflict this curse upon Arthur and his realm."

Even before he had finished Nimue fell to her knees, her fists thumping the wood of the floor in despair. Again, and again she beat the floor until it looked as though blood would seep from her skin. She began to breathe in as though she was choking. In and out each breath seemed to be more laboured. She was building up to a scream of the most guttural and heart-wrenching of her entire life. She had unwittingly supplied the raw materials for Hellekin to murder her unborn child, and the primary ingredient that Hellekin was somehow now using to destroy Arthur and his kingdom. She wailed the most bleak and desolate cry that Merlin had ever heard. Royal guards appeared from nowhere concerned with the safety of their Queen.

They found her crumpled upon the floor screaming like a wounded animal. Merlin's heart felt like it was ripping into two. He knelt down and comforted her in his arms. Tears broke through his clenched eyes as he too was consumed with the emotion. Together they cried and let loose all of the hurt and pain that they had harboured all these years. Clutching each other they became as one. Thoughts and feelings merged together and crossed over from one to the other in a way that only magical beings can share.

Merlin became Nimue, the mother who had known and loved her child whilst still in the womb; now facing the loss of that child anew. It was absolutely heart-wrenching.

Nimue became Merlin, the man who had taken the newborn Arthur and raised him to be a worthy ruler of the land; now facing the destruction of everything that he had worked his entire life to achieve. The desolation that he felt plunged into the depths of exasperation and sorrow. They each were free to explore the intricacies of each-others being.

Chapter 19: Nimue; the Architect of Torment

Together in their embrace the magical force of each being combined with the other and they relived the events that led to this moment. Nimue and Merlin saw through Morgan's eyes as she entered Arthur's room believing it to be Merlin's. They saw through Arthur's eyes to Morgan disguised by Nimue as Gwenhwyvar. The passionate love making that conceived the triplets; King Arthur and Morgan's children. In an instant, they realised that Arthur and Morgan beguiled and in the throes of making love were not alone in the room. King Hellekin was there on the window sill in the form of a pigeon. His eyes watching the scene with interest; able to see through the beguilement disguises that both wore. They could hear his thoughts. "

What game is Nimue playing with these humans?" his magical abilities were able to see the moment of conception, a triple conception. They experienced that too.

Time sped past and they both became Morgan undergoing her vision of the future. Now they were in the brilliant sunshine outside the walls of Caerleon Castle; the three beautiful boys playing together, all unmistakably Arthur's. Nimue and Merlin experienced the horror that Morgan felt when she realised that the children that she was carrying were not Merlin's but Arthur's. They saw through her eyes as she fell down the great staircase in Caerleon Castle and landed in a wrecked heap at the bottom. They felt the agony of her injuries.

Now Nimue could see through Merlin's eyes and feel what he felt as he worked without rest to draw out the two dead babies from Morgan's body and into the sow's womb. She suffered the feeling of loss just as he did.

They were in one of the smaller internal courtyards of the Castle; they were now witnessing the scene of the sow giving birth to the still-born bodies of Morothyne and Morlois. They could feel the awe and disgust of the servant through whose eyes they watched the event. The dead babies were hurriedly covered in a roughly woven sack and were taken to the river Usk nearby Caerleon Castle. Merlin and Nimue could feel the effort of the man throwing the tiny corpses into the river in order to dispose of them.

Now Nimue and Merlin were a faerie that transformed from a fish into a full sized human. He reached over and grabbed the bag. They could feel his confusion at thinking that maybe something had already fallen out of the bag the short time that it had been in the water before he could recover it. Peering inside and seeing the contents he dismissed his earlier suspicion. How could there have been more than one dead human foetus in the bag? The joy that the faerie felt; this is exactly what King Hellekin has been seeking. He will surely use it to help make the faerie people fertile once more and bear more faerie children.

The Faerie Queen and the Sorcerer watched through the eyes of the faerie as he presented his prize to Hellekin in secret. Hellekin thanked the loyal servant and promised him a prominent position in his court as reward.

Now Nimue and Merlin became King Hellekin as he prepared the foetus as part of the spell that would see the end to Nimue's pregnancy. He knew this dead child. He was there when it was conceived; it was of royal blood coming from King Arthur and Lady Morgan.

They could feel the smug self-satisfaction that he revelled in as he worked to murder Ellergia in Nimue's womb. This child will never be born and never be the instrument of his downfall by recovering the fertility spell and sacrificing him to ensure the success of the spell. Merlin clenched his fists so tightly that his fingernails drew blood from his palms. This unbelievably evil faerie had resorted to murdering an unborn child to ensure his own survival and continuance as king. Merlin was feeling the revulsion that Nimue felt for Hellekin, an abomination.

The shared vision continued. Time has gone past, they could not ascertain how much, but it did not feel like a lot. Another faerie in the form of a fox has picked up the scent of something. Tracking it to the edge of the river Usk he came across its source; a deceased human child. King Hellekin has decreed that all faeries should keep a watch for such a thing so that it may be used to aid the faerie people. Just like the faerie that found the first still-born child it was taken secretly to Hellekin. Again promises of stature within the court were promised. But this time Hellekin dismisses his guards and takes the faerie down to the hidden library of spells. They see through his eyes as he recovers the spell that Nimue and Merlin had just been reading. He speaks to the faerie.

"I know this dead child; it is the progeny of King Arthur. Its value to me at some time in the future could be substantial. I thank ye for such a wondrous prize. Here let me give you a reward befitting such great bounty."

They could feel the excitement of the faerie; his reward will surely be generous. King Hellekin searched through the library for another spell. Finding it he took the hand of the faerie that has served him so well and speaks words unfamiliar to the miniscule being.

Suddenly wracked in pain the loyal servant of Hellekin is dissolved into ashes in excruciating seconds. Hellekin feels no shame or regret. Merlin and Nimue are left in no doubt that this is what happened to the first faerie as his reward for assisting the malevolent King. They see him carefully preparing the body of the dead baby and reducing it to a paste that is then dried and stored in a bag that Hellekin keeps around his neck and beneath his clothing, out of view.

The next thing that they see is Nimue using the memory stone to relay to the court her testimonial from Matrona of Hellekin's evil doings. They can feel the rage within Hellekin at being discovered and banished. But it is not the overpowering feelings of revenge that fill Hellekin's mind that Nimue and Merlin are concentrating upon, it is the bag secreted around Hellekin's neck as he is banished from Briton. He had it with him when he fled the country. They have all of the explanation that they need. The sequence of events that brought them to their current situation has been laid out for them to clearly see.

Chapter 20: The Faerie Library of Spells.

Merlin and Nimue felt that they had been away for a long time. They opened their eyes. They were still in a tight embrace. Both were breathing in unison. It was a little disorientating. After having travelled so far and wide and through so much time and inside the thoughts of so many others, now they were back where they had begun, in the faerie library of spells. The guards that had come to the assistance of the Queen when they heard her cry out were still standing there with looks of bewilderment on their faces.

Nimue addressed them in a weak voice that echoed her state of being.

"How long hath we been in embrace?" she inquired.

The guard closest to the Queen replied. "Only a few moments, mine Queen. We heard a cry and came to assist. Merlin knelt down to offer ye comfort and ye both fell silent for a short time, until just now."

It was what both Merlin and Nimue had suspected. Their shared experience had taken a few fleeting moments but it had felt to them like hours. Separating physically from each other, they found that they could still feel the physical state of each other. Merlin knew that Nimue was exhausted by the vision, and she knew that he was too. They both sat quietly on the floor without saying anything. The guards were unsure of what to do other than stand and await orders.

Merlin could feel his strength coming back bit by bit. There was something else too; his individuality was returning. The sharing of Nimue's thoughts and feelings was lessening and becoming a distant light in the core of his being. He guessed correctly that Nimue must be undergoing a similar withdrawal of communion.

Merlin was about to speak but Nimue beat him to it.

"I shall place what we hath experienced in a memory stone and show it to the elders of mine court."

Her words had finality to them. Merlin was taken aback.

"Why?" he asked simply.

"Because" she responded "the faerie people hath been deceived enough by Hellekin; they deserve to know the truth about everything. It was one of mine pledges when I accepted the monarchy."

It had all of the marks of a royal commandment, somehow it suited Nimue, and for the first time he saw her through different eyes. She may have unwittingly started the sequence of events that gave rise to the Green Knight, but the price that she had paid was considerable. Now she was prepared to throw herself upon the judgement of her elders rather than try to cover up the events or assign blame completely to the wicked Hellekin.

Merlin considered her current predicament.

"As ruler ye are duty-bound to find the fertility spell and if so sacrifice…" he began.

Nimue completed his thought, "...sacrifice mine body to ensure that the spell is successful. Just as the ruling King did thousands of years ago."

"Surely then," he said, "the elders..."

Again, Nimue talked over the top of him "...the elders will decide mine fate Merlin. I hath so far been unsuccessful at locating the spell. Mine emissaries hath been dispatched to all of the lands that we are still able to go. They search for any assistance or clue that may help. Matrona hath been unwilling to speak with me further even though our very existence is under threat."

Merlin listened with great compassion for the selflessness that Nimue exuded. He almost wanted to tell her of the spell that he had recounted from his vision of Ellergia in a future that will now never happen. If he concentrated hard enough he was sure he could recount the spell once more.

Merlin was conflicted. He now felt so much awe of Nimue and how decent a ruler she had become that he wanted to help her. But revealing that he knew the contents of the fertility spell would mean that she would be slaughtered to carry it out. He did not want to see that happen. If Matrona is unwilling to help the faerie people perhaps he should be as well. And none of this was helping solve the problem of the Green Knight. At least it did not seem so urgent a problem right now. If the Green Knight can only appear one evening and night per month then they had time to work on a more permanent solution. His scheming mind began to formulate a plan.

"Nimue, offer the elders of thine court mine help in locating the fertility spell if Arthur's Knights and court survive the magical attack that Hellekin hath released upon us."

It was a clever offer. This way he may perhaps garner support from the faerie people to assist in the defeat of the Green Knight.

"I wish ye the best Nimue in receiving the judgement of the faerie people."

He leant forward and embraced her. He carefully guarded his thoughts just in case they could still experience each other's thoughts and feelings, but nothing happened other than the physical sense of togetherness and comfort.

Still wrapped in her own sense of guilt Nimue failed to see that Merlin was hiding something in the back of his mind. She accepted his well-wish and together they helped each other to their feet.

"What will ye do now Merlin?' inquired Nimue.

"I hath sent Sir Guaen to Pen Rhionydd. It is mine hope being surrounded by the Christians will nullify the magic of the Green Knight just as his influence robs Morgan and me from our abilities," he replied

"Ye do not seem too sure" responded Nimue catching the hesitant tone in Merlin's plan.

He looked at her evenly. "I will explore any idea that will defeat Hellekin and ensure the survival of Arthur and his Kingdom."

There was another matter still at the forefront of Merlin's thoughts.

"The spell" he said "does it say how to end it?" It was a pragmatic question that somehow felt awkward in the current circumstances. Nimue recovered the spell from the floor where she had dropped it earlier.

She shook her head. "No Merlin, I'm sorry – it says nothing about how to end the spell!"

Merlin looked exasperated even though he tried his best to hide it. He moved to stand beside Nimue and look at the spell once more in the feint hope that somehow something would be revealed in looking upon the words that he could not read. More than that, he wanted to be able to transcribe the exact wording of the spell once he returned to Caerleon.

"I will leave now. Send me word about what the elders say when they witness what ye will show to them?" Merlin spoke whilst he looked up at the opening and only then wondered how he would get out of the hidden room. Nimue picked up on what the old man was thinking. She sought to offer him some solace and recompense that this regrettable situation began with her wanting to trick him into fathering their child.

She commanded the two guards.

"Bring a step ladder for Merlin. Assist him to the opening of the Hollow and carry him to Caerleon; a falcon should suffice to adequately carry our small friend," she said to the first and to the second she further commanded, "bring me a memory stone and summon the council of elders. I hath much to tell them."

Chapter 21: Tyntagael Village on the Coast of Dumnonii

It was late afternoon by the time Guaen rode into the tiny coastal village of Tyntagael. He had made better time than he'd estimated. It was a small fishing community that like all of the settlements in West Wales was part of Arthur's monarchy. Recognising his attire a small band of villagers gathered together to greet him. From his position on the horse he could see the smiling faces of the villagers turn to frowns of curiosity when they saw that there was a woman tied into a makeshift bed suspended between two horses. Guaen felt as though he should explain but decided simply identifying the object of their vexed expressions would do.

"Please assist Lady Morgan Le Fay, she is weak from conjuring," he announced.

This had exactly the effect that he had hoped, it eliminated any questions from the villagers, who upon hearing that the mysterious sorceress sister of the king was present, were practically falling over themselves to help.

"We will require the king's long boat, provision it for a journey to the far north."

He dismounted as he spoke. His orders were being shouted from one person to the next comforting Guaen that their journey would soon be underway. He moved around the horses to help those that were assisting Morgan. To his surprise her eyes were open. Holding up his hands to stop the clutch of villagers that were untying her he leant forward.

"Lady Morgan" she looked at him. "Sir Guaen, I feel so tired. What happened? Where are we?" she asked.

"After Merlin departed to Caerleon, ye fainted. I tied ye into a bed suspended between two horses for the journey to Tyntagael. We hath only just now arrived." He explained.

She nodded her understanding. "I feel as though I could sleep for a week" she said.

Guaen went on to explain that he had ordered the preparation of the King's longboat for their journey north but Morgan was not listening. She felt that something was missing; something that she had possessed for years. It was the Minotaur's power that she had taken from the beast. She was certain that it was now all gone. The effort of opening another doorway across the country to Caerleon had drained it of its vigour. Morgan tried to focus instead on what Guaen had been telling her. She looked around, the sun was low on the horizon across the water.

"Shall we leave tonight?" she queried.

Guaen nodded. It was unusual to launch a sea-going journey at night. "We do not know how close the Green Knight is? It would be best to leave as soon as the villagers can prepare the boat."

His outline of their hurried timetable made sense to her. "Let us hope that is before sunset," he added.

Chapter 22: Caerleon Castle, Sunset

Merlin was bemused to be carried back to Caerleon Castle in his miniature form by a large falcon. In all of his years he had never before travelled in such a fashion. The guard that was his mode of transportation had transformed himself into the bird of prey but with blunt claws so that they could grip the old man's arms without hurting him. Not that the faerie silk could be punctured, but it was a small courtesy that he'd appreciated anyway. Merlin was deposited back into his chamber without anyone on the battlement lookouts noticing the unusual sight.

Knowing that his new black faerie silk robes would be able to transform with him to his correct size, he had elected to keep them on whilst casting the spell that would do so. Unlike the ease at which faeries took on new sizes and shapes the transformation had been agony for the sorcerer. He felt tired but wanted to firstly transcribe the spell that gave rise to the Green Knight onto a clean piece of parchment before then reporting his findings to the king. It was sunset before he had completed the task of replicating the words of the spell. Whilst he was doing so, he had tried to interpret it with some small success. Nimue was correct. The spell did seem to be an arrow that once fired had no way of being stopped.

It was time to let King Arthur know what he had learnt from the meeting with Nimue. He stood up and giving the spell one more forlorn look he went to find the King.

***

He found the king seated at the Round Table along with all of the knights that were present in Caerleon at the time. It was clearly a discussion of a forthcoming battle, but he was not aware of any such thing. His appearance muted the conversation that was taking place when he walked in.

"Merlin; come join us," invited Arthur.

Merlin took his place in the seat to Arthur's right hand.

"We hath been inventing ways to deal with the Green Knight should it reappear. What news is there?" inquired the king.

"The Green Knight will appear only upon the fullest face of Gaelach," Merlin responded, "so we need only face him one evening and night per month."

This was good news. It garnered a murmur of approval from the gathered warriors.

"Do we know who this Green Knight is?" asked Sir Lyonell.

Merlin waved away the question. "It is an animated corpse given life for one purpose; to disrupt the rule of King Arthur."

Merlin's announcement brought a flurry of "Who dares do this?" in various iterations from the Knights.

"A former faerie ruler; the same one that conspired with King Aelle to ensure defeat in the battle of Anderidae" replied Merlin. Merlin saw no need for secrecy about the faerie populous in front of the Knights. They had witnessed first-hand the damage that Hellekin had unleashed by siding with Aelle in the battle eight years before.

Arthur interrupted the next burst of questions that ensued from the Knights at Merlin's revelation.

"Former ruler…Merlin?' he said.

"Aye; now deposed and in exile from Briton," explained Merlin.

"Then how will we find him?" asked one of the Knights; Merlin did not see which.

"For now, let us journey to meet with Sir Guaen in Pen Rhionydd before the next full moon," he said. "Lady Morgan and I will try to locate our enemy in the meantime."

For Merlin this was the end of the discussion. Clearly however the Knights wanted to know much more about the situation that they were facing.

Questions were directed at Merlin even as he rose to exit from the battle planning meeting. With a knowing look to the king, Merlin felt that it was best that Arthur take over from this point. Arthur understood the expression on his old sage's face and gave the sorcerer leave to depart.

The evening meal was beginning to be set up by the servants in the Great Hall but Merlin was exhausted. He grabbed the arm of a passing servant and asked for a meal to be sent to his room; thinking that this would be preferential to sitting through an extended session with the court.

It took Merlin longer to climb the great staircase than usual, so tired was he. By the time he made it up the Great Staircase and to his room a servant had arrived close behind him with something for him to eat. Sending the man on his way Merlin carried the tray into his room. There was some hot stew of some description and bread and some boiled eggs. He sat down and contemplated the situation whilst eating. Unless Nimue could use the faeries throughout Briton to help locate Hellekin, he and Morgan had only a little chance of doing so.

A wave of fatigue swept over him and finishing the food, he retired for the evening and fell immediately into a deep sleep.

Chapter 23: Avyze Village, Gaul AD495

Merlin and Morgan were looking at each other with vexed expressions. They were standing opposite each other about twelve or thirteen paces apart. Around them the beautiful daylight shone. People in the village went about their daily lives oblivious to the fact that Sorceress Morgana had returned to the village.

"Where are we?" asked Merlin.

"Avyze Village in Gaul," responded Morgan.

"A shared vision," stated Merlin, certain now that that is what was happening to them both. They looked about. It was an idyllic scene. Nothing seemed out of place. The reason for the vision was as yet unclear.

Making the most of the ability to communicate with Morgan, Merlin walked over to her.

"I hath learnt that the spell of the Green Knight was cast by Hellekin, now in exile from Briton. The creature will only appear upon the full-moon so for the time being ye are both safe," he reported.

"That is welcome news. Sir Guaen and I are on a long boat bound for Galloway. Shall we continue?" said Morgan.

"Aye," said the old man, "It is still mine hope that the presence of the Christians will inhibit the appearance of the Green Knight. Arthur and I will join ye before the next full moon."

Nimue interjected at this point; there was something of importance that she needed to relay to Merlin.

"Mine ability to travel between destinations in no time at all is gone Merlin," she said.

"Surely not?" began Merlin, but Morgan shook her head vigorously.

"The last of it was spent sending ye to Caerleon. Merlin, I am certain it is gone" she concluded.

This was indeed bad news thought Merlin. The power of instantaneous travel was one of the rarest ever practiced by magicians anywhere; few ever mastered it. The fact that Morgan had come across it by stealing the ability from the Minotaur was a stroke of luck. He tried his best to console her.

"Do not be concerned with this at the moment Morgan, there are other matters that need our attentions."

While they were still speaking, there was a small gathering of women nearby. They seemed a little excited as they chatted to each other in Gaulish and looked past Morgan and Merlin to something just beyond the borders of the village. Seeing the small commotion Morgan and Merlin turned around to see what it was that had caught the attention of the women. It was Hellekin. He was walking brazenly into the village as if he did not have a care in the world. His trajectory was taking him straight toward Morgan and Merlin. They froze at the sight of him.

"Is this another threat?" began Morgan. But the focus of Hellekin's eyes seemed to be on the women rather than on his adversaries.

Acting upon that information and assuming that he was part of the vision rather than the active proponent within it, Merlin said, "stand fast Morgan."

Morgan could not believe her ears. Hellekin was about to collide with them, he must have been blind or something because he was not slowing or altering his course. Morgan was about to object when Hellekin walked right through the both of them as if they were not even there.

Realising what had already occurred to Merlin, Morgan also satisfied herself to simply watch what was going on.

"Do ye think that this is the future or the past?" asked Morgan.

"The past" answered Merlin.

Morgan did not question how Merlin knew the answer; she simply accepted it as fact. They were experiencing this retelling of a past occurrence for a reason.

Hellekin reached the small gathering of village women.

"Greetings" he said in perfect Gaulish. "I am a weary traveller that is in need of a good meal, is there somewhere that I may eat?"

This invoked a chorus of giggles from the women clearly infatuated with the handsome stranger in the odd clothing.

"Surely sir, there is a tavern yonder" said what appeared to be the youngest of the troupe; a girl of perhaps sixteen or seventeen years. She pointed to the very tavern that Morgan and Gwenhwyvar had spent so much time in whilst healing the sick and injured in the village.

"Mine gratitude lovely ladies; perhaps I shall see ye there later on?" he said shamelessly flirting with all of them at once.

This provoked another chorus of giggles from the women. Hellekin gave them a broad smile and proceeded toward the tavern.

"Let us follow him" suggested Merlin. The sorcerer and sorceress set a pace to fall in behind the faerie and shadowed him to the tavern. Entering they ensured that they scurried in behind him before the door was closed.

Hellekin attracted the attention of everyone in the small tavern. He cut quite a handsome and athletic figure in his faerie silk robes. His flawless skin and perfect teeth, smiling at everyone, ensured that he stood out from the small crowd. Not to mention the unreal beauty that made up the entire faerie populous. He was sure to turn heads wherever he went.

"Some food mine good man," he said with a benign smile to the tavern owner.

"That is Garrone, the owner of this inn" said Morgan, identifying the man for Merlin. Garrone for his part gestured to a free table which Hellekin dutifully took a seat at.

The crowd turned back to their various conversations, and tried to not make it too obvious that the new centre of all of their conversations was the stranger in their midst. Garrone quickly served up some stew, bread and cheese on a tray with a cup of wine and delivered it to Hellekin.

"What is he doing here?" asked Merlin rhetorically.

Morgan was about to admit to her inability to fathom his presence in the village when time dissipated around them. Suddenly it was night and the inn was full of people. Hellekin had long finished his meal and was regaling a crowd of the villagers with the tales of his travels.

"The hideous creatures that inhabit the night in Greece dare not be spoken of…" he said, lowering his voice for effect. He portrayed an expression of wonderment and continued "The Hydra that lives in the sea just offshore from the city of Pireas in Greece is a fearsome creature that swallows long boats whole."

The drama in his voice coupled with the thought of a mythical creature devouring a boat full of sailors produced a collective gasp from the crowd. He had them completely in his thrall.

"Ye hath seen this beast?" asked one of the crowd. "Aye, with mine very own eyes, and lived to tell the tale." He boasted.

"What lies is he spinning?" asked Morgan. "Does he hope to tell children's stories to pay for his food and lodgings?" she said, the scorn obvious in her tone. "Patience," cautioned Merlin. "There is a reason that we are experiencing this vision. Let it sail its course so that we may find its destination," he concluded.

And so it continued for an obnoxiously long time, or so Morgan thought. Hellekin told story after story of his adventures in far off lands that the humble villagers had no hope of ever seeing. Eventually the crown dwindled as the night wore on and only a small clutch of people remained to listen to the self-obsessed former king of the faerie people of Briton. There was one though that was listening more intently. It was the young girl that had given Hellekin directions previously. They were glancing longingly at each other through the story telling. Once more time sped up and the scene around Morgan and Merlin altered.

Now they were in one of the village huts. It was the one inhabited by the young girl. She and Hellekin were engaged in rambunctious sex in her bed. The noise of love-making filled the room.

"It would seem that Hellekin found a warm bed for the night," observed Merlin wryly.

"Hmm," replied Morgan in a disapproving tone. Morgan and Merlin were a little embarrassed to be voyeurs in the current situation. They looked around to see if there was something else in the small dwelling to distract them. The "Oohh's" and "Aahhh's" from the two engaged in sex made it difficult to focus on anything else. Eventually they contented themselves with looking at each other so as not to see the scene being acted out on the nearby bed. After too long a time Hellekin reached climax and the noises settled down to a peaceful deep breathing.

There was some small talk that began, but Hellekin seemed to be more interested in discussing something that the girl had told him.

"Now Mirim; I hath told ye everything I know about monsters in far-away lands; tell me of the creature that haunts Avyze village?"

This got Morgan and Merlin's attention. The young girl, now identified as Mirim sought to tease Hellekin before delivering the closely guarded information to the handsome stranger.

"What more will ye give me to reveal what I know about the beast?" she smiled.

Hellekin stroked her breasts gently and licked each of her nipples in turn.

"More of what ye want the most my dear Mirim" he said, the licentiousness apparent to all in the room. Mirim giggled. "Now tell me" he insisted.

Rolling her eyes and sighing before she began Mirim answered.

"For years, a hideous creature that none of us had seen devoured a traveller or a villager, one per year, but then a great sorceress called Morgana visited our village. She led a band of brave village men and together they slew the beast. Half man, half bull, it was.; horrible to look at, emitting the foulest of odours. But now it is dead and the village has tried to cover up the very existence of it. They want to forget about it like it never happened. But I think that it is a wonderful story to pass on to our children; the day that the Avyze villagers killed the beast in the caves." She finished an over simplified summation of the story.

Morgan was less than impressed.

"The story now seems to favour the villagers that abandoned us in the labyrinth" she observed indignantly.

Merlin tried to give her an insight as to why the story had been altered to favour the villagers.

"Morgan if the story was that the village men ran screaming and left two women to battle the beast..." he did not need to finish the explanation. Morgan knew only too well that the pride of the men in the village would not allow them to tell the entire truth.

Hellekin was insisting that Mirim show him the caves but she was resistant to the very idea.

"No, no, no, the lair of the beast is forbidden!" she insisted.

Hellekin did not want to hear what he could not do.

"I will be there to protect ye from any harm. And what harm could there be? The beast is dead. It will be exciting. We can make love where it once roamed. Think of the thrill" he said enticingly.

He must have been very persuasive because the scene altered around Merlin and Morgan once more. Now they were at the mouth of the Minotaur's cave. It was morning. Hellekin and Mirim were approaching them. They must have left well before sunrise to make it to the caves this early in the morning. The sun had only just risen and was lighting the fields and trees around them. Hellekin was practically dragging Mirim the last part of the way. He was being boyish and teasing her for her fears. The goading was effective because it was overcoming Mirim's better judgement and she entered the caves with Hellekin.

Morgan and Merlin followed them.

"This is not going to end well," ventured Morgan.

"Aye" responded Merlin.

The sorceress and sorcerer shadowed Hellekin and Mirim through the caves. Hellekin had made a makeshift flaming torch from a stick of wood and something that he had produced from his robes. It was uncannily bright for the size of the flame. Merlin and Morgan guessed that it was some sort of faerie spell that made a particularly bright light from a naked flame.

The passage ways turned this way and that, and soon Mirim was fearful of finding their way back to the entrance.

"Hellekin let us go back. We have seen the caves now," she was clearly concerned and was looking back the way that they had come hoping somehow to see a clue that would lead to the exit. Hellekin held her hand tightly and pulled her forward,

"Just a little way more Mirim; do not be afraid." But his tone lacked conviction.

Then they found the arched entrance to the centre chamber of the Labyrinth. Hellekin stopped it looked as though he could hear something. Mirim challenged him,

"Can ye hear something?" she said almost panicked.

"No" he said, "look!"

He pointed through the archway. The glow-worms could be seen lighting the interior. The wondrous sight made Mirim temporarily forget her fears. She gingerly stepped through the archway captivated by the sight on the high vaulted cave ceiling above her. Hellekin followed but his attentions were elsewhere. Mirim had wondered almost to the middle of the chamber before she looked downwards and saw the prone form of the Minotaur lying upon the ground.

She screamed and jumped with terror. Hellekin seemingly embraced her in his arms. The uncharacteristic show of comfort made Merlin and Morgan look at each other in surprise. But all three of them were mistaken. Hellekin was not offering Mirim a sympathetic and reassuring embrace. Instead he lifted her and carried her toward the Minotaur. Realising what was happening Mirim screamed anew. She kicked and struggled against her captor.

"What are ye doing?" she pleaded. "Do not take me near that hideous thing!" but her pleas fell upon deaf ears.

With an almighty push her hurled Mirim down on the ground she landed on her hands and knees just in front of the beast. Its bulging arm struck out and grabbed Mirim around her throat. Lightning shot from Mirim's open and screaming mouth and into the Minotaur. Mirim's scream tapered off as her body wizened and lost cohesiveness. The entire life force of Mirim was drained by the Minotaur in hardly any time at all. What was left oozed out of his hand and dropped on to the floor of the cave.

Disgusted by what they had just witnessed Morgan and Merlin could not help but turn away.

"What possible reason could he hath to do such a wicked thing?" asked Morgan, angry at seeing such a young life extinguished before her eyes.

"It will be to benefit Hellekin, somehow" answered Merlin. He had just finished speaking when the Minotaur's voice filled the cavern. "Come closer" he said to Hellekin.

"Come closer and hath ye drain mine life force?" Hellekin said mockingly to the prone creature, "I think not Minotaur. What if I did, what then? How much longer would ye hath to wait for some explorer to wander into thine labyrinth? What if another does not come for a year; two years? How much longer can ye wait between meals?" Hellekin paused for effect before delivering his reason for being here. "What if I were to supply ye with as many humans as ye require to regain thine strength. What reward would I receive?"

Still unable to move the Minotaur managed to open its eyes and try to look in the direction of Hellekin. "Ye are a faerie" he boomed. "Aye" confirmed Hellekin. "I hath heard stories of the Minotaur since I was a child. The faerie turned into a human-devouring beast. I did not think them to be true before coming to Gaul. But there are so many that speak of the legend of the man with a bull's head, I knew that it had to be true."

"What do ye want in return for more people so that I may feed?" asked the Minotaur without any feeling in his voice whatsoever. Hellekin crouched down so that the beast could see him.

"I want help in destroying the Sorceress that nearly destroyed ye, and her lover, and her brother King Arthur, and his entire court!" Hellekin spat the words forth vehemently.

Hellekin's accomplice was revealed. He had forged an alliance with the critically injured Minotaur. Hellekin would see to the beast's return to health by feeding it unsuspecting prey, in return for help in his revenge against Morgan, Merlin, Arthur and his Knights; and it was all starting with Sir Guaen. Merlin thought quickly.

"With the Minotaur returned to vigour, we do not know the extent of its power? And now allied with Hellekin, they could be too much for us to overthrow!" he was not ashamed to let Morgan know how worried he was about the situation facing them.

He did not have time to elaborate upon his fears. It was morning in Caerleon and the light was streaming through his window. Merlin sat upright in bed. The vision was over. He had spent the entire night in it with Morgan. Now he was alone in his chamber high up in Caerleon Castle.

Realisation dawned upon him. Merlin was facing the most powerful magical enemies of his entire life. Morgan's powers were depleted; his own, no longer the force that they once were. What was he to do?

Chapter 24: Pen Rhionydd; One Week Later

Sir Guaen had proven himself to be an excellent leader on the boat journey up the coast from Tyntagael to Galloway. He had successfully navigated, with favourable winds, the coast past Mynyw castle in Wales and up past Northumbria, North Rheged and to the coast of Galloway. Then skilfully entering the mouth of the river Deea, he had managed, with the help of the oarsmen to push the boat half of the way to Pen Rhionydd. Eventually though the current of the river proved too much and they had to make land-fall, walking the rest of the way.

Sir Bors De Ganys was acting as Arthur's representative for this part of the year. He was surprised to see Sir Guaen approaching the township, but more surprised to see that he was with Lady Morgan Le Fay and a troop of oarsmen wearing the Cellewig coat of arms. He'd listened with awe as they described their adventures beginning with the appearance of the Green Knight and the ensuing race to Cellewig and then Tyntagael. The part of the recounting of the story that encompassed the Lady of the Lake was omitted completely.

They were in Maelgyn's house, just the four of them. Sir Bors De Ganys was struggling to understand some of the detail surrounding the situation.

"So, this corpse can only appear when the face of Gaelach is at her fullest?" he asked, describing the full moon.

"Aye," answered Guaen and Morgan in unison.

"And when this next happens the Knight will appear once more to try again to slay Sir Guaen. And if it is successful then he will turn his revile against another of Arthur's knights?" he finished off his questions realising that he was the only of Arthur's knights currently present.

Easily guessing his thoughts Morgan interjected.

"King Arthur will be here before the next rising of the moon and the Green Knight."

Her words helped settle the feeling of ill in Sir Bors De Ganys. Maelgyn was listening intently to all of this with wide eyes.

"A magical creature called a…faerie, has allied itself with a creature from Greek mythology and caused a long dead Knight to rise in order to topple King Arthur by murdering his Knights one by one."

Maelgyn's sudden interruption startled everyone. He'd been so intensely quiet since they'd entered his home and took seats to discuss the reasons why Sir Guaen and Lady Morgan had come to Pen Rhionydd. The expression on his face gave everything away. He didn't believe a word of it.

Guaen and Morgan looked at each other as if to say, who is going to answer his scepticism? Sir Guaen attempted to do so.

"Maelgyn, Merlin and Lady Morgan perform feats of magic all the time….in any place other than Galloway."

He spluttered his explanation to its conclusion. Suddenly the good intention of his clarification seemed to lack veracity. He groaned at hearing the silliness of his own words.

"Would the dear lady care to perform a feat of ....*magic* for us?" asked Maelgyn looking at Morgan for a response; clearly not convinced of the existence of any such thing.

She tried her best not to roll her eyes. It was going to be impossible to persuade anyone here in Pen Rhionydd that she was capable of such feats when the very presence of so many Christians seemed to nullify any magical abilities.

"Maelgyn please; have faith that we are speaking the truth. It is Merlin's hope that the Green Knight will suffer the same magic suppressing circumstance that pervades life here in the township."

Her response carefully integrated the use of the word *faith*, in the hope that it would prevent him from simply disbelieving because he could not see proof with his own eyes.

She was correct in her assumption. Maelgyn held up his hands as if to surrender his active disbelief. Instead he altered the subject to one that he was sure that he could cope with.

"King Arthur will be joining us; excellent. We shall make preparations to greet him...before the next full moon." He winked at the trio. Standing up he made his way to the door and turned around. "We look forward to seeing our King again. It has been quite some time since he came to visit us."

With a genuine smile, he gave a small courteous bow to those remaining and exited.

The trio all looked at each other wondering what to say next. Sir Bors De Ganys broke the silence.

"One thing is certain Sir Guaen – until the next full moon ye are safe."

Both Morgan and Guaen each breathed an audible sigh of relief.

Chapter 25: Pen Rhionydd, the Evening of the Full Moon

King Arthur had arrived only two days before the next full moon, with six of his knights. At first Sirs Guaen and Bors De Ganys thought that it was too few. But Arthur explained that the news of the Green Knight had spread throughout his kingdom and beyond. Most of the other Knights were on short errands to the far corners of his domain spreading the word that King Arthur was still king and would find a way to defeat the Green Knight. He wanted to assure his people that there was nothing wrong, at least nothing that he couldn't deal with; and that he was still a strong ruler dedicated to uniting the land.

Merlin accompanied them as he said he would. He had dedicated his time since last communicating with Morgan to searching his scrolls for any assistance that he could. Nothing he found could help. He had sat through endless planning sessions with Arthur and his Knights on potential ways to restrain or otherwise stop the Green Knight from killing Sir Guaen and then turning on one of the other Knights.

Some ideas had to be set up. First, a boat had been prepared for Sir Guaen it was hoped that the Green Knight could not swim and would find the river running through the township unpassable. A rope tied to it and spanning the entire width of the river ensured that a willing band of helpers could pull Sir Guaen into the middle of the river if required, and back to shore if necessary.

Morgan and Merlin had spent a lot of time talking together. Sir Guaen was initially interested to join them but as the day of the full moon approached he became more and more distracted and agitated. It was difficult to tell if he had slept the previous night at all, he looked so ragged. Both tried over and over to calm him with the thought that the Green Knight, animated by magic, was almost sure to not be able to appear in the midst of a Christian settlement.

The day sped by in a way that none of them had encountered before. It was still Elembiuos, or as the Christians insisted, the month of Julius. The days were meant to be long and warm and sunny. But no matter how pleasant the weather none of the visitors from Caerleon seemed to notice. The day began and suddenly it was late afternoon heading into evening. Soon Gaelach would appear in the soft evening light of the sky and the terror of the Green Knight would begin again.

It seemed all of the Pen Rhionydd inhabitants were outside. They were curious to see this dead Knight for themselves, although almost all of them doubted that such a thing could exist. They were almost patronisingly reassuring all of the anxious visitors from Caerleon. Sir Guaen was standing with King Arthur, Merlin and Morgan on the stone bridge that straddled the River Deea, which divided the township into two equal halves.

"It won't be long now," observed Arthur. They all looked up at the sky, searching for the first sign of the moon. With his expert knowledge of astronomy, it was Merlin that was looking in precisely the correct spot for the appearance of the moon. The smallest bent line of glowing yellow could be seen on the horizon.

"There!" he shouted pointing with his finger and outstretched arm. Sir Guaen's heart missed a beat. They followed Merlin's direction. For sure, there it was, creeping up slowly above the horizon, now clearer than before.

"Be on guard, Gaelach rises!" shouted Arthur to his Knights.

They were positioned either side of the bridge. The rising of the moon took an amazingly short time. Being on the horizon as it was, it was large, much larger than any of them had seen for many months. Bit by bit it made its presence clear. Soon over half of it was visible.

There was silence in the village. The people had stopped moving and talking picking up on the uneasiness of the Knights and the King. Everyone stood as if transfixed with the image of the moon becoming fuller and fuller with every passing moment.

Then it was done, Gaelach fully visible, her bright face shining across the horizon to the township. There was a moment of absolute nothingness, then a shout from one of the Knights. The head of the Green Knight had broken the surface of the River Deea close to the shore of the left-hand bank. A crowd surged forward to see what was coming out of the river. Sir Guan felt his heart sink down into the pit of his stomach. It walked out of the water the same hideous Green

Knight that had terrorised them a month ago. Now it was here in the middle of Pen Rhionydd with only one objective – to kill Sir Guaen.

Chapter 26: The Second Apparition

Knights drew their swords in anticipation of another spirited battle with the daemon. The Knights that had been on the right-hand side of the bridge ran to the left and down the embankment to meet the threat head-on. Together the Knights, minus Sir Guaen, formed a semi-circle around the decaying corpse. It paused looking at the wall of humanity stopping it from reaching its prey.

In a moment that sent shivers up the spines of everyone watching, it turned its head to cast its dead eyes upwards on the bridge directly at Sir Guaen. With sword at the ready and with a blood-chilling scream it lunged at the nearest Knight with superhuman strength and speed and slashed the shoulder of the man. He screamed in agony as the sword penetrated his chainmail and cut a bloody gash in to his anterior-deltoid. With a mighty push the Green Knight knocked over the injured man and ran past the defensive band of Knights toward the bridge.

Arthur turned and pushed Guaen the other way.

"The boat!" he screamed at the terrified Knight.

It was poor judgement in the horror of the moment. Arthur had somehow convinced himself that the Green Knight would not be able to come into the land of Galloway, for the same reasons that Merlin and Morgan's magic did not seem to work here. If he had been thinking correctly he would never have sent Guaen to the boat and the perceived safety of the river from which their enemy had just arose.

Sir Guaen ran in the opposite direction faster than he had ever run before. He covered the half-span of the bridge in seconds. Behind him the Green Knight was being chased by the remaining Knights. However, the creature seemed more agile and faster than their first encounter. One of the Knights, frustrated that he could not catch up with his supernatural quarry, resorted to hurling his sword at him as if it were a spear. The throw was perfect. Had the Green Knight been a human it would have pierced his spine and been a deadly blow; but the Knight's well aimed sword bounced off the hardened-body of the hideous thing.

People everywhere screamed at the terror that they were witnessing. The townsfolk ran away from it in every direction. Sir Guaen slipped on the muddy embankment of the river and fell face first into the mud, sliding the remainder of the way to the moored boat. A foot soldier ran forward and helped the fallen Knight to his feet and into the small boat. It was barely big enough for two or three people.

"Cast off!" shouted Guaen through his muddied face. The soldier pushed the boat with all of his might. It slid into the rapidly moving waters with ease.

"Pull!" shouted Guaen to the men on the opposite side of the river that were manning the rope.

With a perfectly timed team effort the troupe pulled the boat containing Sir Guaen directly out to the middle of the river. A contra-team on the side of the river with the Green Knight ensured the stability of the boat in the rapidly moving waters, holding tight their side of the rope.

The Green Knight ran effortlessly into the water, not tripping or sliding on the wet slippery earth. It waded noisily into the river and was soon submerged. All the people that remained collectively held their breaths. Was it going to be swept away by the force of the river?

Guaen stood on the boat watching the creature submerge. He was panicking. He could hardly breathe. Suddenly, not being able to see the Green Knight was more terrifying than looking directly at it. He looked down into the water. He couldn't see anything. The water was clear enough, but in the diminishing light, it was not so easy to see through.

He looked from one side of the boat to the other; nothing. For just a single moment he felt as if the plan had worked and the river had taken the creature. Then it erupted from the water in a display of unbelievable strength, jumped clear of the water and landed in the boat with Guaen.

He stood paralysed for a second facing the greatest fear he had ever known. Instinct saved him. The Green Knight went to cut off Sir Guaen's head with a single blow, but Guaen automatically countered with a thrust that took all of the effort that his muscles could give. It was clear that the Green Knight was much stronger than the last time they'd fought. Thinking in a split-second that he would stand no chance against the stronger enemy on a rocking boat in the middle of a fast-moving river, Guaen looked for another way to extricate himself from the situation.

Again, the Green Knight made a sweeping blow and by ducking it, Sir Guaen was inspired in that brief moment on how to achieve his goal. He felt the swing of the blade swoop over his head and shoulders as he neatly ducked it. He was in a perfect position to grab one of the ankles of his adversary so he did so; and with a huge pull, pushed the Green Knight off his balance.

The fearsome warrior tumbled backwards into the water. A huge splash followed. Momentarily relieved, Guaen looked around for inspiration on what to do next. He could n't swim back to shore. He was wearing chainmail and would sink to the bottom of the river.

The fracas, however, had distracted him from what was happening onshore. Merlin had ordered the men to pull him over to the left bank so that he could at least receive help from the other waiting Knights. It took Guaen a moment to realise that he was in fact much closer to the shore than he had been when the Green Knight first jumped into the boat with him.

Merlin and Arthur and the Knights were shouting various things to each other, but it was lost on Guaen. The blood was pumping in his veins so hard that it obscured his hearing with the sound of the pulse in his head. Merlin was signalling frantically to Guaen, beckoning him from the boat and pointing to something further up the embankment.

He was almost ashore by now and the beating of his heart returning to a level that allowed him to hear once more.

Again, Merlin was shouting. "Guaen, the horse escape route!”

He followed the pointing arm and finger of the frantic old man. A steed was waiting for him. The second contingency plan dawned on Guaen like the brightest day. On their way to Galloway, Arthur and his Knights positioned a series of horses, tended to by foot soldiers, each of them positioned a hard ride from the other. There were not enough to get him all the way back to Caerleon, but there were enough to give him rapid egress from the immediate area of the Green Knight. And certainly, enough to ensure that he could ride almost continually throughout the night until the moon was no longer able to be seen; and the Green Knight would disappear for another month.

As Guaen jumped off the boat and sloshed onto the mud, he briefly entertained the thought that this could be the way that he would have to spend the remainder of his days. Riding away from the horror of the Green Knight; it was a soul-crushing idea.

"Hurry; hurry; to the first horse!" Merlin was shouting at him. "Leave the Green Knight to us.”

Guaen needed not further encouragement he ran up the hill almost slipping over twice but made it safely to the horse. The horse's attendant assisted the Knight onto the steed. Grabbing the reins tightly and digging his heels into the flanks of the horse Guaen bellowed a loud "HAAA!" to the horse as he forced it into motion.

At that very moment, the Green Knight came charging out of the water. The Knights formed a line between the departing Guaen and the Green Knight. The sound of the horse's hooves pounding the earth could clearly be heard. All of the Knights steeled themselves for another epic battle. The Green Knight looked at the rapidly departing Guaen and then at the line of Knights between him and his quarry. It was angry and being denied its prize yet again and let out a scream that lasted longer than human lungs would be capable of producing. It was actually shaking with rage.

"Hold true!" called out one of the Knights to his compatriots.

The Green Knight looked around at the scene. There were the three soldiers nearby that had pulled the boat ashore. They were unarmed. Racing forward the Green Knight bellowed again and raised his sword. In a stomach-churning feat of super human strength he swung his sword at the nearest of the soldiers and split the man from head, straight down the middle, to his testicles and into two equal pieces. The two halves of the man separated and fell one to each side of where he'd stood.

A couple of the Knights actually screamed with shock. The remaining soldiers scrambled to get as far away from the Green Knight as possible. But there was no need. The Green Knight had become absolutely still.

Merlin was flummoxed. The Green Knight was supposed to only attack Sir Guaen and then when he was killed, the other Knights of the Round Table one by one until there were none left. This action did not make sense.

Then something happened that nobody could have possibly predicted. The Green Knight turned his sword upon himself. Holding it firmly with both hands, he did the exact opposite cut upon his own body that he had just inflicted on the unsuspecting soldier. But this time it was slow and deliberate. Starting at his crotch he pulled the sword up and began to sever himself.

Everybody was absolutely aghast at the horrific sight. It seemed to take longer than it actually did because the scene was so incredibly revolting. The sound of the dead flesh being cut filled the air. The Knight had cut now up through his stomach and into the centre of his ribcage. Repositioning his arms on his sword handle so that he could get better leverage, he continued to cut upwards through his neck and head. The Knight's metal helmet covering his decayed face split perfectly into two at the bridge nose piece. The final push of the sword breaking through the top of the head and helmet of the Knight produced a spray of black blood that spurted upwards in a small grotesque fountain.

Just like the soldier, the Green Knight fell into two halves. Unlike the soldier whose blood and internal organs were red and normal looking, the interior of the Green Knight was a mixture of black and green ooze. The lichens and moss that covered the exterior of his hideous body continued through to the interior of the creature.

There was absolute shocked silence from everybody. Merlin was stunned beyond his own comprehension. He was just allowing himself to think that the beast had self-destructed out of anger for the inability to achieve his goal, when the now familiar columns of light appeared, dashing his foolish hope. This time though, instead of attracting the fallen pieces of the Green Knight, the right-hand side shot a column of light to the left-hand side of the murdered soldier, and vice versa. Merlin and Morgan shot a knowing look to each other. They realised immediately what was happening. The right-hand side of the Green Knight formed with the left-hand side of the sacrificed soldier. The left-hand side of the Green Knight did the same the with the right side of the soldier's body.

Watching in a horror that none of them had before experienced, the parts came together to form two beings. Both twitched and made and effort to stand up. The ring of Knights began to walk backwards unable to face the fear of what was happening. One of the creatures made it to his feet. The soldier-side of the body was changing before their eyes. The Helmet grew from one side of the Knight's face and covered the side that was bare. This happened to the clothing and chainmail too. Before they knew it there were two exact images of the Green Knight standing there with them. Somehow the side that did not have a sword now possessed one.

This was too much to handle. Both of the Green Knights moved toward Arthur's Knights. Merlin was almost too stunned to shout orders to them. He kept shaking his head as if to deny what he had just witnessed. Arthur saved him the bother of trying to take charge of the situation.

"Stand aside, Knights, stand aside!" he shouted from his vantage point on the bridge, from where he had witnessed all of the happenings.

The Knights did not need much encouragement from their King. Holding their swords as best as they could to fend off any surprise attack, like the one they had just seen, they allowed both of the apparitions to begin their pursuit of Sir Guaen.

Merlin ran back up to the bridge to Arthur and Morgan. For a moment, they were all at a loss for words. How could they deal with what had just happened? Merlin was still occasionally shaking his head in disbelief. Arthur had never before seen Merlin so completely at a loss for words or action. It worried him deeply.

Morgan broke the brief stunned silence.

"Did Nimue say anything about the Green Knight being able to…to…replicate itself!?" She said.

"No; no, no" was all that he could say in reply.

"Now we hath two of these evil things chasing Sir Guaen," observed Arthur trying to face the situation in the way that a good military commander would – assess the situation and find the best course of action.

"But, the escape route of horses will keep Guaen ahead of them until morning at least, and probably more if he is not too sore to keep riding." Arthur finished his summation. It was strangely comforting to both Morgan and Merlin.

"Aye" said Merlin. "No matter how sore Sir Guaen is from nearly constant riding, he will endure it rather than admit defeat and allow the Green Knight…Knights to catch him."

Morgan joined in. "Then we have only one more month to find the whereabouts of Hellekin and the Minotaur so that we may have at least some chance of ending this evilness." That was the key to the matter.

Morgan's words seemed to give them all relief. A lot can happen in a month. They may have a vision of the whereabouts of the evil doer. But if not, what then? Merlin gave his thoughts to them,

"I shall return to the faerie forest and see if Nimue hath survived the judgement of the faerie elders; if so she may yet be able to assist us with finding our enemies."

It was a faint hope, but it was all that he could manage to think of in the circumstances. What he did not let on was that if Nimue was able somehow to help them locate Hellekin and the Minotaur, what then? Only Excalibur could pierce the flesh of the beast, and now in league with Hellekin, who knows what they would be capable of.

"The magic that Hellekin and the Minotaur are using is so powerful that it can walk amongst these Christians."

He stopped himself from continuing to voice his concern. He was worried that it would reveal to Arthur and Morgan that he was in absolute fear of having no idea how to fight these two powerful enemies. Instead he opted to distract them from his unguarded sentence.

"We should return to Caerleon at first light tomorrow." Arthur nodded his agreement and moved off to give directions to his Knights.

Chapter 27: Caerleon Castle, Four Days Later

The comparative safely of the remaining days before the next full moon gave Caerleon an air of restored calm. People went about their business as if nothing had happened, but everywhere, there was talk in low tones about 'it' and when it would return.

Merlin and Morgan were in Merlin's chamber wracking their brains for solutions to the problem. Merlin had not yet had the opportunity to seek out Nimue to find out her disposition and scavenge for further information about the Green Knight, especially any ideas she had about stopping it. Merlin was half-listening to Morgan's latest suggestion about restraining the daemon in a custom-made iron cage and sinking him in the sea between Briton and Gaul. She completed outlining her plan and waited for a reaction; nothing.

"Well Merlin?" she said snapping him out of his thoughts.

"Ahhhhhhh!" he said in reply, realising that he had not heard enough of the detail to form a suitable opinion.

Morgan guessed that he had had his mind on other things and looked cross.

"Merlin, we are facing a problem that will repeat until it destroys Arthur's entire court; at least *try* to listen to mine suggestions." Morgan's scalding had the desired effect. He looked apologetic.

"Forgive me Morgan" he said, "I hath been thinking more and more that if Nimue cannot help us with more information about the Green Knight or the whereabouts of Hellekin, then we may not find a solution to the problem in time."

Merlin was about to end his procrastination and announce that he would this very minute leave for the faerie forest when a loud knock at his door interrupted him.

"Come!" he shouted.

The door opened and standing there was one of the soldiers. He looked a little nervous at having to disturb the Castle magicians during their deliberations.

"Merlin, King Arthur hath received a messenger from Humber; he wishes ye to join him at the Round Table."

The soldier delivered his communication and waited for a response. This was interesting news thought Merlin; a dispatch from a peninsula to the east of Northumbria that had long made noises about abdicating to Arthur's rule and joining his Kingdom.

"I shall come immediately," he responded and made to stand up from his wooden stool.

"Shall I accompany ye?" asked Morgan.

Merlin answered by pulling out a blank piece of parchment from a pile on his desk. He deposited it in front of Morgan and said,

"Draw me the cage that ye were speaking of; we shall ask the ironmonger how long it would take to construct."

Morgan reached for the parchment whilst nodding and saying that she would do as he instructed.

***

By the time that Merlin made his way to the ground level and into the Round Table room the knights were in a furore. The tone was one of shock and disbelief. Some of them were shouting and banging the table. Arthur saw Merlin enter and called for quiet.

"What news King Arthur," asked Merlin as he made his way to his normal seat.

"King Pellehan of Humbor hath sent a messenger."

Arthur held out the scroll for Merlin to take. Merlin unfurled it and read it. There was a brief silence. The Knights in the room watched the expression on Merlin's face turn from concentration to incredulity.

"He will no longer join thine Kingdom?!" he said half way through the text.

"Fear of the reprisals from the Green Knight?!"

Merlin dropped the scroll to the table and clutched his face in his hands. Arthur summarised the situation.

"The Green Knight hath not yet succeeded in killing Sir Guaen, but he hath succeeded thwarting mine attempts to further unite our land!"

Arthur slammed his hand down in anger on the table surface.

"The damage that this dead Knight is now doing reaches beyond his appearances every full-moon. This was to be an easy assimilation; peaceful and with the blessing of a king that although he hath blood from an Angle mother, is a king of Briton; ruling native people. Pellehan's Knights were to join us here in Caerleon, and he was to act as regent for the land representing mine rule. Now it is all gone. He will live out his days independent from us."

King Arthur was still talking when Sir Alynore spoke up.

"We should invade sire, and take the land, they could not hope to put enough of a fight to resist us."

This only served to make Arthur angrier.

"Invade a land of Britons!? Are ye mad! I will not hath Britons killing Britons for any amount of land or conquest. He should want to be part of a united kingdom; not subjugated to be so!"

Arthur turned once more to Merlin hoping that he would offer some solace.

"What further damage will the Green Knight do Merlin?" Although a rhetorical question Merlin felt compelled to answer and to try and say something that would calm Arthur down.

"I shall leave immediately for the faerie forest Arthur and seek further information from Queen Nimue. There must be something more that she can tell us about how to end this nightmare."

He had just finished his sentence when a white dove came flapping loudly down from somewhere above them. It shimmered with light and turned into a beautiful woman. This caused the Knights and even King Arthur to jump up from their chairs in fright. Some even reached for their swords. But the woman held up her hand to quell them.

Merlin was equally surprised.

"Nimue!?" he said.

Knights looked from Merlin to the woman. Arthur was at a loss for words.

"Greetings King Arthur, I am Queen Nimue of the faerie people of Briton."

It was a formal greeting meant more for the gathered Knights than for the King. Arthur had met Nimue years ago when Morgan and Gwenhwyvar recovered Excalibur. Merlin had presented her with a memory stone of information provided by the Lady of the Lake, Matrona. Of course in those days, Nimue was not the Queen of the faeries.

He did his best to nod an acceptance of her greeting and to return the salutation.

"Welcome Queen Nimue. It would appear that ye hath saved Merlin a journey to thine forest."

It was not much of a reply but it was the best that Arthur could do under the circumstances.

"What brings ye to Caerleon Castle?" he asked.

"I hath come to offer the assistance of the faerie people of Briton. We recognise that our former corrupt leader is responsible for the appearance of the Green Knight, and I share a personal measure of accountability in this state of affairs."

Her tone was regal and her gaze unyielding. The part about her own blame in the situation would have raised more questions from everyone except they were so astonished at what they were hearing. She continued without pausing.

"Although there is no magical spell that we hath found that can defeat the Green Knight, it is mine belief that the combined magic of Merlin, Morgan and myself can locate the villain. Find the perpetrator of this heinous crime and ye shall find the answer to defeat it."

It was a tempting thought. Merlin wanted to know so much at this point, but did not want to talk openly in front of the Knights.

Something occurred to him. He had not felt Nimue's presence in the room with them before she appeared. Surely, she was watching them in the shape of a dove for a while before making herself known.

Maybe this was part of being Queen; her abilities may very well have evolved to a point where she can hide her presence from him. That too was a tempting thought; to combine her powers with theirs, it may be the only viable solution that they would have.

"Nimue, hath none of thine subjects seen Hellekin in the land, anywhere?"

"Not a single one Merlin" she replied, "He hides somewhere that only our magic can uncover."

The stunned silence of the Knights helped Arthur think through the pros and cons of the offer. He did not answer immediately. Instead he offered Nimue the chair to his left-hand side.

"Please Queen Nimue, be seated."

The Knight that had been sitting there, pulled out the high-backed chair allowing Nimue a graceful seat. She sat and looked directly into Arthur's eyes, now moving to sit in his usual chair. Arthur was thinking that he would take Nimue up on her offer, but continue to plan for the next appearance of the Green Knight anyway.

"Ye are a persuasive orator Queen Nimue and the offer is too enticing to refuse," he smiled his acceptance.

"Good," replied Nimue, "Call for Lady Morgan and send the Knights away, there is much to do."

Although somewhat abrupt, Arthur could think of no reason to not do exactly as she had asked. He signalled to one of the soldiers standing at the doorway to fetch Morgan. It was the same one that had gone to fetch Merlin only minutes before.

The Knights of the Round Table however were not going to be dispatched so easily. They began to murmur their resistance to leaving the King with this faerie Queen that had appeared from nowhere. But the scowl on Merlin's face and the gentle shake of Arthur's head was enough to stymie their collective objection. They exited bowing to the King and giving a stiff nod to the visiting Queen as they did so.

Chapter 28: The Three Magicians

Morgan looked like she had run all of the way to the Hall upon hearing the news. It was true; sitting at the Round Table was Nimue. Strangely Merlin and Nimue looked like a matched pair in their faerie silk robes. Morgan was not quite sure how she would react to seeing Nimue once again. She was dealing with mixed feelings. On the one hand this was the selfish faerie that had tricked her into sleeping with Arthur and conceiving Mordrede eight years ago. However, Merlin had told her that now that Nimue was Queen of the faeries, she was prepared to give up her life if it would save her people and once more make them fertile and able to produce their own offspring. That was a quality that she did not expect from Nimue. In fact, it was the complete opposite of selfishness. The selflessness of her monarchy was to be admired.

Nimue too, was anxious at once more speaking with Morgan. The last time they had met was charged with negative emotions. Morgan was then, still very angry at her for the deception, the pregnancy, the loss of two of the three boys that would have been born from that union with Arthur. Now of course it was revealed that had two of the triplets not been aborted then Hellekin would not have had the raw material to cast the spell animating the Green Knight. Morgan had even more reason to blame her for the situation that they all found themselves in.

Morgan walked calmly up to the table and said hello to her brother. Then she turned to the visiting Queen.

"Nimue; what brings ye to Caerleon?" There was no note of anger or vitriol in Morgan's question.

"It is hoped that our combined powers can uncover the location of Hellekin so that he can be brought to justice."

The simplicity of Nimue's answer resonated with Morgan. In return Morgan's acceptance of the offer was equally as simple.

"The let us begin at once."

"Move the chairs so that three of us can face each other in a circle and hold hands" said Nimue.

Merlin and Arthur stood up and pushed and pulled their chairs over toward Nimue's. She turned hers around to face theirs. Arthur stood aside knowing that he would not be a part of this magical circle. Merlin and Morgan took their places. They held hands.

"Now we must share our power to see beyond the veil of this place and to that where Hellekin is hiding."

Chapter 29: The Minotaur's Labyrinth - Gaul

It was difficult to place the time of day, or night, or whether or not this was the past or the present. But the combined vision of Morgan, Merlin and Nimue somehow told them that it was the past they were seeing. This was the central chamber of the Minotaur's labyrinth. The stone altar was bathed in the unearthly light from the ceiling full of glow worms, their light impossibly bright for such tiny creatures. Hellekin was having rambunctious sex with a naked woman on the stone. Their animal cries of lust echoed in the chamber.

Morgan, Merlin and Nimue stood only a few paces away comfortable in the knowledge that they were witnessing a vision and would not be able to interact with anybody that they encountered.

"He makes me sick," commented Nimue. It sounded like she was talking to herself and that she had accidentally verbalised her thoughts. Merlin and Morgan did not respond.

At that point Hellekin reached climax and puffed and panted his sweaty body to a halt. Behind them the Minotaur had stealthily entered the chamber. He was only noticed by the three magicians when he walked directly through them and crept up to the altar out of sight of the woman.

"Now, I hath a surprise for ye mine pretty," said Hellekin a malicious smile upon his face. Misinterpreting his smile for one of benevolence the young woman asked eagerly for it to be presented to her.

"What is it Hellekin?" she said.

Hellekin responded by looking up at the Minotaur now only a step away. The woman had to crane her neck at an awkward angle to see what he was looking at. Just as she brought into view the hideous apparition of the Minotaur and began to scream the beast reached out clutching her twisted throat and began the process of draining her life-force forcibly from her body. Her scream stymied, she died in writhing agony as the beast took his fill of her precious energy. The liquefied remains ran over the surface of the altar and down the sides.

Disgusted by having to witness this atrocity the three magicians regarded the pair with distain.

"How many more?" asked Hellekin to the Minotaur.

It growled its response. "Two or three and I shall have repaired mine body completely and replaced the magic that the Sorceress stole from me."

Nimue looked directly at Morgan for an explanation of the Minotaur's words.

"Magic stolen from the Minotaur?" she said incredulously.

She had never heard of such a thing. But Morgan seemed distracted. She was squinting at the Minotaur. Unbeknown to Merlin and Nimue, Morgan could even now see the shimmering outline of the Minotaur's power. His words were true. It was not as bright as it was when she had first seen it, but it was only a few shades duller. Knowing that it would take more human sacrifice in order to get it back to its former glory put Morgan into a dark mood almost instantaneously.

The scene changed around them. They were somewhere in the labyrinth now. Hellekin had a young woman, naked and pushed up against the rock face. He was entering her from behind. There was a repeat of yet another frantic sexual encounter and his eventual gratification. However, this time the scene did not play out entirely the same as with the previous victim. The Minotaur was approaching from behind Hellekin. Checking that the beast was in place Hellekin delivered his sarcastic promise of a surprise once more. But this time instead of simply draining the woman of her life-force the beast took Hellekin's place, and with his huge erection raped the terrified woman. It was a mercy when the Minotaur had finally had his fill of her and ended her life, extending his own.

"Let us depart immediately," said Hellekin, the liquefied remains of the woman still oozing down the cave wall.

Hellekin had put on his faerie silk robes in the blink of an eye. The Minotaur too now was wearing a Greek-style wrap around his waist, also made of faerie silk. Invoking his newly restored power the creature opened up a portal to a place where the sun was shining. The contrast to the darkness of the cave was striking. The Minotaur walked through followed by Hellekin.

The three magicians walked toward the rectangular opening in the fabric of space. In an instant, they were standing on the side of a very steep rocky face, but it was covered with narrow terraces of grass and wild flowers. There was a single stone cottage ahead. This was no-doubt their new lair. It was like a long-house but with walls that looked as if they could withstand a siege from an army. Not that any army could attack them this high on the rock face. It was practically a cliff. Only the various levels of rock acting as terraces along with the grassy parts saved it from being completely unscaleable.

It was windy. The sea far down at the base of the rock-face was turbulent. Even at this distance it could be heard crashing against the rocks below. Various birds normally associated with the coast squawked and flew above them. Merlin and Morgan looked around them in confusion.

"If this is the hiding place of Hellekin, then there is a problem; I do not recognise it," said Morgan.

"Nor I" added Merlin.

They were saved from ignorance by Nimue.

"This is the island of Skellig Mhor" she said identifying the craggy rock.

Now it made sense to Morgan and Merlin.

"Off the coast of Hibernia," said Morgan using the Latin name associated with the land. This was the land of the Gael and the Scotti. "This is a perfect stronghold from which to launch an attack on Briton," said Merlin." Too steep for an invading force by boat to surprise the inhabitants – too remote from the main-land for the Gael or the Scotti to be bothered with. They hath chosen well."

He was still speaking when the three of them found themselves back inside the walls of Caerleon Castle, with Arthur looking at them somewhat vexed.

"Skellig Mhor?" he said. The three magicians realised that they must have been speaking aloud whilst enveloped in their collective vision.

Merlin stood up to summarise what they had learned for Arthur.

"The Minotaur is at full strength. Together they hath taken sanctuary on a rocky outcrop off the cost of the land of the Gael and Scotti. That is why none of Nimue's subjects hath seen Hellekin anywhere in Briton, because he hides outside of its borders. We cannot attack by sea, it would be impossible to land safely on the island; the sea-facing rocks are too dangerous. Besides any attack by sea would be seen long before we could land. They hath the Minotaur to provide instantaneous escape should it be necessary. No…no….no...what we must do is attack him magically and in force."

Merlin was energised. He no longer felt completely helpless. Now that the lair of the enemy was exposed his mind was already working on ways to overthrow their shared adversary. It was impossible not to get caught up in his excitement. Merlin continued his theoretical battle strategy.

"If we can surprise Hellekin, and separate him from the Minotaur then any hope of Hellekin escaping through a portal can be minimised. But we must also stop him from taking on the form of a bird and simply flying away."

He stroked his beard fiercely trying to come up with a solution to the obvious problem.

"And then there is the Minotaur itself. We do not know the depth of its loyalty or gratitude to Hellekin for seeing to its recovery. What if he elects to fight us instead of abandoning Hellekin?"

Morgan interrupted everyone with finality in her voice that sent a shudder through Merlin.

"Leave the Minotaur to me!"

They all looked at her. Morgan had a resolve on her face that seemed to be unquestionable. But it did not stop pragmatic Arthur from wanting to know the details of how she planned to accomplish this miraculous feat.

"Dear sister, how can ye hope to stand against the Minotaur? The last time had it not been for Gwenhwyvar wielding Excalibur, ye life would hath been forfeit. Unless this plan involves me somehow accompanying the invasion force to Skellig Mhor, then how else can the Minotaur be subdued?"

It was another problem that seemed to be insurmountable at first. How indeed could they get Arthur on to the island? It was then that Merlin, Morgan and Arthur realised that they may have made too many assumptions already. Nimue spoke.

"I'm not certain that the faeries will follow me into battle." The news was devastating.

"Why?" asked Arthur and Morgan in unison.

"If it were Hellekin alone, then I am sure that they would attack. They hath me to protect them. Mine powers are greatly increased now as reigning monarch of the faerie people. But his alliance with the Minotaur changes everything. Remember that it is the oldest known faerie other than Matrona. Powerful beyond anything that even I or any other faerie could dream of. They will not want to attack knowing that the beast is involved."

This altered the situation completely. Without a supernatural force to command, Merlin could not see any other way to rid themselves of Hellekin and in turn the Green Knight. Nimue in the meantime had stood to face Morgan.

"How Morgan? How can ye hope to engage the Minotaur in battle? How did ye *steal* power from it previously?"

The questioning was shining a light upon Morgan's own plan forming in her mind. She was planning how to deal with the Minotaur. But it meant revealing more to Nimue than she had wanted to. Looking from Arthur to Merlin to Nimue and realising that in order for the battle plans to progress, she would have to contribute her not yet fully resolved idea. Steeling a breath, she spoke to the trio.

"I saw the power within the Minotaur in our vision, the very same way that I did in Gaul all of those years ago. If the beast can just be distracted briefly, then that is all that I will need to once more strip away its power and make it more open to attack. Will this help ye convince the faeries to join our battle?"

The twists and turns of the planning session were as jagged as the rocky face of Skellig Mhor. Nimue was contemplative. She had never-before heard of any one being able to take powers from another magical being. Yet, she knew better than to question the veracity of this Sorceress. If Morgan said that she can do such a thing, to one of the oldest and most powerful faeries that had ever lived, then she believed her. And yet in her heart Nimue knew that it would not be enough to convince her people to follow her on this quest for justice.

Merlin could see the hesitation in Nimue's face.

Shooting a worried glance at Arthur as if asking for permission for something, he said, "I can give ye the spell of fertility Nimue."

Three shocked faces turned to Merlin.

"How?!" demanded Nimue raising her voice too loudly for the small gathering.

"I saw it in a vision and copied it down, but destroyed when it seemed that the faeries hath had a part in Arthur's defeat at Anderidae. But I could recall it once more. It would take time, I admit, but it could be done. Only if we win in our allied battle against our foe, of course," Merlin added a caveat to the end of his offer, one that he hoped would ensure complete cooperation from the faeries.

Nimue could scarcely believe her ears. The very spell of fertility lost to the faerie people for over two thousand years. Its recovery would be invaluable to the faerie nation.

"And ye would cast the spell for us?" said Nimue leaning forward in anticipation.

"No," he responded. Nimue was exasperated. Merlin was tempting her with the one thing that she as Queen had vowed to spend her reign trying to find. Yet he pulled back the most crucial part of the offer, a sorcerer powerful enough to cast the spell.

"But ye would hath the spell in thine hands once more. That is my final offer Nimue do not presume that ye can ask for any more from me."

Merlin was stern. He secretly regretted needing to offer this to Nimue. If the faerie people found a Magician powerful enough to cast the spell it would mean that Nimue must sacrifice herself in order to supply the raw materials for the spell. Merlin did not want to see that happen. Nor did he really want to give them the spell, as the Lady of the Lake herself seemed to have abandoned the faerie nation; he believed that she had done that for valid reasons.

But he was reticent to face both Hellekin and the Minotaur with only himself and Morgan to battle against their physical and supernatural powers. Having a faerie force on side would tip the odds of victory in their favour, he hoped. Merlin looked into Nimue's face to try and ascertain what she was thinking. The silence had gone on too long. Nimue looked absolutely tortured. She seemed to come back from her deep thoughts and nodded almost imperceptibly.

"It is too tempting an offer to refuse Merlin, I accept on behalf of mine people." Nimue knew only too well that the faerie nation would agree to anything at this stage in order to retrieve the spell. She was confident that there would be no dissenters when she told them the price that they would have to pay in order to get it.

"Then it is done" declared Merlin. "Consult with thine people and then we should gather to discuss our plan of attack." Merlin turned to Arthur, "I am afraid King Arthur that this time the Knights of the Round Table will not be able to be involved. This battle will be one of wits, magic and cunning."

Just as he finished his sentence, Nimue transformed into a dove and flapped away to one of the high-up open-shuttered windows and into the sky beyond.

"It would appear that our audience with the faerie Queen is at an end," observed Morgan.

Arthur chimed in. "The audience yes, but our battle strategy planning session; no. Let us adjourn to mine study and speak more about how best to achieve victory in this magical battle."

Morgan and Merlin were taken a little by surprise at Arthur's insistence. They had both assumed that because there would be no non-magical beings in the battle that there was no need for him to involve himself in the battle plan. Of course, he had just as much to lose as both Merlin and Morgan should they not be successful in their new alliance with the faeries.

"Aye," said Morgan obediently, and looked to Merlin for a similar show of accession.

"Aye, aye," he said quickly realising that he should have agreed immediately and not hesitated.

Arthur led the way from the Round Table and out of the hall. None of them turned around to look at the empty room behind them. But if they had, they would have seen the Lady of the Lake standing where they had just stood moments before. She watched them leave. It was impossible to gauge anything from her expression. She looked serene. Turning her head, she looked in the direction of the faerie forest as if she could see through the thick stone of the walls and through the distance to the Queen's hollow. Slowly, she faded away into nothingness.

Chapter 30: Caerleon; the Following Day

Arthur, Merlin and Morgan had spent the entire rest of the previous day going through possible scenarios on exactly how to successfully attack Hellekin and the Minotaur on Skellig Mhor. They were so involved that they missed the evening meal, and worked together through a lot of the night before calling a close to their strategy meeting.

It was late in the morning, almost noon, before Merlin's eyes opened. He yawned and stretched and pushed the blanket off of himself. Slowly rising he walked over to the closed wooden shutter and swung it open. Resting on the deep ledge was a grey pigeon. He looked at it and acting on a guess he said, "Queen Nimue, I hope that I hath not kept ye waiting."

His assumption was correct; the pigeon took flight and flapped past him into the room before taking on Nimue's full-sized human form.

"Ye surprise me Merlin. I thought that mine powers were now so strong that I could hide mine presence from ye."

Nimue looked a little disappointed. "However, I can see that I need more practice at masking mine faerie powers from other magical beings."

She sat on a nearby stool. In fact, that was just what had happened. Merlin had not detected her at all; it was just a guess that the pigeon was indeed a faerie. But not wanting to dispel the mystique that he had unrightfully earned from her he simply said, "There are dimensions to me that ye do not yet know Nimue."

Walking over and taking the stool next to her he asked the question that he knew the answer to already.

"The faerie people will help us?"

Nimue gave s single deep nod, "Aye Merlin. Mine people were of one voice; although scared of the Minotaur, the price that ye will pay for victory is greater than any fear that we possess." This pleased Merlin enormously. "Excellent Queen Nimue, I am glad. We should choose the appropriate time to attack; before the next full moon…." he was really just thinking aloud but Nimue corrected his presumption. "No Merlin. We hath cast the runes and determined that we cannot attack until one week after the full moon of this month."

Merlin was horrified. This meant that they would have to endure another full moon and the terror of facing two Green Knights and not just one.

"This is bad news," he said summarising his many thoughts into a short sentence. Nimue went on to explain the detail surrounding the decision. Although Merlin gave the impression of listening, his thoughts were with Sir Guaen and how to best protect him from two marauding daemons instead of one. He did not want to seem rude so he did not interrupt nor question Nimue's explanation on the choosing of the date of attack. Instead after her overly long explanation he smiled and indicated that he understood.

"The Green Knights will attack when Gaelach is full once more. Is there anything that is contained in the faerie library of spells that can help us protect Guaen from them?" he looked eagerly at Nimue hoping for an answer to the looming problem. Instead she looked at him as though he were mad.

"Them?" she said. It occurred to Merlin that Nimue did not know that the last attack had resulted in the Green Knight doubling his number by sacrificing some poor soldier.

"Of course Nimue, ye were not in Galloway to see the dread that we faced. The Green Knight cut into two a soldier and then his own body. The two halves of the Green Knight joined with the two halves of the soldier producing two of the wretched creatures. Now our trouble is increased beyond anything that we can hope to battle for long. Sir Guaen is in more danger now than ever before." He was distressed and it was showing in his voice and his face.

Nimue was shocked at hearing the news. Battling with one of these unbeatable creatures would be difficult enough; the thought of two was not worth imagining. She thought quickly and offered a simple magical solution.

"Transform him into an owl before the rising of the full-moon and the onset of the magical suppression spell. He can fly away and evade the daemons."

She looked pleased at here simple solution to a complicated problem. Merlin was not convinced.

"Even if I thought Sir Guaen could survive being transformed into a bird and then back again, there is nothing to say that when the Green Knights appear that their magical suppression will not undo the transformation. Imagine if he were to turn back into a man whilst in mid-flight. He would fall to his death for sure. The Green Knight's work would be done and they could then turn their revile upon the next of Arthur's Knights; whichever that will be? No Nimue, it must be something more imaginative; something rare, a spell or idea that hath not been seen or thought of for many years, if we are to outwit the cunning forces that we face."

Nimue was apologetic. She'd offered what she though was an obvious solution to a man that had clearly already dismissed it as a viable option long ago.

"I am sorry Merlin; ye are correct of course." She said.

Merlin spoke, "Nimue, but I must think of any ideas that can help us through another encounter with the Green Knight, both physical *and* magical. As the Queen and with access to such a vast library, there may be something of value?" he looked like a boy begging for more time to play with his friends.

"I shall consult the library once more and send news to ye if there is anything that may be of assistance. But we remain resolved, no attack on Skellig Mhor until we are past the full moon of Edrinios." Merlin agreed. There was little choice in the matter.

"We should have strategy planning meetings regularly between now and then to resolve the finer detail of our attack." He looked at Nimue hoping that she would agree to that. She did. "Twice weekly I shall come to Caerleon with mine head soldiers and oldest advisors. Between us, we can formulate a suitable plan that will rid us of the Minotaur and Hellekin."

Nimue gave Merlin a warm smile.

Merlin breathed a sigh of relief. This had softened the news about the delay in the attack; and it would give them plenty of time to plan an intricate strike. However, between now and then there were still the Green Knights to consider. Merlin sensed that his current visitation from Nimue was over. He was correct, without any further word she glimmered into the shape of a wren and flew out the window.

He stood and watched her fly away into the bright daylight. Now he had a more pressing matter to attend to. His first thought was to enlist the help of Morgan to get as many ideas into action as they could to ensure Guaen's safe passage through the next meeting with the Green Knights. He had Nimue working on any potential magical solutions to the problem. Arthur and his Knights could therefore help implement any worldly solutions that they could come up with. This thought gave him hope.

He practically ran from his room; his pace was so fast. Along the corridor, he came across Sir Lyonell.

"Ah good, Sir Lyonell," said Merlin "Please see if the King is able to once more begin another planning session, I shall fetch Lady Morgan, we should begin at everyone's earliest convenience," he finished his request, although it sounded more like a royal command to the Knight, and hurried off in the direction of Lady Morgan's chamber.

Sir Lyonell stood almost stunned by the unexpected interaction with the wizard; then deciding that he had best do exactly as he was told by the wise old man, went to ensure that Merlin's request was carried out.

Chapter 31: Preparing for the Green Knights

Arthur was suitably horrified to discover that they had to endure another visitation from the Green Knights before any attack on Hellekin could happen. But he was glad to have all of his knights involved in the planning sessions. He felt as though together they could all achieve more. They had had many now and the results were being put into action in various sections of Caerleon.

Arthur was supervising the digging of a particularly large hole in the middle of the main courtyard.

"Not long before the end of Edrinios men, this needs to be much deeper to catch the horrid things; dig!"

Although said in an almost light-hearted tone, the underlying message was clear, and the soldiers and servants assigned to digging the hole redoubled their efforts.

***

Next to the stables was the ironmonger's workshop. He had been assigned the duty to construct a cage that could hold at least one of the Green Knights. It was large and heavy. The thick iron bars looked as though nothing could penetrate them. But it was at Morgan and Merlin's insistence that they be so thick. The magicians were present for the finishing touches to the device. The ironmonger was busy hammering in the last bolt around the far side of the cage. Merlin was testing the hinged door on the front.

"What about carrying it when we hath captured one or both of the Green Knights?" queried Morgan. "It is enormously heavy, and without our ability to levitate it we are reliant upon the strength of numbers."

Morgan had a point. Merlin considered for a brief moment and gave the solution.

"We shall levitate it onto a cart before the Green Knight's arrive. Then the only problem will be to get one or both of them into here."

He swung the gate of the cage closed and it gave a solid and resounding clang as it shut. They both smiled.

"Now, the brew for the horses; do ye hath all of the ingredients?" asked the old man.

"Aye" said Morgan, "I shall mix it up the day before the full moon so that it is fresh and when fed to the horses, still pleasant to taste. If I do it now, I fear that it may spoil before we get a chance to use it."

Morgan's reasoning pleased the Sorcerer. He signalled his approval of the proposed method.

***

Sir Guaen and his brothers were busy erecting a large post into the ground near the entrance to the main hall. Garethe and Galahallt were helping him lower it into the pre-dug hole. It was a close fit.

"Now as we keep it steady, fill the hole, it must be secure and fetch the ropes, they will need to be nailed to the top of the post," instructed Guaen to the nearby soldiers.

Some hurried forward with buckets of dirt and began to pour it down into the hole and stamp it into place in order to sure-up the post. Another two went to fetch the ropes and nails.

***

A small contingent of Knights was returning through the main gates of the Castle with horses that were pulling along wooden trolleys full of large rocks. Sirs Degore and Lamorak and Pellus had hunted through the nearby quarry for rocks large enough to carry out their plan. As they entered one of them signalled to the waiting servants.

"Bring the nets and the blankets to wrap the stones in." He shouted to them. Then turning to his fellow knights, he said, "let us set the carts down near the stables but not too far from the hole. We can begin the next step of the plan there."

***

Gwenhwyvar and Amhar were watching the activity from just inside the main doors. Amhar looked up at his mother and asked, "Will the Green Knights be defeated this time?"

It was an innocent question, but one which Gwenhwyvar felt unable to answer with any certainty. Summoning her most regal tone she smiled confidently down at the eight-year-old Prince and said, "We shall all do our very best to see that Sir Guaen is not harmed by them."

At that moment, Lady Florie appeared from behind them holding Wigaloith's hand. She bowed to the Queen and followed on from her words addressing both of the young boys, "we are brave and strong and there is nothing that can stand against the combined will of virtuous people. Do ye understand?"

She looked from one to the other. Not actually understanding at all but feeling more comforted by the words they nodded obediently.

***

In the kitchen of the Castle, Lady Lyonors was busy trying to feed young Akhera who was having nothing to do with what she was offering her daughter, as well as keeping the servants busy with the preparation of the oil.

"How much more oil Lady Lyonors?" asked the head kitchen servant. Lyonors gave up attempting to get Akhera to eat the pungent piece of cheese. She looked up and reaffirmed the instruction.

"All of it!" The head servant looked exasperated and waved her arms frantically at two nearby girls "Ye heard, fetch the last of the oil." The two girls scurried away to the storage cellar to get the last of the oil. Looking around she could see that every bucket and bowl in the kitchen was already brimming with the stuff. She was going to need more containers.

***

All around Caerleon castle people were working toward a single goal, to stop the Green Knights from harming Sir Guaen.

Chapter 32: The Third Apparition

The full face of Gaelach was only moments away. It was still light and the air of dread and excitement filled Caerleon Castle and Caerleon Village. Even though there had been a small exodus from the village because of the impending visitation from the hideous Green Knights, for the most part the villagers believed that King Arthur, his Knights and Magicians could defeat the daemons.

Villagers tried to go about their normal duties for the sunset hours, but most of them had gathered in groups and were watching the sky for the first sign of Gaelach.

Teams of soldiers and servants were gathered in groups. All had assignments that they had to concentrate upon. It was helping the general mood of everyone. The infectious optimism from Merlin over these past weeks had helped stave off the onset of fear and panic. But now was the time for the rising of the full-moon. People watched the sky. It was slightly cloudy; the weather was perhaps a bit too cool for the time of year.

Merlin was watching from the battlements. He knew exactly where to look and was the first one to spot the moon. He did not point it out to anyone. He knew that it would only be seconds before someone else did. He was correct. From somewhere in the courtyard he heard a muffled shout.

"There!" followed by a brief moment of absolute stillness, and then a collective murmur from all around as people spotted the full face of Gaelach. It was time for the terror of the Green Knights to once more befall them.

Merlin motioned for the Knight on duty to ensure that the soldiers all kept a lookout over their respective areas, and not to concentrate upon looking at the moon. He saw that his non-verbalised instructions were being carried out.

From his vantage point high atop the Castle he could hear the scream coming from the village. It must have been a very loud scream to carry so far up the hill. Rushing to the edge he leaned out over the top of the main gate and peered down the hill toward the village. There were two horsemen riding through the outskirts of the village and heading toward them up the hill. How had he not seen them before? He had a perfect line of sight to see any horses enter the village. To suddenly find that they were already through the village and beginning their ascent was difficult to reconcile. Had he been too engrossed with the sky to take notice of such a significant happening?

He shook off the self-deprecating analysis for the time being. This was no time for self-doubt. He needed to be strong and to show how confident he was to all of those around him. It was important that everybody believed that they had a real chance of stopping the Green Knights this time.

The figures on the horses were unmistakable even from this distance. It was the Green Knights. There was something else too, the horses looked odd. As they approached Merlin could see why.

The horses too were clearly deceased. This was a turn of events that he had not planned for. The Green Knights apart from getting stronger each time they appeared, seemed to have become more cunning with each appearance. To ensure that Guaen did not escape on horseback this time they rode horses too.

The anxious jostling and mumbling from the crowd rose. Realising that it was uncertainty what was happening that was contributing to the overall disquiet; Merlin elected to address the crowd. He ran to the side of battlements which was above the gates so that he could lean over and address the people below.

"The Green Knights approach, on horseback; be ready they shall be here soon." As an afterthought and confidence builder he shouted, "we shall prevail."

The sentiment was picked up by King Arthur who gave a rousing motivational talk of his own to the assembled people.

Merlin did not hear any of it he was busy monitoring the rapid approach of the daemons. They were closer now. The horses were a sight to behold just as the Green Knights were; decaying flesh and bone showing through the rotted hides of the animals. He wondered how the muscles worked to propel the hideous beasts at such a frightening pace.

Within moments they had reached the front gate that was left open to greet them. The sight of the rancid horses being ridden by the decomposing Green Knights was too much for some of the large number of people present. There were loud screams from here and there followed by an order from the King to hold their positions. The enemy rode brazenly through the front gate and surveyed the scene ahead of them. There was a large hole in the courtyard. There was absolutely no attempt to disguise it. The ground ahead of it had been shaped to slope down toward the hole from where they were. As if sensing that something was wrong the two Green Knights looked down at the ground upon which their mounts were standing. They were in the groove that led to the large hole.

The combined crowd could almost see the look of puzzlement upon the putrid faces of the Knights through their helmets. There was no way that they would willingly ride down the carved slope and into the hole.

"NOW!" shouted Merlin at the top of his lungs. From behind the stone battlements above the gate a plethora of servants stood up from crouching down. Each pair held enormous buckets of oil. In a well-rehearsed motion the two openings above the Green Knights were used to target the enemy and two by two, the buckets of oil were poured over them. Each load hit its mark squarely on their green iron helmets. As one set of buckets was emptied they were replaced with the next four servants in the queue who similarly emptied their two buckets each of oil onto the Green Knights and their horses. The speed and precision of the pours was so fast and accurate that the Green Knights had endured two and a half pairs of buckets of oil being poured upon them before they simply motioned their horses forward and out of harm's way.

This didn't deter the remaining servants who continued to pour the buckets over the edge of the battlements and onto the ground. Soon there was a growing mess of dirt and oil sliding underneath the hooves of the Green Knight's horses. The Green Knights themselves seemed to be trying to ascertain exactly what was going on. At first glance it did not seem like pouring oil onto the ground and having it cause a small river beneath them could possibly result in the Knights sliding down the gentle groove and into the waiting pit.

On the other side of the deep hole Sir Guaen stepped forward and away from the crowd bravely showing himself to the creatures. He positioned himself at the edge of the hole on the opposite side to the Knights. They instinctively drew their swords and dismounted. The ground was slippery, but not so much as to make their steps too unsure. Just at the point that they both touched the ground there came a loud shout from Merlin above the main gate.

"NOW!"

Six of Arthur's knights to the left of the oily ramp stepped forward as did six to the right. They reached down in unison to what appeared to be the dirt ground of the courtyard. Out of nowhere, and apparently buried or covered lightly with dirt, they lifted two ropes. The ends were attached to a large rope net also buried only slightly beneath the ground, but where the horses and Green Knights were standing right now.

With a mighty heave they pulled the rope, bracing the net and causing the two Green Knights and their horses to falter on the moving ground beneath them. The horses having longer legs were able to bound out of the way before the net caused them to completely fall over. The Green Knights were not so lucky. The slipperiness of the ground conspired to thwart them and they both fell into a mess upon the ground and now fully exposed net.

Arthur's Knights pulled backwards digging their heels into the ground of the courtyard and further enveloped the two Green Knights in the net. With the ground so completely covered in oil sliding them down the gentle ramp toward the hole was easy. Realising at this point that it would be less of a chore than they had anticipated Sir Garethe shouted for the two teams of Knights to go "Faster!"

Both teams heaved on the ropes and pulled the two Green Knights to the very edge of the hole and over the precipice. At the point where the entangled Knights were too far over the edge to possibly recover Merlin shouted the order to the two teams of Arthur's Knights.

"Let go of the ropes!"

The Green Knights, enveloped in the oily rope net and covered with a mixture of dirt and oil, fell into the hole with a loud thud. It was accompanied by a frustrated growl from both of the creatures. With limbs flailing they tried to untangle themselves from the ropes. But the oil that had helped slide them into the trap was making it more difficult to grip the ropes and thus to tear them with their superhuman strength.

From above a further order was given, this time by King Arthur "The rocks!" he bellowed.

The throng of people gathered in the courtyard bent down to retrieve the rocks that were hidden behind their lines. Each person had been allocated a number of rocks that they now had to lift and race as quickly as they could to the edge of the hole to bombard the Green Knights with them.

The effect of now being stoned by rocks the size of a person's head had a detrimental effect on the escape plans for the Green Knights. It seemed that the people hurling the rocks were very accurate marksmen. Rock after rock hit both of the Green Knights, each resulting in a howl of frustration from the daemons.

The people were well organised and upon throwing their rocks returned to their own small stash for the second and then third. The Green Knights were unable to get to their feet to defend themselves and were soon partially covered in a growing pile of large stones. But unexpectedly the bombardment from above stopped. The initial part of plan was complete. Now the Round Table Knight's horses were brought into play. Three horses were lead up to the edge of the hole and then turned around. Men hurled ropes from the far side of the hole and towards the tails of the horses. Each of the horse's minders caught the ropes and attached them to harnesses that the horses were wearing.

With the ropes securely attached, each of the minders gave a signal of preparedness and together urged the horses forward and away from the hole. It was then apparent what was happening. The ropes were attached to large cluster of rocks wrapped in blankets and rope nets. Far more than individuals could hope to thrown into the pit in a short timeframe. But the horses were dragging these considerable packages deliberately toward the hole and the unsuspecting Green Knights. They never saw it coming.

Three large packets of rocks tipped over the edge of the pit and the ropes that tied them to the horses tensed. At that exact moment Knights nearby to the horses, with raised swords, swung their sharp blades and severed the ropes allowing the parcels of rocks to plummet into the hole unabated.

The sound of metal helmets being crushed was barely audible over the thud of the rocks hitting the stones that were already in the pit.

There was yet another signal from Merlin from his vantage point above the gate.

"The carts!"

Out of the stable came three wooden two-wheeled carts. Obviously, normally pulled by horses, these had soldiers pushing them from their wooden beam frames. The rear planks had been removed. Each of the three carts was carrying a load of large stones, similar to the ones that had just been thrown onto the Green Knights by the crowd of people. It was hard going trying to push the heavy loads but in a well-rehearsed motion the first of them made it to the point where the soldiers could stop pushing the cart and lift the frame thus tipping the load of rocks into the pit. The first cart was then hurriedly pulled out of the way to allow the next cart to offload its pile of rocks into the pit; then the third. The pit was now almost full of rocks, the Green Knights crushed at the bottom of the incredible load.

There was a palpable sense of joy in the air. The sense of relief mixed with achievement and the feeling that the horror was now at an end manifested itself as the loudest cheer that anyone in Caerleon had ever experienced. Soldiers, servants, Knights, members of the court, and royalty cheered together as one. Some of the people near to the pit actually jumped in to the rocky mess and began to jump up and down as if to spite the vanquished daemons below them.

There was applause and laughter everywhere. People turned and hugged those closest to them regardless of rank or stature. Arthur bent backwards and breathed a huge sigh of relief to the evening sky. As he regained his posture he looked over to Sir Guaen who was doing exactly as Arthur had just done. He must be more relieved than any man in history though the King. Lady Florie and Wigaloith ran forward to embrace him. The scene was perfect, husband, wife and child in a three-way embrace of love.

Only Merlin was not rejoicing with everyone else. He stood at his post watching the surface of the rocks, suspicious that the problem was taken care of too easily. Morgan was making her way along the battlements trying unsuccessfully to avoid as many spontaneous embraces from the crowd as she could. She was smiling broadly. But she could see even in the soft evening light that Merlin was not.

By the time she reached him his eyes had narrowed. Either he was finding it difficult to see some small detail in the distance or he was not happy with something that he did see. She was about to say something when he reached out and grabbed her arm. Locking their arms together he worked his hand down her forearm and then tightly clasped her hand.

"See, there!" he said pointing straight out with his other hand and finger.

She followed his instructions. The surface of the pile of rocks in the hole was moving at one corner. A single rock rose up and then rolled away from its place. This alerted the three people still rejoicing on the surface of the rock pile. They stopped rejoicing and looked over to see what was happening. Sure enough, another rock rose up pushed from below and then reaching a critical height rolled away; then another and another. There was a pronounced bulge of rocks rising up from one corner of the pit. It grew large. The people in the pit let out various cries of panic and hastily scramble out of harm's way.

The ebullient joyfulness subsided. People stopped what they were doing and looked at the surface of rocks in the pit. To everyone's absolute horror the gloved hand of one of the Green

Knights shot up and clawed at the edge of the pit. This was followed by the crushed helmet and head from the Knight. Then the second arm was freed from the pile of rocks that had been entombing him. With two arms free the Green Knight was able to get a better grip upon the ground. Fingers dug into the solid dirt giving him enough adequate hold to pull his torso free of the pit.

Once more there were screams from within the gathered crowd of people. By this time, the Green Knight had managed to push away the rocks surrounding him and had raised a leg out of the pile. With that free, he brought it down on the surface of the pile and used the leverage to extricate himself fully from the trap; now liberated from the pit he scanned the crowd for his target. Bit by bit, unnoticed by all except Merlin and Morgan, the Green Knights crushed helmet pushed itself back into shape from within. Now complete once more it was able to see Sir Guaen clearly through the slits in its helmet.

Sir Guaen was frantically giving his wife and son instructions, "We must enable the second part of our plan; take refuge inside the Castle." Even though Lady Florie objected she wanted to ensure the safety of Wigaloith. Almost in tears she gave Guaen a peck on the cheek and grabbing the boys hand hurried him away from his father and toward the entrance to the Castle.

The Green Knight was still unsteady on his feet, but that did not stop him from inexorably walking around the pit toward his goal. Sir Guaen backed away slowly, looking occasionally over to this left to ensure that he was heading in the right direction. Step by step he made towards the pole buried near the entrance of the castle.

At that moment, the hand of the second Green Knight also surfaced from his rocky prison. Just as the first one had done previously, he grabbed the edge of the pit and used it to pull himself up and out of the rocks. The second Green Knight stood there looking angrily around for his prey.

Chapter 33: Dusk

The second Green Knight followed the first clockwise around the pit toward Sir Guaen. The embattled Knight could be heard breathing in anxiety even over the growling of the creatures and the general panic from everyone that was happening around him. At the point where Sir Guaen felt that he would lose the advantage of being behind the pit and now assured that the two adversaries were approaching from his right, he ran toward the entrance to the main hall. More specifically he ran toward the pole that had been erected near the entrance and took up a standing position behind it.

To the casual onlooker, the scene would have seemed absurd. The wooden pole did not offer nearly enough width for Sir Guaen to hide behind. Yet he was standing there peering around from the girth of the pole to check on the progress of the advancing Knights. Neither of them had broken into a run. It was unknown if that was because they were still trying to repair themselves after being crushed under so many rocks or if it was apparent to them that Sir Guaen was no longer trying to escape.

Both of the hideous things were getting closer. Sir Guaen stood his ground. Another shouted signal from Merlin watching the proceedings from his vantage-point.

"Now Sir Guaen, Climb!" was heard across the courtyard.

Sir Guaen began to ascend the pole. Although not visible to anyone at a distance, the pole had large iron nails driven into it on the far side. The nails were in an off centre stepped pair from the bottom to the top. They barely held his weight as he grabbed on to the highest within his reach and then turned his attention downwards to guide his feet onto the correct point. He had barely gone two levels of nails up when he misplaced his left foot, causing him to slip off the pole and crash to the ground gashing his arm in the process.

He let out a cry of pain. Gathering himself up, he saw that the Knights were only five or six paces away. He knew that if he panicked now his life would be forfeit. It took all of his nerve to once more concentrate upon the task before him.

He reached up to the highest nails and then carefully placed his feet on the nails near the bottom of the pole. He concentrated; right hand up one nail, left foot up one nail, left hand up one nail, right foot up one nail. He pushed every other thought out of his head. Soon he had traversed half of the length of the pole

He was so immersed in the mechanical process of climbing he did not hear the guttural growls emanating from the Green Knights. They were only three steps away from him now, swords drawn. Had he not climbed with absolute precision he would have been within reach of their sharp blades by the time they made it to the base of the pole. They stood their looking up at him. One of the Knights began to climb after Sir Guaen using the same iron nails that he was using. The other elected to re-sheath his sword and use his hands and feet.

With inhuman ability, he gripped the pole with his hands; his feet pushed against it like an impossible simian from a far-away land.

Sir Guaen had reached the top of the pole and clambered to the flat and very small round apex. He had to stand with one foot on the other in order to balance. But balance, he did with the ability of a stork. Once more Merlin's voice could be heard across the courtyard.

"Jump!"

Sir Guaen looked over at the dangling rope for which he had to aim. It was swung over an iron pulley that was connected to a jutting out pole above the front door of the main hall. It was a good distance. But this had been practiced and he had failed in only the first few attempts. But he had mastered it eventually.

Looking down he saw how close the two Green Knights were to him and it gave Sir Guaen all of the motivation that he needed to bend his knees and hurl himself at the target rope.

The adrenalin pumping through his body ensured that he nearly over-shot his destination. Under any other circumstances, he would have been applauded as a miracle athlete worthy of the ancient Greek Olympic Games. But those that were watching were more carefully monitoring the progress of the hideous creatures that were pursuing the good Knight. Sir Guaen grabbed the rope and his weight pulled it down. From all around the pole another hidden rope net arose with smooth precision. It enveloped the pole and the two Green Knights. Sir Guaen made a resounding thud upon the ground as he came down. The net closed over the two pursuers. They growled, tightly bound within the structure; one unable to reach for his sheathed sword; the other trying to get any sort of movement in his constrained arm in order to make his sword an effective cutting instrument.

King Arthur bellowed out the next order "Chains." From above the pole, four chains that were somehow connected by a large circular ring to the rope that had pulled the rope net into place were thrown from the battlements above. The chains sprawled over the top of the pole and down the sides. Big burley men raced out from the crowd to fulfil their part of this devious trap. Like a May-pole, the muscle-bound men each grabbed a length of the chain and dragged it out as far as they reach of the chain would noisily extend. Then they ran in circles around the pole causing the chains to wrap tightly around the pole and the trapped Green Knights. The top of the chains had each in turn caught the highest of the nails, thus anchoring it and beginning the spiral downwards the length of the pole.

Soon the Green Knights were even more encased than they were with the rope net. The chains were pinned with u-shaped nails to the point of the pole where they finished their spiral down the shaft. This point was around head-height for the men. Hammers were brought and the nails driven into the post securing the four chains so that they would not come asunder.

A further order from King Arthur was heard.

"Chop them down!"

With that, two of the burley men were presented with axes and they began to hack away at the naked part of the pole beneath where the chains were anchored. Some of the rope net was sacrificed in the action but it did not matter, the chains were holding the supernatural creatures captive now.

With a cracking of wood and a maniacal snarl from both of the imprisoned creatures, they came crashing down like a felled tree. Sir Guaen gingerly walked up to look upon the confined Knights. They were so locked in to their positions that they could not even turn their heads to look at him. But they did continue to howl in frustration.

He looked up and gave a signal to someone across the courtyard in the stables. A twin horse-drawn cart holding the previously constructed cage was brought out of the shadows. It had to be navigated around the hole, now filled with rocks and over to the ensnared Knights. King Arthur organised the nearby men to lift the pole. It was a huge effort. The weight of the now shortened pole, along with the four chains and the two Green Knights made it nearly impossible. But they were motivated to get this done.

The cage door was opened. Looking at it now, it was clear that the contraption had been made to fit a thick post through the top of it and allow it to poke out the top whilst still covering and jailing the chained Knights. The swarm of men that were pushing and pulling and heaving it into place looked like an army of ants over a ripe piece of fruit fallen from a tree.

With much cajoling and puffing they managed to get the pole into place and slam the thick cage door shut. The ironmonger hurried forward with a still glowing iron pin to hold the door shut. He slotted it into place using his long tongs and then discarded them, drawing out his hammer and bending the shape of the pin so that it could not be undone. Lastly his apprentice raced forward with a bucket of water. When the ironmonger was happy that the pin was now so distorted that it would effectively lock the cage door, the young man threw the entire bucket of water on the pin cooling and hardening it.

It was done. The Green Knights were once more trapped. It was only now that Merlin and Morgan made their way down from the battlements above the main gate.

"Excellent, excellent, everyone, an outstanding job!" he was beaming as he and Morgan walked up to the cart holding the imprisoned Knights. King Arthur joined them as did Sir Guaen and his brothers Galahallt and Garethe.

The crowd that was gathering around them gloated at the captives. There was a mixture of cheering the success of outsmarting and outmanoeuvring the adversaries along with a good deal of jeering the incarcerated creatures. Arthur was impatient though to see the next phase of the plan put into action.

"If the creatures can escape from the pit of rocks, then we should not be complacent that this cage will hold them for ever. Bring the horses and we shall begin the journey to the coast."

Arthur's command was obeyed immediately. Stable hands rushed forward with the horses for Morgan, Merlin and Sir Guaen. This was part of the plan. Sir Guaen was originally meant to remain at Caerleon but insisted that he remain within sight of the creatures throughout the entire full-moon. At least he would know exactly where they were, he argued. And that would make him feel more at ease.

Similarly, horses were provided to Arthur, Galahallt and Garethe. They all took their mounts. People were still giving their congratulations to the party as Arthur gave the signal for them to move out. The two horses that were pulling the cart had a bit of difficulty beginning as the contraption was so heavy. But Merlin had taken their reins and motivated them into motion.

Once more the rock pit had to be carefully navigated, but soon they were out of the gate and heading down the gentle slope to the Village of Caerleon.

Chapter 34: On the Road to the Coast; Night

The night had come. The party had faced a similarly raucous and happy crowd when they traversed the village. But now they were well away from the village and heading toward the mouth of the estuary where a long boat was awaiting them. The entire group except for Merlin took turns in riding beside the cart to look at the captive daemons. They were vocal the entire time. Growling and hissing in frustration at not being able to free themselves and kill Sir Guaen. Yet it was weirdly fascinating to see them up close and apparently contained and no longer harmful.

"Merlin, are ye sure the deepest part of the sea will be enough to hold them?" asked Sir Galahallt. It was a question that had been asked many times in the various planning sessions that had led to the successful capturing of the Green Knights. Merlin did not believe for a moment that the Knights would stay caged for very long, but was not willing to let on what he actually thought.

"The deepest part of the sea, which is within a reasonable distance from the shore, will be enough to hold them for the time being." His response had an edge of impatience to it. They continued their ride toward the waiting long-boat. Arthur was the next to ride up next to Merlin for a chat.

"Half an hour more and we should be at the coast Merlin" he said.

Mentioning a fact that Merlin knew all too well was simply a conversation starter. Merlin correctly guessed that Arthur had something on his mind.

"What troubles ye, King Arthur?" he asked, easily seeing the real reason that Arthur wanted to talk.

Arthur smiled, he should have known better than to verbally dance around the subject. He was surrounded by his closest Knights and his sister. There was no need for him to be coy. He changed his attitude and approached the subject head-on.

"Ye think that the Green Knights will escape from this prison; so it is the attack upon Skellig Mhor that consumes thine thoughts." Arthur's summation was completely accurate. Now that Merlin's real thoughts had been laid bare before the small crowd he somehow felt more at ease.

"Aye Arthur," he said. "Where such powerful magic is involved I cannot believe that any cage, or cave or hole filled with rocks will imprison these two things for very long." He turned to motion to the captives on the cart.

The admission garnered a surprise reaction from the three brothers, but not from Morgan, who like Arthur had suspected it throughout all of their Round Table sessions. All of Arthur's Knights were part of the strategy meetings prior to the full moon that involved how to best deal with the next appearance of the Green Knights. But there were other battle strategy sessions taking place at

Caerleon. The ones that Queen Nimue and her counsellors attended. These meetings were solely concerned with the forthcoming attack on Hellekin and the Minotaur. None of Arthur's Knights were in attendance to any of those.

"The faeries want what I have to offer more than they want to not get involved with this situation. That gives us an advantage. But how to apply that advantage in such a way as to ensure our victory is what keeps me awake at night. Make no mistake" he said now turning away from Arthur to address the entire troop, "We are up against a foe of power that I can only imagine. It will surely take all that Nimue and her people have to give in order for us to succeed."

The three brother Knights had not been privy to the battle strategy sessions that Nimue had attended at Caerleon. So they were unaware of any such misgivings that Merlin harboured. Their complete exclusion because they were not magical beings also meant that they were putting all of their faith in Merlin and Morgan to produce a resounding victory against their enemy across the sea. It was now clearly written on their faces that they had doubts that he could achieve the victory that they assumed he would deliver.

There would have been more conversation on this very subject except for a loud cracking of metal. One of the links on one of the chains near the base of the pole where it had been nailed into place broke. Sir Guaen rode up close to the cart to confirm what they all feared.

"One of the links has broken on one of the chains," he said, worry filling his tone. "Now only three chains and the ropes hold the Knights to the pole."

In unison, the Green Knights let out an incredible howl, unlike anything that they had emitted before, and certainly unlike anything any of the party had heard before. It cut through the air like shrill squawk from a falcon mixed with a guttural growl from a wolf-hound.

Chapter 35: Near the Coast

Another of the chains made a loud surrender to the inhuman force the Green Knights were subjecting them to. With no need to regain their strength, the supernatural beings were relentless in their struggle against their captivity. What had seemed like a flawless plan when proposed was coming apart before their eyes.

"If they break free of the chains, how will we load them on to the boat and then throw them overboard and into the sea?" shouted Sir Guaen to Merlin. He'd taken up position directly behind the cart so that he had a clear view of his feared enemies.

The moon washed the land with soft light. Under other circumstances it would have been considered a soft and even romantic light. But illuminating the angry creatures it instead looked eerie and disturbing. Sir Guaen could feel his heart begin to pound with fear once more. How was he going to survive another attack from these unstoppable monsters?

"Come away from there Guaen," advised Morgan. "Ride with us here at the front of the cart."

It was good advice. Perhaps seeing their quarry and not being able to attack was aggravating the Green Knights. Sir Guaen dutifully obeyed the Sorceress. He prodded his horse into a small gallop to overtake the cart.

Arthur spoke first. "Sir Guaen is correct; we cannot hope to load them on to the boat if they are able to move about freely within their cage."

The description did not really do justice to the actuality. Even if they freed themselves of the chains and ropes, the cage was barely bigger than the two of them. They would still be imprisoned. But the point was that they could poke their swords through the cage and thwart any attempt to move them.

Merlin was completely practical about a viable solution. We shall load the entire cart onto the boat and thus maintaining a safe distance from the Green Knights."

His eminently simple solution quelled the rising tensions in the party but only momentarily. The third of the four chains gave way. They could not see where, but the sound was unmistakable. Fear gripped them all, including Merlin, but he was the best at hiding it.

"The coast!" said Arthur. They all looked at where he was pointing. In the bright moonlit night they could see the final slope down to the estuary and the waiting long-boat. The tantalising closeness of their destination and the subsequent promise of soon being able to dump the Green Knights into the sea gave them all the motivation that they needed to carry on.

The king-tide had swollen the water to a height that they had not witnessed in years. It would be easy to navigate the boat out of the estuary in these conditions. The prevailing wind would assist them.

The fourth and final chain gave way with a clang. The Green Knights were free to tear at the rope net covering them. It took only a few precious moments for them to tear it to fibres. Now free of the pole but still imprisoned in the thick iron cage, they turned their strength and attention to the bars. Their hands grabbed at the bars and they could be seen to push and pull at them with little signs of success.

This continued for the remainder of the journey down to the waiting boat. The party of oarsmen surged forward to greet the King and his party. Arthur was busy giving instructions to them, and as curious as they all were about the caged freaks that were growling on the cart they hurried to obey his instructions. Two of the thickest and flattest planks were recovered from within the boat. These would be used as a ramp to push the cart up the side of the boat and into its belly.

The men were still trying to comply with the King's orders when the sound of galloping horses interrupted them. People looked around to see who else was coming down the slope toward the boat. To everyone's shock it was the Green Knight's skeleton-like horses. They were neighing, nostrils flared.

The sight of the angry and disgusting creatures scared everyone. "What shall we do Arthur, fight them?" shouted Galahallt.

Arthur did not have time to answer. The Green Knights had started to rock the cage that held them. Left and right it was being pushed and pulled from within by the captives. Soon it unbalanced and tumbled off the cart and onto the stony shore. Oarsmen panicked and screamed.

"Hold ye ground!" bellowed Arthur trying to restore calm.

The Green Knights' horses galloped up to the fallen cage and began to assist the Green Knights by kicking at it with their front feet.

The combination of the horses and the Knights soon proved too much for the strength of the bars and they began to give way.

"We need a new plan!" shouted Sir Guaen at Merlin. Merlin was pointing to the cliff face over to the right of the estuary. The mounted party guessed that Merlin was indicating that they should ride back up the way that they had come and then turn to make their way into Cliff Wood and towards the cliff face.

"Ride up there with everything that ye horse can muster!" he shouted at the party.

They collectively forced their horses into a charge; the six of them bolting away from the water and back the way that they had come. None of them looked around to see the progress of the Green Knight's escape. What Merlin was thinking was to somehow get out of the range of the magical inhibiting influence emanating from the Green Knights, so that a magical escape of some-sort could be enabled.

The boat crew all ran away from the horror that they were seeing. Bar by bar the iron cage was peeled away as if it were a straw basket. Soon the two hideous creatures were free and mounting their gruesome horses. They pursued their quarry. The Caerleon party had a good head start but it was not enough to get them out of the range of the magical suppression force. Reaching the point of the road where they had been only a short time before, Arthur bellowed for them to turn and take the road toward the wood.

Each of them was breathing as hard as their horses. The dash was exhausting for both rider and mount. With the sound of hooves pounding upon the dirt road they made their way toward the woods. Dust kicked up and covered them all. Soon it became apparent that the King's horse and those of Sirs Galahallt and Garethe were slowing. Their horses were absolutely exhausted. Had it not been for the special mixture that Morgan had prepared and fed to Merlin, Guaen and her own horse, theirs too would have been faltering.

"You go on!" screamed Arthur at Merlin.

He could see that the old sage was looking worriedly behind him at the King and his two Knights. King Arthur now concerned himself with ensuring that he gave the other three a good chance of escaping. Together with Galahallt and Garethe he formed a line across the road and the three of them drew their swords, ready for battle.

Chapter 36: The Road to Cliff Wood

Arthur looked to his right and left at Sir Galahallt and Sir Garethe. If there was anyone that he would want to face battling these evil daemons with it was them. They were agile, thinking fighters that did not rely on their brute strength to overcome an enemy.

The Green Knights were riding side by side up the hill at break-neck speed.

"Unless we challenge them in motion we run the risk of them simply riding around us," advised Arthur.

The statement made it very clear that Arthur intended to rattle the Green Knights and their mounts by riding head-on towards them forcing them to stop. Even if they were unsuccessful at engaging them for very long it would be enough to put more distance between the creatures and Sir Guaen, Merlin and Morgan. And that was the real aim of this particular manoeuvre.

There was no more time to contemplate, Arthur prodded his horse forward. The Mare, although exhausted, complied. The two flanking Knights did likewise. Together they raced downhill to close the short distance between them and the Green Knights. The time it took raced by faster than they were moving.

Now they were upon them. Any ordinary foe and their horses would have reared up at facing a potential collision. The Green Knights and their horses did not even react. With a precision that was as unearthly as the creatures themselves, they deftly slipped between the thinnest of margins separating the three brave fighters.

The plan had completely failed. Arthur's own mare took fright and reared up, after the Green Knights had already passed them. So did the horses ridden by Garethe and Galahallt. They all struggled to calm the frightened beasts.

"Steady," "Down" and "Quiet" could be heard coming from the three riders as they attempted to stop themselves from being thrown, and regain control of their mounts. By the time they had managed to compose themselves and their horses, and look back up the road, the Green Knights were disappearing into the edge of the wood covering the cliff top.

***

Progress through the dense forest was slow. The thick canopy of trees was blocking out most of the obliging light shining down from Gaelach. Although enlivened by Morgan's mixture, the horses were beginning to show signs of exhaustion. Merlin's mind was racing. Even if they could get out of the range of the Green Knights, what exactly could he do magically to assist them? They could not pull-off the instantaneous travel spell anymore. Levitating them all to someplace safe seemed the only viable option.

"Make for the edge of the cliff, the trees are thinnest there," ordered the old man. Morgan could just make out the tree line ahead of them. Along with fewer trees to navigate around, came more light from above. It was a wise decision under difficult circumstances. They broke through the edge of the forest and faced a small tract of land that then disappeared over a sheer drop. The land curved gently around and off to the left. They could see a section of the cliff that had become eroded beneath it and was jutting out over the swollen waters of the estuary below.

"Still nothing Merlin," shouted Morgan; Merlin guessing correctly that she was referring to their magical abilities. She must have been trying to conjure up a simple spell to see if they were yet out of range of the Green Knights. No luck.

The horses were sweating profusely. There was no hope that they would be able to go further. They were trapped with the cliff to one side and the Green Knights approaching from somewhere behind them in the woods.

Just then a flock of cormorants appeared from somewhere behind them and briefly hovered above them squawking loudly. It was enough of a racket to attract the attention of the three of them. Even under these circumstances it was peculiar enough to warrant notice. This went on for far too long for it to be a coincidence. Then the flock flew off and made toward the section of the cliff that jutted out over the water. They took up position hovering above that point of the land and began to squawk loudly again.

A thought crossed Merlin's mind. If they jumped off the cliff it may give them the precious distance that they needed to elude the

Green Knights' dampening influence. The cliff edge was high, but the fall into the deep waters of the king-tide would not be fatal.

"Morgan, Guaen; ride to that point of the cliff. We are going to jump into the water below!" ordered Merlin.

Morgan and Sir Guaen looked at him as though he had gone completely mad. He did not need to see their expressions to guess what they were thinking.

"The water is deep, we *will* survive; and it may give us the distance that we need to evade the Green Knights influence" he further explained.

The situation was desperate and it called for a desperate action. Guaen knew it, he was a fighter. Morgan trusted Merlin and his judgement. Resigned to take the extraordinary step, they rode to the point marked by the noisy cormorants, and dismounted.

Each gave their horse a hearty slap on the rump to send it on its way. They obeyed but slowly, nearly unable to comply from the absolute fatigue that they were suffering from.

The three of them walked up to the cliff face together and looked over. The moon-light was reflecting on the water making it easy to see how far down it actually was. It seemed a much greater distance than any of them had anticipated.

"No time for fear, nor for contemplation. Jump!" he said whilst pushing Sir Guaen with a mighty shove.

He hollered as he fell forward over the precipice. Merlin turned to Morgan. She guessed that he was about to do the same to her so she took the initiative and hurled herself into the air. Merlin then jumped forward with all of the effort that his legs could muster.

Their hearts were in their throats and their stomachs were where their hearts should have been. The exhilaration and fear combined to slow the perception of time. All three of them were screaming. Wind pushed on their faces, rushed past their ears. Hearts pounded so hard that it felt like they would explode from their bodies. Hitting the water brought a sound more akin to a crack of thunder than a loud splash of water. It was nowhere near as gentle or soft a landing as any of them could have guessed. Water rushed over their heads and foamed up with bubbles all around them. It felt as though they had sunk to the very bottom of the estuary.

Clambering to the surface they coughed and spluttered the water from their lungs and noses. It took a few moments for them to gain their composure and look around them. They'd jumped close together but somehow landed further apart than would have seemed logical.

"Merlin!" shouted Morgan.

He looked over to where she was adeptly treading water. She had managed to give a shrug of her shoulders punctuated with the brief raising of both her hands. He knew exactly what she was communicating to him; still no magical abilities. This was an absolute disaster. What possible course of action was open to them now?

The flock of cormorants all dived into the water at various points around the trio. But they did not surface. Nimue broke through the water at the central point between the three of them. The trio all let out a nervous yelp and then shook their heads in disbelief as they realised who it was that was now with them.

"Merlin, thank goodness ye understood our instruction. I was worried that ye may not be able to hear our voices whilst in the form of the cormorants," said Nimue.

Merlin looked at her with complete bewilderment. "What?" he said, unable to come up with anything else under the bizarre circumstances. A pod of dolphins broke the surface and clicked and made odd sounds. This too caused a minor stifled scream from the trio.

"Mine people will take ye to the far side of the estuary or further if ye require. Grab onto the fins of the dolphins," she instructed.

Morgan, Merlin and Guaen looked at the nearest dolphin to each of them. Sure, enough the odd looking creatures were each was offering them their fins. The surreal situation ensured that the party did not argue or even question the offer. Merlin, Morgan and Guaen reached out and took hold of the fins. The dolphins began to swim away from the land and across to the other side of the body of water.

The strength of the dolphins in the water was incredible. None of them had ever encountered such a thing before. Nimue transformed into a dolphin too and accompanied them. It took all of their effort to hold on to the dolphin's fins. Both hands had to be clasped around the base of the fin to ensure that they did not slip off. The water rushed passed them and soon they were a fair way away from where they had so unceremoniously tumbled into the water.

A series of loud splashes in rapid succession came from somewhere behind them. Sir Guaen was in the best position to swing his head around to see what had fallen into the water. As he did, the faces of the Green Knight's dead horses broke the surface of the water. The Green Knights were next to rise from the water, their helmets glinting in the moonlight.

"The Green Knights hath followed us into the water!" screamed Sir Guaen to Morgan and Merlin.

They both craned their necks to see what was happening. As they looked, they could see the two Knights' take their mounts and ride their swimming horses in pursuit of them. Merlin looked around for the dolphin that was Nimue. There were so many he could not tell which was her. He shouted at the top of his lungs.

"Nimue, take us to the long-boat, we may yet make sail and out run these things."

It was clear headed thinking in a fantastic situation. His instruction must have been heeded because the pod of dolphins turned and made toward the point where the long-boat was still partially beached. This was a calculated gamble. If enough of the oarsmen had remained with the boat then they would have a good chance of setting sail and making good their escape. If not, then...Merlin did not want to think about the alternatives.

Spurred on by the new goal, the dolphins carrying the trio pushed through the water even faster than before. They were more than a match for the slow moving swimming horses behind them. It took about fifteen or more minutes but they were soon in sight of the boat. "I cannot see if the men are still there," shouted Morgan back to the two men. It was impossible to tell from this low in the water. They may have been around the shore side of the boat. Hopefully some were taking shelter within it.

At last they were there. The dolphins could only take them to the point where they could stand up. It was surprisingly difficult. Their legs were shaking from a mixture of the coldness of the water, their general fatigue and the excitement of the race away from the Green Knights carried by these skilful creatures of the sea. Morgan, Guaen and Merlin stumbled their way to the shore. Nimue appeared beside Merlin. He was very glad to see her again. "Mine thanks Nimue, I do not know what I would hath done...." he began, but she waved away his gratitude.

"I could not let our commander be injured before our victory over Hellekin," she said.

All around them faeries that had formerly been in the shapes of dolphins appeared in shimmers of light; until they were a small band of about a dozen men and women. Looking to Nimue as their guide for what to do next, they gathered that the Queen was determined to see Merlin, Morgan and Guaen safely on to the boat. They rounded the bow of the boat. There was nobody there.

"Men?" shouted Merlin.

Gingerly two faces peered over the top of the side of the boat to see who was calling for them. Merlin spotted their white faces in the pale moonlight immediately.

"How many others are there?" he said quite gruffly.

One of the nervous pair stood up and looked behind him doing a quick count of how many men were there. It did not take very long.

"Five of us Merlin" said the man. Merlin audibly groaned with displeasure and exasperation. That was not nearly enough to tow the boat to deeper water so that it could raise sail and make good their escape.

"We shall crew the boat Merlin," said Nimue. She gave instructions for the men in her troop to take hold of the ropes at the stern of the vessel. Merlin was grateful but didn't have time to show it.

"Out, give them assistance!" he commanded the oarsmen cowering in the boat. He turned to Morgan and Nimue and motioned that they should board.

The oarsmen were jumping over the side and splashing in the water racing to give the strange newcomers help in pulling the boat out of the shallow water. Nimue briefly took the form of a wren and flew up to take position comfortably inside the long-boat. Merlin and Sir Guaen had to give Morgan a leg up in order to get her aboard. When that was done Guaen dutifully went to give the men a hand with re-floating the craft.

It was surprisingly easy to do, there was so much assistance. Soon the boat was floating freely in the water. Merlin directed from his viewpoint at the stern of the vessel.

"Half of ye get aboard now, the other half turn the bow of the boat to face the entrance to the estuary."

The order was easy enough. Executing it in near neck-deep water was not. It became apparent that only the tallest of the men need bother try this manoeuvre and the shorter men started to climb up the ropes to board the longboat.

With a lot of pushing and puffing from the workers they managed to get the nose of the boat pointed in the general direction of their escape route. Merlin had taken up position at the rudder and was assisting as best he could.

"Climb aboard!" he bellowed from the stern of the boat. Men and women reached over the side to give the others a hand to clamber aboard. "The wind is picking up!" exclaimed Morgan. This was just the turn of luck that they needed. When the last of the drenched faeries and oarsmen were aboard Sir Guaen took over directing the crew.

"Raise sail," he said.

The motley crew effortlessly raised the sail as if they had been working together for a lifetime. It soon showed signs of being puffed-up with the increasing wind. The thrill of making sail in the bright moonlit night filled them all with glee. The oarsmen could be heard engaging the strangely dressed newcomers with obvious questions like "Who are ye?," "Where did ye come from?" and similar. However they were nearly frozen rigid with fear when they discovered that they were trying to escape from the Green Knights who were in the water on their horses and swimming toward them.

"Keep a lookout for the Green Knights and their horses" bellowed Sir Guaen. A flurry of men rushed to the edges of the vessel and looked down into the water fearing what they might see. A piercing scream from the stern of the boat alerted everyone to the presence of the Green Knights. The man standing beside Merlin was pointing down at the water. Morgan and Nimue raced to the stern and looked over to where the horrified man was pointing. The two Green Knights were close. Merlin realised that the ropes used to pull the boat back into deeper water were still dangling off the stern.

He was about to order that they be pulled in when one of the Green Knights managed to grab onto a rope close by him. The rope tensed as he heaved himself off his horse. With hand over hand he deftly climbed up the rope.

Sir Guaen drew his sword and pushing the women away from the side of the boat slammed it down onto the rope. The Green Knight fell with a loud splash into the water. Merlin felt a sudden strain on the rudder. "Something is wrong with the rudder" he shouted. Before anyone could react to what he said, the same oarsman that had spotted the Green Knights before let out yet another mortified scream. The people at the stern of the boat leant over to see what he was looking at. The Green Knight had managed to take up a standing position on the slim but sturdy rudder. He appeared to be standing up in the water.

"Throw something at him!" screamed Morgan. People looked around for anything that may be of assistance. But it was too late. The Green Knight had crouched down and with a superhuman push jumped off the rudder and onto the stern of the boat.

He drew his sword, his dead eyes looking directly at the ill-fated Sir Guaen. Just as a sword battle seemed inevitable an oar flew through the air as if it had been tossed like a Greek javelin; the flat end of the oar neatly hitting the Green Knight squarely in the face. Simultaneously and completely coincidentally the boat lurched on a wave and the Green Knight lost balance and tumbled overboard.

He hit the water and angrily splashed about still trying somehow to catch the boat whose speed was increasing every moment. People let out a collective sigh of relief.

"Pull in those ropes!" ordered Merlin, not wanting to take a chance that they may be used again to assist the Green Knights. "Did anybody see what happened to the other one?" he inquired of the crew.

Nimue answered. "The second Green Knight could not get close enough to the boat Merlin. We should be safe now."

"Merlin, were shall we make sail? We must stay ahead of the Green Knights until the Gaelach disappears from the sky." Morgan was stating what they already knew but it helped Merlin focus upon what to do next.

"The prevailing winds should take us around the coast and to the north. We will make for the bay near Mynyw Castle. By the time we reach there the moon should hath nearly set."

Even as he spoke the words Merlin was calculating whether or not he was correct in his estimations. It seemed to hold true. By the time they reached Arthur's most recently-built Castle, it should indeed be time for Gaelach to disappear from the sky. The Green Knights window of opportunity to kill Sir Guaen would be at an end.

"We need to get word to King Arthur, Galahallt and Garethe," said Sir Guaen.

Morgan turned to Nimue and continued Guaen's thought. "We left them on the road leading into Cliff Wood. They will be concerned for our safety."

Nimue reached out and gave Morgan's forearm a reassuring squeeze.

"I will fly back and tell King Arthur of thine plans." She offered. Turning to her faeries she further commanded "Mine people will assist ye in safely reaching Mynyw Castle before returning to the faerie forest."

There was a general nod and acknowledgement that they would do exactly as they had been directed. Morgan looked Nimue right in her large beautiful brown eyes.

"Mine thanks Queen Nimue," she said with genuine feeling. Merlin too offered his gratitude as did Sir Guaen. Nimue took the form of an owl and flew off back the direction that they had come. It caused a minor fracas in the small contingent of oarsmen who had no doubt had their fill of magical occurrences for a lifetime.

Chapter 37: Caerleon Castle; Four Days Later

Merlin's plan had come to fruition. The boat had made good time around the coast. He elected to land north of Mynyw castle instead of trying to traverse the River Alum. Even though this would have cut-off time traveling to the castle, the object of their sea faring voyage was to outlast the full moon, not find the most expedient passage to their destination. By the time they had anchored around the peninsula the full moon had disappeared for another month, and with it the threat of the Green Knights.

King Arthur, Merlin, Morgan, Nimue and three of her closes faerie advisors were in conference in the King's study in Caerleon. Nimue was summarising the overall objectives of the forthcoming attack on Skellig Mhor.

"The object is to ensure that Hellekin and the Minotaur do not escape using magical means. Mine attack force will engage Hellekin and prevent him from using his abilities. Morgan and Merlin and I shall attack the Minotaur. Our combined power will surely be enough to give even that ancient beast pause for thought." It all sounded very easy when spoken so succinctly.

King Arthur, however, wanted to know more details about exactly how the three magical beings would combine their powers to attack the Minotaur.

"What spell will ye use to disable the beast?" He looked at the three of them in succession. There was no answer forthcoming. "Surely ye hath thought of how to best defeat this foe?"

He once again engaged the three of them in eye-contact, each in turn. When they failed to respond, Arthur knew that they did not have a completely resolved plan at all. He caught Merlin's gaze and gently shook his head. Merlin knew that he was indicating that the failure to answer such a fundamental question about their strategy meant that it was not a plan that should be implemented.

Arthur quite dramatically stood up from his chair, attracting the looks of all seated around him.

"Until ye can answer that question, the plan is incomplete."

There was no scorn in his tone, but it was clear that he did not approve of the vagueness of the component that he considered to be the heart of the battle.

"The Minotaur must be dealt with; with the greatest possible chance of success; and even then, there must be a back-up plan should the initial one fail." They were words of wisdom from a seasoned fighter.

Merlin was disappointed in his own performance thus far. He of all people knew that Arthur was correct in his derision of their plan. He felt ashamed of his lack of a definitive strategy for such an important battle.

"King Arthur is correct" he said, "If we cannot devise a decisive way to incapacitate the beast, then all of our planning will be for nothing. I suggest that we retreat to the Queen's Hollow and scour the faerie library of spells for anything that we can use to categorically deal with the Minotaur." He looked to Nimue for her support.

"Aye Merlin, we need to be as sure as we are able that there is a way to immobilise the creature at least long-enough for Lady Morgan to strip it of its powers. We should gather ourselves and reconvene at this time tomorrow, in mine Hollow," offered Nimue.

Nimue's advisors all nodded in agreement.

"Then it is done," she proclaimed. She stood from her chair, which made her advisors follow her lead. "Until tomorrow King Arthur, Lady Morgan, Dear Merlin."

With those words, they all transformed into doves and flapped out of the open window into the cloudy sky.

Chapter 38: The Queen's Hollow; the Next Day

Morgan had been given faerie silk robes when she transformed herself from a wren into a miniature version of herself in the Queen's hollow. Merlin had taken to wearing his faerie silk so often now that he could easily have been mistaken for one of Queen Nimue's elderly advisors. The three of them were in the faerie library of spells, and had poured over hundreds of scrolls searching for anything that could give them the advantage over the powerful Minotaur.

"Here is another that will need translating Nimue," said Morgan, handing the flat piece of bark to the Queen.

It was written in a particularly obscure dialect of Lindisfarnish which was well beyond Morgan's capabilities. Nimue took the spell and studied it frowning at the syntax and general poor construction of the directions that it contained.

She shook her head and announced, "tis a spell to prevent milk from going sour."

"Why not just throw a piece of silver into it?" said Merlin almost absent-mindedly.

The two women gave him a look of semi-exasperation which he did not notice. Merlin was intrigued with the spell that he was reading.

"This one is how to take the wool from a sheep without using a blade," he said to nobody in particular. "Each of the woollen hairs is severed at the level of the skin of the sheep and the wool can then be lifted from it as one complete fleece; fascinating."

"Interesting but not very useful on a Minotaur Merlin; his body does not have much hair," Morgan's rebuke fell upon deaf ears. They had been scouring the library for anything useful for the entire afternoon. Morgan and Nimue were hungry and tired and just about fed up. Nimue summoned one of her aids and ordered food and wine to be brought down into the library. The young woman hurried away to do as she was bid transforming into a moth to fly out of the hidden room.

There seemed to be little to do whilst waiting for the refreshment other than continuing the search. Morgan and Nimue each took yet another spell from a niche in the wall of the circular room. The spells that had been ascertained so far were neatly piled into small columns directly in front of the alcoves in which they were found. This way it would be easy to return everything to its rightful place once the search was completed. The room still had over two thirds of the bulk of the spells still in their places. There was much yet to do.

They all quietly read the pieces of bark that they were holding and almost in unison placed it in the pile of other spells that offered them no solution to their problem. Again, and again they repeated the action; sometimes verbalising what the spell did, other times not bothering because it was so completely unable to assist them in defeating the Minotaur. Eventually the Queen's aide arrived with a tray of food and wine. She signalled from the entrance to the library.

Morgan took the initiative and levitated the tray from the hands of the aide and down to the beautifully patterned floor.

Morgan and Nimue took up a position at each side of the tray, sitting on the floor. Nimue called out for Merlin to join them.

"Merlin, please eat and drink something, we could be here for a long time yet."

It was good advice. He agreed and placed the spell that he was reading in the pile ready for refiling when the time came. Sitting between them they now formed a triangle around the tray. Nimue handed Morgan and Merlin a cup of wine. It was clear when they tasted it that it was surprisingly good.

"It is very rare that faeries farm our own food, as ye know we prefer to steal grain and supplies from villages and castles across the land; but this is a wine made by faeries. The grapes are grown to the south of Warwick in a rolling valley as yet unpopulated by anyone. The wine-making process is a secret, but I can tell ye, that this wine was only pressed within the last few days." She was proud of the reaction that this news caused.

Merlin gave a very satisfied yum sound and took another mouthful savouring the exquisite flavour. Morgan too simply had to have another sip.

"Queen Nimue, it is wonderful. It tastes as though it is finest of wines," she said. The compliment pleased Nimue immensely.

"Nimue, with such skill, the faeries could all turn their hands to wine making and create a prosperous industry that the rest of the country could benefit from" observed Merlin. Nimue gestured with her hands "It is not for the want of trying Merlin, but mine people hath lived by raiding the stores of others for a millennia, change is difficult," she explained. Merlin was about to continue with is point when a piece of bark from one of the top most niches fell to the floor attracting all of their attention.

"I must hath disturbed it somehow" said Morgan, although she was wondering exactly how she did. While she was working the closest to where the spell had fallen, she was not close enough to it to have disturbed it. Maybe it was precariously balanced for ages and chose this time to give way, she mused to herself. Morgan reluctantly put down her wine and stood up to walk over and recover the piece of flattened bark. Bending down she took it in her hand and returned with it to her seated position.

"What is it?" asked Nimue. "A spell in Greek" replied Morgan. "Something about purifying gold when it is molten. A spell for jewellers no doubt," observed the sorceress. She was about to put it to one side when she noticed that one of the edges had peeled back. Inspecting it closer Morgan realised that there were actually two pieces of bark in her hand. One had been concealed behind the other and bonded to it somehow. The expression on her face caught the attention of both Nimue and Merlin.

"What is it?" asked Merlin.

"There is another piece of bark on the back of this one," she said. "It's bonded to it somehow."

Whilst she spoke Morgan was using her fingernails to see if the backing piece could be safely separated from the front. It could.

"Whatever it is, it is coming loose now," with deft fingers and much skill she managed to gingerly detach the two pieces. Looking at the formerly hidden piece Morgan could see the faintest of writing.

"There is writing, but it is so faint that I can barely read it; I think that it is Greek, but a very old dialect from the look of it." She squinted at the words recognising some of them from her languages studies.

"Here show me," said Merlin. Morgan handed it over to Merlin who similarly squinted at the writing. "I shall need more light if I am to interpret this; but ye are correct Morgan, it is indeed ancient Greek."

"Perhaps an old Greek spell to rid us of an ancient Greek monstrosity," said Nimue in jest.

Morgan laughed at the implausibility of the suggestion. But Merlin had become very quiet and his expression one of intense concentration.

"Perhaps we should give Merlin some more light, Morgan" suggested Nimue. They both held out their hands and produced flaming balls of fire neatly contained in their grasps. Each extended it over to Merlin to give him the light that he required.

"Oh, mine thanks," he said, briefly looking up when he realised how light it had become around him. "Debilitating the most powerful of magical beings!" he exclaimed almost jumping to his feet in the process.

"No! Surely Not?" said Nimue, "Ye are making fun..." but Merlin interrupted her.

"That is the title of this spell Nimue" he said forcefully, and then reiterated his interpretation of the writing. "Debilitating the most powerful of magical beings; there is no mistake, that is what it says."

Morgan and Nimue leant in closer trying to see what he was looking at. He was correct. They both studiously interpreted each of the words that formed the title of the spell and when done turned at first to each other and then to Merlin. They simply could not believe their fortune.

"I hath never before even heard of such a spell," said Nimue. "Imagine if any of the previous rulers had known of this spell, they would hath been able to rule in perpetuity. There would be none to challenge them. That must be why it was hidden!" Nimue said, trying to summarise her thoughts in as few sentences as possible.

"What does the rest of it say?" asked Morgan eagerly.

Merlin squinted. Even in the bright light provided by the two women, the writing was so faded that it was still very difficult to read.

"I… Hmmm, let me see…ummm….I shall need a specially ground lens to view the writing, preferably in the light of the sun rather than of fire. But I can see that it's a spoken spell requiring no mineral or other ingredients to initiate. If the three of us can learn to invoke this spell then the Minotaur will be bereft of his powers." He stopped speaking and held his chin as though he were struck by a sudden thought.

"What is it, Merlin?" asked Nimue.

He looked at them. "How can we test this spell before the attack?" he said weakly.

The answer was obvious. One or two of them would have to use the spell on the other. It was the only way to be certain of the veracity of the spell. It was an uncomfortable thought. Which of them would allow the others to deprive them of their magical powers?

Nimue spoke up.

"Practice the spell on mine person Merlin, Morgan" she said looking at both of them in turn. They were amazed, unsure what to say.

"This entire situation is of mine making; it is the very least that I can do. It is temporary?" concluded Nimue in an afterthought.

"Aye," assured Merlin, "from what I can see, it will last a day. But I need time to study it more carefully. Think now Nimue. If we discover that this can be used against magical beings, and it lasts one full day, will ye still submit to Morgan and I casting this spell upon ye?"

Nimue dismissed the flaming ball of fire in her hand. She reached out and took Merlin's forearm with one hand and Morgan's with another.

"Aye," she said earnestly. It was decided.

"If this is successful, then we cannot fail in our attack upon Hellekin and the Minotaur," said Merlin just about bouncing up and down on the floor. He was so overjoyed that it was impossible not to get caught up in the moment. Morgan similarly dissipated the fire in her hand and they all shared a group hug.

When they separated, Merlin offered the immediate course of action.

"Queen Nimue, bring this to me at Caerleon tomorrow morning. I shall ensure that it is interpreted correctly and we shall arrange a secret test of the abilities of the spell. If all goes well, then the attack on Skellig Mhor may proceed with all haste."

He handed the treasure to Nimue. They all stood up.

"Until tomorrow morning then," said Nimue. "I shall arrange for mine guards to fly ye back to Caerleon, to save the trouble of transforming into the shape of birds. I know that taking on other forms is painful for ye."

It was an offer too good to refuse. Nimue loudly summoned her guards.

Chapter 39: The Queen's Hollow, Four Months Earlier

It was dark inside the faerie library of spells; there was nobody present, the hatchway beneath the Queen's throne was in place, therefore nobody could enter. At one end, there appeared a rectangle of light. It looked like an elongated painting of a scene with a steep-sloping grassy hillside and blue sky above. Hellekin stepped through the opening and into the room. He looked around. The opening that he'd come through, that led directly back to Skellig Mhor, was providing ample light for him to see. He walked around the circular shape of the room as if trying to decide something.

He stopped at a point and reached up to the limit of his ability and took down a flattened piece of bark and read it. It was a non-descript spell of no consequence. Taking a similar sized shape of bark from beneath his faerie robes he carefully held them together to check that they were roughly the same size. They were. He rested both pieces of bark on a niche in front of him and then produced a small vial of liquid from his robes. Uncorking it, he took his piece of bark and emptied the liquid onto the face of it, spreading it around with his finger, careful to not cover one of the corners with the liquid. Then taking the other piece of bark with the inconsequential spell written upon it, he glued his spell to the back of the first.

Admiring his skilful work, he stretched up and put the two joined pieces of bark back on the top niche from where he found it. Then looking around again he waked to the opposite side of the room and produced a small red stone from within the many hidden pockets of his robes. Once more he had to stretch up high. He got to the very top niche and pushing himself up on his toes was able to just reach the small arched top of the carved-out niche. The wood was soft enough for him to press the stone into the dark wood. It was done. He stood back to check if it could be seen. But the dark coloured wood and the dark coloured stone worked in unison to camouflage the tiny rock from view. Even in the room still quite brightly lit by the portal to Skellig Mhor, he could not see the stone. His work was done. Giving the room a final cursory look including the hatchway in the ceiling of the library, he stepped through the rectangle of scenery. It dissipated after he was through, and soon the room was again empty and dark.

***

Hellekin walked through the instantaneous travel aperture and onto the ground of Skellig Mhor. Before him the Minotaur towered above him, enormous. Hellekin transformed himself to his full sized human form. The Minotaur was still quite large but now he was more in-scale with his conspirator and the surroundings.

"It is done," said Hellekin. "There are seeing stones planted throughout Caerleon castle, and now there is one in the faerie library of spells. We will be able to see everything that happens in the main rooms of Arthur's castle including Merlin's room and Morgan's too." His self-satisfied tone was evident.

"What of the false spell to deprive powerful magicians of their abilities?" asked the Minotaur, his voice booming.

"It is hidden in the library," Hellekin responded. "We shall simply need to choose a time when Nimue is scouring the library in search for anything that will help her in defeating us, and then make it fall from the top niche. I will rely on her astuteness to see that there is another spell surreptitiously concealed behind it."

"Ye are a conniving faerie Hellekin," complimented the Minotaur. "By not making it obvious, ye are giving her the impression that it is a spell that may hath been hidden for an eon." He then laughed long and loudly. "Excellent, mine evil friend; excellent. But what of Merlin and Morgan? Are ye certain that they will uncover our allegiance and attribute the Green Knight to us?" The Minotaur looked evenly at Hellekin.

"I have every confidence that Morgan and Merlin are magicians of such calibre that they will uncover our alliance. They are both prone to visions of the past, present and future. Believe me, they will find out that we are working against them and try everything in their power to stop us. Nimue will find out about Merlin's dilemma and will give him the spell. They will find our hiding place and attack, believing that they will be victorious. And ye can feast upon the life force of Caerleon's sorcerer and sorceress." Hellekin was so pleased with himself he couldn't help bursting into maniacal laughter at the end of his summation.

Chapter 40: Skellig Mhor, the Present

Hellekin and the Minotaur couldn't believe their luck; Nimue, Morgan and Merlin all together in the faerie library of spells. They watched them for hours. From within the stone hut on the side of Skellig Mhor Hellekin was using magic to see through the stone that he'd planted in the room. The scene was hanging in mid-air just in front of the fireplace; the roaring fire behind it providing a flickering consistency to the scene. Just as the three magical beings were sitting down on the floor to eat, the Minotaur used his power to open the smallest of instantaneous travel-ways in the room. The Minotaur then used the tiniest amount of magic to make the planted false-spell fall from its niche to the floor.

With the small travel-way safely closed, they did not have to hold back their laughter as Morgan uncovered the false spell. They listened to the conversation being transmitted from the eye stone. Merlin was speaking.

"If all goes well, then the attack on Skellig Mhor may proceed with all haste." Merlin handed the spell to Nimue. They all stood up.

"Until tomorrow morning then" said Nimue.

Hellekin imitated Merlin. "The attack on Skellig Mhor may proceed with all haste," and then laughed loudly, the Minotaur joining in. "

Ye death too may proceed with all haste Merlin," again he was unable to hold back the vicious laughter, the two villains slapping their thighs with mirth; their smiles twisted into snarls.

Chapter 41: Caerleon Castle; the Next Morning

Merlin had been awake since long before sunrise. Although tired from the previous day, and drained from transforming into a very small version of himself, so that he could fit into the Queen's hollow, he was still unable to sleep properly. The very thought that this uncovered spell could do what it claimed was giving him energy and preventing restful sleep.

The roosters in the village could be heard crowing in the early morning light. Merlin pushed the blanket off himself and swung his legs over the side of his bed. The flagstones were cold. He looked around for his sandals. Finding them exactly where he had placed them the previous night, he put them on and stood up.

"I may as well go to the kitchen and get some food" he said to nobody.

***

When Merlin arrived at the kitchen, he was surprised to see Morgan sitting at one of the workspaces normally occupied by a kitchen-hand. She looked up as he came into the capacious room.

"Trouble sleeping?" she inquired, knowing the answer before it came.

"Aye" replied Merlin "and ye?"

She nodded. "Here, have some bread and cheese. There is some roast pork left over from last-night's meal."

She pointed to a neatly cut side of well-cooked pork that had been left on the table. It was there for the night-watch to avail themselves of, but there was still plenty left.

Merlin gathered a small pile of nourishment and sat down opposite Morgan.

"If this spell works, then our victory over Hellekin and the Minotaur is assured. It is what happens after that sits heavily upon my mind," he said.

Morgan cocked her head slightly in wonderment, but he continued.

"The faeries will possess the spell that they have searched for…for an age. It will cost Nimue her life."

He looked down at the plate of food unable to continue. Morgan understood why he was depressed. She offered him some solace.

"It requires a magician of your abilities to do so. The faeries will not be able to find any such Sorcerer easily. Nimue may reign for another hundred years before another of thine ilk is born in the land." Her logic should have been enough to brighten his mood but it did not.

"Morgan, ye could cast that spell for the…" Merlin began. Morgan interrupted him.

"I will not." He looked at her and was sure of her genuineness. This pleased him. He smiled and nodded a silent thank you to her.

She reached out and squeezed his hand. Just then the flapping of a white dove broke the silence. They both looked up it had landed on the sill of the kitchen window. In a shimmer of light it had transformed into Nimue.

"I gather that we all could not sleep in anticipation for this day. I went to both of ye rooms and found them empty."

She studied them both. Merlin and Morgan stood and moved forward to greet her.

"Welcome Queen Nimue," said Merlin, he gently embraced her. Morgan too gave Nimue a similarly warm hail.

"Are ye ready?" asked Morgan. Nimue looked nervous but resigned. She blinked slowly and shook her head. "No, but it must be done. I did not bring any of mine aides with me. I shall rely upon the kindness of King Arthur and his court to host me when I am without mine powers."

"Nimue ye will be safe here with us," said Morgan she took Nimue by the shoulders and gave her a reassuring look.

Merlin looked around him, there were three of the kitchen hands entering from the far side of the room.

"Come, let us retire to mine chambers. We will work there. It should not take more than an hour for me to completely interpret the ancient Greek writing. Then the spell may be cast and we can see immediately if it does all that it claims."

They exited from the room with the curious gazes from the staff following them.

***

In Merlin's chamber the three of them were opening scrolls and trying to find the exact interpretation of one of the words that had this far vexed them.

"Here," said Nimue "I think this is it."

She handed the scroll to Merlin pointing to the part that she believed was relevant. Morgan and Merlin squinted at it.

"Aye!' shouted Merlin. "Indeed that is the word. Excellent, it is interpreted."

He looked down and finished off transcribing the spell from ancient Greek into Welsh. He held up the results for the two women to see.

"It is done, a simple spoken spell that requires nothing more than the ability to push forward the words onto the subject and have them drain the magic from the being. It should last one full day." He was obviously pleased with the results.

As Merlin had predicted, it had taken less than an hour.

"When should we try it?" asked Morgan.

"Why not right now?" he responded and then looked to Nimue. If that is acceptable?" he added.

Both Merlin and Morgan knew what a sacrifice this was for Nimue. She had been a magical being since birth and had never been without her powers. Now, if successful, she would effectively be a human for the day. Unable to take on the form of animals or do anything that she had become accustomed to over her entire lengthy life. Nimue breathed in and out deeply trying to steal her nerves and face what was to come.

"I see no reason to delay Merlin. Should I stand; or sit," she said suddenly showing her nervousness. Merlin reached over and put his hand on her forearm…

Chapter 42: Skellig Mhor; that Same Moment

Hellekin had had a sleepless night; he had elected to watch Merlin in his room through a skilfully hidden eye stone that he had planted there months before. It was a calculated decision. Hellekin was sure that it would be Merlin to cast the false-spell upon Nimue and he wanted everything to be ready when the time came. He'd watched Morgan and Merlin's early morning breakfast in the huge kitchen, once again through a very cleverly hidden eye stone. He had observed Nimue arrive and their eventual retreat to Merlin's chamber.

"Wake!" shouted Merlin to the sleeping Minotaur.

The beast was snoring loudly in a large bed on one side of the stone hut. The interruption to his slumber caused a gulping and broken snore. "Wake, it is time!" shouted Hellekin louder this time. The Minotaur shook himself awake and sat up on the bed, looking over to Hellekin with his bull eyes. He loudly stirred himself and stumbled over to where Hellekin was pointing at the vision floating before the fireplace. The Minotaur assessed the scene in an instant. Merlin was speaking the words of the false-spell to Nimue, Morgan was present also. "Now quickly before the moment is past!" hissed Hellekin to the large beast.

The Minotaur raised his left arm and pointed at a spot to the left of the floating vision. There opened the smallest of instantaneous travel portals. The creature could be heard mumbling something beneath his breath. When he was done, he snapped his large fingers and the surreptitious portal closed.

***

Merlin, Nimue and Morgan were completely unaware that the tiny portal had opened somewhere near the pillows on Merlin's bed. Even if they had been looking at it, it would have been difficult to see. A mosquito could have barely used it to travel from Skellig Mhor to Caerleon. But it was not a physical transposition that was required. Only a variation of the spell of magical inhibiting 'fog' was needed to be sent through the opening. The spell found its intended victim and silently descended upon Nimue, enveloping her like an invisible blanket.

Merlin finished speaking the words of the spell. He looked into Nimue's eyes.

"Do ye feel different?" he inquired.

She looked to the ceiling and around her as if expecting to see something.

"No" she replied. "Try transforming into a mouse," suggested Merlin, making a cheeky reference to the first time that she had entered his room all of those years ago.

She understood the reference and let out a small laugh. Then just as quickly her mirth turned to puzzlement. She looked to Morgan and to Merlin an unmistakable note of panic in her voice.

"I cannot.... I cannot change mine form!" She stood up from the stool panicked by the experience.

Merlin however was ecstatic.

"It worked!" he said also jumping up from his seat.

Morgan joined them standing, it seemed the correct thing to do in the situation.

"It works, Nimue, it works Morgan, we will be undefeatable!" exclaimed Merlin; he was actually jumping up and down with glee. Nimue although mortified at losing her magical abilities knew that it was the key to their battle strategy. Even in the position she now found herself, it was hard not to be infected with Merlin's joyous revelry. She leaned forward and warmly embraced him; the three of them just as quickly embraced once more.

"The attack may proceed as soon as the faeries are ready!" shouted Merlin.

"Victory will be ours!" joined in Morgan.

Nimue's comment was not in keeping with the general demeanour of the room nor the direction of the conversation. "Ye are certain that mine powers will return in a day. A single day was all that it said the spell would last." Nimue knew exactly what the spell said, but sought re-confirmation anyway.

"A day is much longer than we will need to defeat Hellekin and the Minotaur," smirked Merlin not wanting to detract from his idea of how successful the forthcoming attack would be. But he could see the worry written on Nimue's face. He put his arm around her.

"Ye will be safe here with us Queen Nimue, and treated as is befitting a monarch of thine stature."

It was a gracious thing to say, and it went a long way toward calming Nimue's apprehension.

"Fear not, by this time tomorrow morning ye will be restored to thine wonderful magical self," he concluded.

Morgan too offered Nimue comfort. "We will do all of the things that visiting royal women do. Twill be a day of falconry, and entertainment for ye our royal visitor from…"

Morgan paused. Would it be proper to let the general populous of Caerleon know that they were entertaining a royal faerie. Merlin anticipated the reason for her hesitation and finished the sentence for her.

"A royal visitor from the faerie forest to the north of Caerleon." He said exactly what Nimue had hoped he would.

There was no further need for secrecy about the faeries. The castle dwellers and the Villagers had seen more than their fair share of supernatural events this year. It somehow seemed silly to continue denying the existence of the faeries, especially now that an alliance had been formed with them to fight for a common goal.

At that moment, there was a knock on Merlin's door by a servant summoning the wizard to the morning meal. He marched over to the door and flung it open. The startled servant looked at Merlin, Morgan and the strangely dressed woman in the room.

"Inform King Arthur and Queen Gwenhwyvar, that Queen Nimue of the Faerie People will be joining us for the morning meal and visiting us for the entire day. Chambers will be required for tonight for our Royal guest. Queen Nimue will be leaving us tomorrow morning."

He announced loudly and deliberately to the man. Almost quivering with shock at the news the man at first stood still unsure of what to do.

"Well?" asked Merlin "Off ye go!' he said quite loudly and with mock impatience.

The servant turned and hurried away, clearly bursting to tell the first person that he came across the extraordinary news that he had just been entrusted with. Merlin swung around and laughed at the reaction that he had caused; the two women joining into the merriment.

"That news will spread throughout Caerleon before we can descend the great staircase," observed Morgan.

"Aye, that it will," agreed Merlin. "Shall we join the court for the morning meal?" he asked turning and offering both of his arms for the women to take, one each side.

They dutifully took his raised hands and somehow managed to exit the narrow doorway in a most exalted fashion.

***

The Minotaur and Hellekin watched the three exit Merlin's room. Hellekin turned to the creature.

"The spell that ye used, will last the entire day?" he wanted assurance that the final point of his intricately devised trap was going to succeed. "It is a variation of the magical inhibiting aura that I hath surrounded the Green Knight with. I gave her just enough of it to last a day and a night. Nimue's powers will be restored by first light tomorrow."

Hellekin gave a single loud clap of his hands.

"Perfect. Now all we need to know is when they plan to attack us?"

Chapter 43: Caerleon Castle, Nightfall

The day had indeed been one full of activity as Morgan had promised. Queen Gwenhwyvar was as usual the perfect royal host. News of the visiting Queen, and the fact that she was a faerie no less, spread faster than falling rain across the valley. Everywhere that the visiting royal went, she found herself surrounded by admiring and curious onlookers; much more so than a normal royal visitor would have invoked from the people. The ladies of the court giggled at the curiousness of the villagers.

Morgan and Merlin were acutely aware that a number of faeries had arrived at the castle in the form of pigeons or doves and taken up residence in vantage-points throughout the grounds. It was to be expected, they were naturally concerned with the safety of their queen. But as the day wore on, and the friendly activities and benevolent nature of the crowd that Nimue drew became obvious, their numbers dwindled. They were under their queen's orders to not interfere with the testing of the magical inhibiting spell. But she did not blame them. Nimue recognised some of her closest advisors and guards amongst the birds that littered the trees and battlements. She was not angry with them for showing such caring concern for her.

Nimue was in conference with some of her advisors and her guard commander in her beautifully prepared chamber. He advisor was speaking.

"This news is both welcome and vexing, mine Queen. We now possess the means by which we can achieve victory over the beast and Hellekin. However, Merlin, the most powerful sorcerer in the land now has possession of a spell that can rob us all of our magical abilities."

It was a valid point, but one that Nimue was careful show that she had little concern over. "Merlin is an honourable man. We will be assured of receiving from him the spell of fertility at the conclusion of our current alliance. If the spell of fertility is to be invoked then we need to show Merlin that we do not fear or distrust him. He is the only one that is powerful enough to cast the spell for us." Her logic was flawless.

Feeling somewhat rebuked, although in the nicest possible way, he continued with his concerns.

"Yet he hath so far refused to be the sorcerer to invoke the fertility spell for our people?" Nimue knew this all too well. "For now it is enough that the fertility spell will once more be in possession of the faerie nation. We are a long-lived people. I hath hopes that Merlin will relent and perform the magic for us, but if he does not, there will be others in time that will equal or surpass his great powers."

That was an end to the discussion as far as Nimue was concerned.

Nimue's guard commander was just opening his mouth to voice his concerns about the very same things, but was skilfully headed-off by Nimue.

"Soon, I will be summoned for the evening meal with King Arthur and his court. Return to me tomorrow with specific plans for the attack on Skellig Mhor. There is no more reason to delay. Mine powers will be restored by the morning, and I want to present King Arthur, Merlin and Morgan with our final attack and battle strategy before I leave Caerleon."

It was a royal command from Queen Nimue. Clearly the queen had spoken and was no longer entertaining the fears of her advisors. They all bowed in unison and transformed into various birds flapping their way across the room and through the open shutters of the window.

Nimue walked over and watched them fly away. Although she had enjoyed her day as a human, she could not wait to once again be a faerie and fly through the air. Watching them she felt the pang of desire to regain her magical abilities. Her contemplation was distracted by a knock at the door.

"Enter" she called from her position by the window.

Morgan opened the door. "Would you like me to accompany ye to the banquet?" she asked.

Nimue was very grateful for the offer. "Thank you, Lady Morgan, that would be wonderful," she replied.

"Then let us depart, the horn is about to sound." And as if by magic the sound that announced the beginning of the meal could be heard coming up through the stairway and halls.

Nimue joined Morgan and they regally walked together toward the great staircase. "Did ye enjoy the day with us here at Caerleon?" politely asked Morgan. Nimue turned to meet her gaze and said with absolute honesty, "Aye."

Chapter 44: Caerleon Courtyard; Day of the Attack

It was a further three days before all was finalised with the attack. The main courtyard of Caerleon was awash with faeries, all in their human form. The Castle dwellers and many of the Villagers had come to see the spectacle. Word had got out that something big was happening on this day; but nobody knew for sure exactly what it was. It was four hours after sunrise. A sense of expectation filled the air. Farmers and artisans mingled with the faeries trying unsuccessfully to glean some information from them.

King Arthur stood with Queens Nimue and Gwenhwyvar; he was deep in conversation with the both of them. Merlin and Morgan appeared from within the Castle and looked at the throng of people and faeries before them. They would have quite a time negotiating their way through the crowd toward the royals. They could have been mistaken for the faeries, as they were both wearing their faerie robes. Some of the servants nudged Merlin and asked him what all of the fuss was, but he waved his hand dismissively and continued to gently push his way toward Arthur. Morgan followed closely behind him.

Eventually they managed to arrive at their goal. Arthur, Gwenhwyvar and Nimue greeted them as they approached.

"All is in readiness, mine King, we hath nothing more to do other than to travel to our destination and subvert our enemy." Merlin reported.

It was welcome news to King Arthur. The next full-moon was only a week away now. The very thought of having to endure yet another attack from the Green Knights filled Arthur with dread. Hearing Merlin's cocky summation of their objective gave the king a sense that all would soon be well again.

"Good work Merlin, Morgan and of course Queen Nimue," he said gently nodding to the faerie Queen.

"Time is marching on like the legions of Rome," observed Merlin, "we should depart."

He looked to Nimue for confirmation. She agreed and held up a hand, which immediately got the attention of all the faeries in the courtyard. There were easily one hundred.

"We await our small travellers," said Nimue with a mischievous smile directed at Morgan and Merlin. As planned, they would travel in their miniaturised human form, it would have been impractical to take on the shape of the pink-footed Geese that the faeries would use to travel the long distance to Skellig Mhor.

Morgan and Merlin found the act of transforming into another species painful and it took a long time to enable. However, being each carried by a Goose as a small version of themselves would mean that they could transform back more readily when they reached the island. Two of the biggest and burliest of Nimue's guards would do the honours. They stood nearby awaiting their instructions.

Merlin was not shy about practicing magic before the people of Caerleon. They had seen him for the most part construct the walls and towers of the Castle. Morgan however was a little shy about shrinking her form using magic before such a large crowd. Merlin noticed her hesitation and decided to lead by example.

He summoned his strength and mumbled the spell that he had taught Morgan. Within seconds he had begun to shrink. His magical faerie silken robes shrinking around him. Morgan suddenly felt that her modesty was holding up the entire plan. She bowed her head in concentration and mumbled the words beneath her breath that would shrink her form to one tenth of her original size. The effect was immediate. With both Merlin and Morgan now a tiny version of themselves, and amidst the ogling of the human crowd, the faeries were free to take on the forms of the long-distance-flying geese.

Queen Nimue gave a final acknowledging nod to Queen Gwenhwyvar and King Arthur and then transformed in a shimmer of light. All around her the faeries took upon the form of the pink-footed goose. Caerleon's courtyard was suddenly full of Geese. With an unspoken, or un-squawked order the two geese assigned to carry the miniaturised Morgan and Merlin took flight and flapped down toward their charges. The webbed feet of the geese wrapped around the biceps of the two small humans and after the geese took flight they drew their legs up into the feathers, so that Morgan and Merlin were effectively cosseted by a the feathery underbelly of the birds. It was going to be a long, but cosseting ride for them to Skellig Mhor.

The flock of geese took to the air with frenetic flapping of wings and to the uplifting cheer of the amazed crowd. Merlin and Morgan had a unique perspective of the entire departure. Warm against the bellies of their geese-guards they watched the courtyard of Caerleon fall away beneath them. It was exhilarating. Within seconds the entire vista of the Castle could be viewed. Then, in what seemed only a few short moments after they had left Caerleon behind they were flying across the green rolling hills of North Wales. The view was spectacular and served to hide the true reason for the flight across the land. Morgan and Merlin were revelling in the experience. This was higher and longer than they had ever been carried before, as passengers of bird-faeries. The sky was blue, littered with white clouds that picked up the sunlight and radiated it from within, making each of them glow with light.

Watching the flock ascend there was a sole figure on the highest battlement of the tallest tower of Caerleon. Nobody noticed her. Matrona, the Lady of the Lake watched the attack force fly into the sky and head northwards. Her clear eyes followed the flock with far more precision and clarity than was available to those below in the Courtyard. She looked down at the throng of people below. Piece by piece she faded away from sight until she was gone.

***

Nestled in the feathers and against the stomachs of the geese, they could feel the heart-beats of the bird through the soft feathers. It was calming, mesmerising and exciting all at the same time. The scenery flew past. The flock of geese flew for mille passuum after mille passuum. The coast was now visible. They flew north following the coastline. The wind rushing past them and the altitude did not affect Morgan and Merlin. They were content to be held tightly as if in a mother's bosom. As impossible as it seemed, the flight and the length of the journey served to make both of them tired. Soon, Merlin and Morgan had completely lost track of time. They both succumbed to the gentleness of sleep.

***

Suddenly they were only a second away from landfall. Morgan and Merlin awoke with a fright. Gently deposited on the firm ground they looked above them as their carrier-geese made landfall beside them a wing-span away. In a blur, they had transformed into the small version of their human-selves. Geese were flapping noisily to the ground all around them. The entire flock transformed into their small-faerie-selves upon landing.

Nimue had somehow managed to land between Merlin and Morgan and in her small form drew the both of them to her. She addressed the gathered faeries.

"Mine people; we have arrived at the Island of Mann. It is here that we will rest before our final assault on Skellig Mhor. Find nourishment in the surrounding land and take what rest ye are able. We leave for battle in two hours."

The faeries almost simultaneously transformed into animals of all shapes and sizes and scurried away to find food to fortify them before the forthcoming battle. Nimue tuned to Merlin and Morgan.

"This is the only place upon the Island that we are able to land; the southernmost tip." Merlin understood the inference immediately.

"Because the Christian Monks hath taken up residence upon the Northern point of the Island?"

It was a statement made in question so as to confirm Merlin's understanding of the relationship between Christianity and the faeries.

"Aye Merlin," responded Nimue "The faerie people are unable to exist near the Christians. We find them a hindrance to our powers as much as ye find the Green Knight a hindrance to yours. It is best that we avoid any place where they proliferate." Nimue stated the situation as if it were something that annoyed her, but was to be endured as it could not be changed. She produced some dried-flat-white substance from within her faerie robes and handed a piece to Morgan and then to Merlin.

"Eat this. It is compound of flour, water, cheese, oats and dried meat, combined with various herbs and spices to ensure that it does not easily spoil. We use it on long-distance journeys like this one. It will sustain ye for the remainder of the day and more."

Merlin and Morgan took the pieces of food from Nimue, gingerly sniffing them before tasting a small portion. It was surprisingly good, given the dour description that Nimue had endowed it with. They contentedly ate without much conversation above and beyond their immediate objective. The battle plan was so well rehearsed that it seemed second nature. As if all they had to do was land, transform and enable their plan, thus defeating Hellekin and the Minotaur. It all seemed deceptively simple. And in that self-assurance, one of them should have felt some uneasiness. But Nimue, Merlin and Morgan were so assured that they could pull-off a victory against a much more powerful foe, that they were blinded to how easily they had been led down the path of destruction.

Chapter 45: BC 3579: The Minotaur's Labyrinth; Greece

The Minotaur moaned and bellowed. It was impossible. He had devoured a plethora of virgin girls to enhance his powers, yet he still could not transform his head and neck back into that of his human-self. No matter how much of the life-essence of others that he consumed it made no difference. Nothing would restore his once handsome looks to their former-regal beauty. A thought occurred to him. Perhaps he should be absorbing the life-force of young men instead. Maybe that would make a difference to his abilities to transform.

With renewed vigour he set out to ensnare the young and curious men of the nearby village from which he had taken almost all of the girls.

***

One hundred years later the Minotaur found himself standing at the edge of the sea. It was night. The full-moon shone above him. Nothing that he had tried over the preceding century had worked. No amount of sacrifices to his powers whether they were men or women had enabled him to regain his rightful-form. His ability to take on the shape of any animal had long-since vanished. He was trapped in this hideous hybrid of a creature's body. It had been so long since anyone had even said his name that he had to think about it before his memory would reveal it once more to him. Anger and resentment for his own inability poisoned every fibre of his being. The only solace that he found was his own increased magical abilities. It was the ultimate insult. He had become more powerful than any faerie before him, save Matrona, that elusive former faerie Queen that had vanished into the world so totally as to be nothing more than myth herself. Yet all of his powers could not give him the one thing that he wanted above everything else. To be restored.

His now almost limitless life would be a prison for him endure his misshapen body. Any vestige of decency had long-since died within him. Now there was nothing left but the hollow-pursuit of more power to serve as recompense for the one thing that was denied him. And pursue it he would, through thousands of years. He accumulated thousands of spells, inventing many of them himself, growing in power year after year, decade after decade. He was for all intents and purposes, invincible, yet still incomplete.

Chapter 46: Skellig Mhor, the Present Day; Mid Afternoon

Hellekin stepped through the portal leading from the mainland. He was hand-in-hand with a young wide-eyed maiden. Stepping through the rectangular opening that led from her village to this far-away island, she stopped.

"Indeed, ye are a powerful magician," said the young lady.

She was about to tell Hellekin that in all of her years she had never seen such a feat of magic, but he pressed his lips to hers and kissed her roughly. She did not resist. How could she? So impressed was she with the handsome stranger that had strolled nonchalantly into her village that all thoughts of sensibility were gone.

He started to pull at her clothing. Modesty made her pull back. She looked around as if to warn him that somebody could be watching.

"There is nobody else on mine island my dear, just the two of us," he said in what sounded like a warm reassurance.

The thought of making love in the open air in the afternoon sunshine aroused the lass. Hellekin grabbed both of her breasts. He could feel her nipples harden. Again, he forced his lips onto hers. He pulled her closer to him so that she could feel his erection growing in his loins. He broke the almost brutal kissing of the hapless woman just long enough to sneer.

"Would ye like to see some more magic?" Without waiting for a response, he mumbled something beneath his breath and suddenly the clothing on the woman fell off. It was impossible to tell where it had split, if indeed it had, but it fell from her body as if it were shredded, yet remained whole.

She was amazed. The broad smile of lust and mischief covering her face pleased Hellekin. He used magic to make his own faerie-silk robes disappear completely. They stood naked on the grassy slope, the sun shining on their bare skin. She admired the perfect physique of her chosen lover; his healthy erection and handsome features. She reached out to fondle his bulging pectorals. Leaning in she bit one of his nipples with her front teeth. Hellekin groaned with pleasure and excitement.

He dragged her to the ground. It felt soft beneath them. Thrusting himself into her, she initially drew a sharp breath but let out a moan of pleasure rather than pain. This continued with frenetic energy and much panting and satisfied whimpering. Hellekin caught a sign of movement out of the top of his eye. It was the Minotaur coming out of the hut. Hellekin disengaged himself from the woman and stood up.

"Let's stand" he commanded. He helped her to her feet, she was now facing directly away from the beast and would not see him approaching.

He kicked her legs apart to spread them wider. Then he pushed his penis into her vagina again. The naked Minotaur approached from behind without making a sound. His large penis was now fully erect and dripping with pre-seminal fluid. Hellekin slowed the pace of his pumping pelvis.

"There is one more surprise for ye, mine Dear," he said breathing heavily.

The woman rolled her eyes from back in her head to try and focus upon him and what he was saying. She managed to say the beginning of the word 'what' but was cut short by a searing pain in her vagina. She could feel somebody pushing up against her from behind. She screamed in fright and agony as both erect penises pushed their way into her simultaneously. Twisting her head she could see the broad shoulders of a large burley man. She screamed again, she was in absolute agony and shock.

Somehow, she managed to twist her head to the other side between the two broad chests pushing against her. Her muscles must have been more flexible on that side of her neck because she could angle her head just a little further to see the face of her unwelcomed attacker. It was hideous. A bulls-head with dripping nostrils and grunting mouth greeted her field of vision. Again, she drew breath to scream all the more loudly. It was exhilarating for Hellekin who reached climax and ejaculated in the woman. Perversely the injection of semen helped to lubricate her vagina and gave her a small relief from the unbelievable pain that she had so far endured.

Hellekin finished his orgasm and withdrew his penis from the victim. He breathed a huge sigh of relief and morbid satisfaction.

Death was a merciful relief for the young woman. The Minotaur began to seep the life-force from her just as he too ejaculated within her vagina.

Soon there was nothing left of the poor girl but a liquefied mess upon the sloping grassy hill.

***

From their vantage points in the sky swooping downwards, the faerie attack force saw the last few moments of the latest victim of Hellekin and the Minotaur. It made Nimue sick to the stomach to see how cruelly the poor girl had met her death. The attack would come too late to save her, but it would certainly stop any further women falling victim to the merciless faerie and his cohort.

Flying in a line of three across, not a perfect formation but one that attracted the attention of Hellekin nevertheless. They could see the look of confusion upon his face even as they approached the ground. Hellekin waved his hand and reinstated his faerie robes. The Minotaur did the same. Geese flapped down toward the ground all around them. Unseen by Hellekin and the Minotaur, the two Geese carrying Merlin and Morgan landed on the far side of the stone hut. They gently released their charges to the moss-covered ground. Merlin and Morgan wasted no time.

"Quickly," said Merlin to Morgan. "The spell to restore our rightful stature."

They both said the words aloud. Within seconds they had transformed to their full-sized selves once more.

The two geese that had carried them changed into their burley human forms. They would act as the personal guards of the sorcerer and sorceress during the operation. As one they marched around to the far side of the hut. The sight of nearly one hundred faeries greeted them. They had almost engulfed the Minotaur and Hellekin such was their force. Now all that was needed was the spell to rob the Minotaur of his powers so that he could not fight back and their victory would be complete.

At that moment, the pile of faeries that had overrun the Minotaur went flying, screaming in all directions. They were hurled from the muscular form of the beast with the ease of a man throwing off his cloak.

"Arrrrrrrghh!" rumbled the Minotaur as he did so. "What treachery is this?" he shouted to the sundry faeries that he had just flicked away.

"No trick Minotaur, this is thine end!" responded Morgan. This attracted the attention of the beast and he swung around to see who had spoken the words.

"Sorceress!" he bellowed, recognising the woman who challenged him.

"Release me!" screamed Hellekin. He had been bound by three faeries with ropes made from faerie silk. If Hellekin chose to alter his form the three nooses around him would similarly alter and keep him ensnared. The beast saw that his fellow conspirator was incapacitated. He raised both of his hands and with a gesture flung the ropes off the pleading former ruler. Hellekin shook his head to try and clear it. He looked around to ascertain what was happening. Nimue was there, so was Merlin and Morgan.

"How dare ye set foot upon mine island!" he shouted, pointing at Nimue and then Merlin. "Be gone before we incinerate ye all with ancient magic that ye hath never before encountered."

"An empty threat, Hellekin, from a small man trying to believe that he is great," Nimue's rebuke made Hellekin's eyes narrow and glow with anger. "We do not fear this misshapen faerie, twisted by his hatred of life itself. We know exactly how to defeat ye" she said; her confidence oozing into a smile of growing satisfaction.

She gestured at Merlin, who stepped dutifully forward. Both Hellekin and the Minotaur looked from Nimue to Merlin. There was just a moment of silence then the bellowing of laughter from the both of them. It resounded up and down the hill. Hellekin pointed at Merlin.

"This old man is thine weapon against us?!" he managed to say catching his breath. "Ha!" he said with spite.

The Minotaur took up the jeering. He spread his arms as if to give Merlin a free shot at him. "Let us see what this puny Human Sorcerer is capable of?" he said, in a malevolent and mocking tone.

Merlin stepped forward, and the faeries surrounding them moved back to ensure that nobody was between Merlin and the beast. Raising his right hand and pointing at the large Minotaur with his index finger he spoke words beneath his breath, one maybe two sentences. He finished and lowered his hand looking with satisfaction at the beast.

"And Hellekin too; just to be safe," instructed Nimue. Again Merlin pointed and spoke the words beneath his breath. He finished and smiled at Hellekin.

"What was supposed to happen, old man? I feel no different." Hellekin's sarcastic question jarred Merlin slightly, but he was too gracious to let it upset him. Instead he replied in his polished and cultivated manner. "If mine best was not good enough, then perhaps the both of ye would like to retort?" It was his turn to open his arms in a gesture of welcome to whatever they would direct toward him.

Hellekin and the Minotaur looked at each other. "What should we do to this stupid old man?" badgered Hellekin, poignantly ignoring Nimue, Morgan and the others in the process. The beast answered. "Perhaps we should use the spell that robs great magicians of their powers?"

Merlin, Nimue and Morgan froze. "Aye, what a good idea; just like the one that I wrote onto a piece of bark and planted in the faerie library of spells for ye to find, mine Dear," he spat the final words toward Morgan.

It was a trap and was being sprung around them. The Minotaur reached and with both fists shouted some words that none of them could understand. A wave of air moved out from around him and in all directions. It felt as though it was going to knock them all to the ground. They managed to stay upright with some difficulty, but as they recovered their wits, each of them knew something was seriously wrong. There did not seem to be any words to describe the feeling.

The Minotaur reached out and grabbed the nearest faerie by the face and drained the life-essence from the man in a matter of seconds.

"Retreat!" shouted Nimue. But then the realisation of what had occurred dawned upon them. They were all powerless. None of them could transform into anything. The faerie powers that they had taken for granted their whole lives were gone. They were trapped on the island with a beast of unbelievable power with no way to escape.

Mayhem erupted. Faeries ran screaming in all directions, there was the vain sense of hope that if they could simply put enough distance between them and the Minotaur that they would be alright. It was a foolish assumption. The Minotaur rounded them up with a dramatic sweep of his hand. It was almost as if invisible ropes bound themselves to the panicking group. Suddenly they were pulled backwards toward the Minotaur. Some of the faeries were just frozen in their tracks. They seemed to be trying to move but incapable of it. Others were able to move but it looked like they were wading through snow that was waist deep. Their movements were exaggerated and sluggish.

Hellekin too was using his powers to cause grief. He was assisting the Minotaur by rounding up the faeries that the beast had not managed to retrieve, ensnare, or delay. Using the spell of levitation he was dragging them back and into a manageable group. From out of thin air he produced faerie silk rope of his own and with a flick of his hands it coiled around the group like a worm coiling around a root. He repeated the manoeuvre a few times until he had four groups of faeries now bound and awaiting sacrifice to the insatiable beast.

Merlin and Morgan had watched the entire scene with mounting horror. There was no alternative plan to enable. They were taken completely by surprise. An attempt to escape the line of sight of both evil doers by making toward the hut and circling around to the far side was thwarted by the Minotaur.

"No Merlin; ye will not escape me!" he shouted as he dragged them and Nimue back toward him with his invisible influence. "Come Morgan, come closer to me, I hath not finished with ye yet mine beautiful Sorceress."

As he spoke he beckoned with his hands. Unable to resist the powerful pull they were dragged across the stone and grass toward the hideous creature.

"Shall I devour thine subjects before ye Nimue, and save Merlin and Morgan for last, or shall I absorb their essence now and see what effect it has upon mine powers?"

Merlin, Morgan and Nimue didn't know it at the time but they were all thinking the same thing. This was the day that they were going to die. They were doomed.

Chapter 47: Llyn Callyfyrth

Merlin looked around him. He was standing on top of the water at Llyn Callyfyrth. He did not feel like he was levitating himself. He looked down at the surface of the water. He could feel it beneath the sandals on his feet. It was most unusual.

This was a vision. No. It couldn't be. There was always something in the back of his mind that let him know when he was experiencing a vision, and this felt completely real. He stopped to think about the recent happenings. He did not remember trying to invoke the spell of instantaneous travel. Even if he did, his powers were blocked, or impeded somehow by the Minotaur.

"This could not be a vision. But how did I escape Skellig Mhor?" he said to nobody.

Matrona's voice answered him.

"Your body is still on the island of Skellig Mhor Merlin. I hath removed everything that is not of ye body and reconstructed it at mine lake."

Merlin was surprised to hear the Lady of the Lake's voice. But her explanation did not actually explain what he was doing here or how he came to be here. He wanted much more information than she had provided.

"But I can feel the water beneath mine feet?" he said.

"Merlin, I would strike a bargain with ye."

Her words came from all around him. It was perhaps the most intriguing thing that anybody had ever said to him. Immediately all of the questions about how he still felt like he had a body and how she had brought him to the lake whilst leaving his body at the island did not seem important anymore. He answered cautiously.

"Another bargain. It hath been many years since we struck our first bargain Matrona." His tone was cautious.

She gave a small laugh. "Merlin ye hath fulfilled the terms of our first agreement to mine satisfaction. I gave ye a sword so that the people of this land could rally behind it. Ye tested Uther and directed him to be a fair and just leader. When that failed, ye raised Arthur to be the King that Uther was not. More of the land is united beneath Arthur, Gwenhwyvar and Amhar than it hath experienced in its entire history. I am pleased."

Merlin grabbed the opportunity that the Lady of the Lake was presenting him. "Aye dear Lady, but that rule is in jeopardy now from the Green Knight; a supernatural power that I am powerless to combat."

He hoped that she would be able to offer the solution to the problem that had plagued them for these last months. However, she appeared to have not heard him; her reply made no reference to his assertion at all.

"A second bargain, wizard. There is something that ye must never do, and ensure that Morgan does similarly." Her voice had a stern quality to it. It gave Merlin the feeling that he had better not try to change the subject or argue the point.

He paused only for a moment. He knew that the Lady of the Lake had the best interests of Briton in her heart. Excalibur was proof of that. Subsequently learning that she used to be a faerie had not altered his respect for her at all.

"Aye dear Lady; ye hath mine word...What is it that I shall never do?"

"Do not enable the spell of fertility for the faeries. This is the time for humanity, not faeries. Although they give me hope with their actions, helping ye in thine struggle with Hellekin and the Minotaur; I do not wish for them to be able to perpetuate themselves. Swear this to me Merlin, by all that ye hold dear!"

Merlin was in a spot. "I hath agreed to provide the spell to the faeries if we were successful in our campaign against the beast and the former faerie ruler."

The absurdity of his situation dawned upon Merlin even as he finished the sentence. He had no hope of overcoming the evil duo, there would be no need to honour his promise to Nimue and the faeries.

Matrona interrupted his dour musings.

"Give the spell to Nimue if ye must but never invoke it for them. Swear it to me, sorcerer, as once ye swore that ye would find a king fit to rule the land." Her words sounded urgent and somehow unfitting for a being of such stature.

Merlin let out a sigh of capitulation. He did not know what good it would do, but he was not going oppose the wishes of the Lady of the Lake.

"I swear it Matrona; neither Morgan nor I shall cast the faerie spell of fertility for them whilst we live." Adding the caveat of *'whilst we live'* was his way of trying to begin to come to terms with his impending death back on the island of Skellig Mhor.

The water in front of Merlin bubbled and formed a column that became the body of Matrona. She stood before him on the surface of the Lake. Although it had been almost thirty years since he had last spoken with her she had not aged a single day. She looked different. Her hair was pure white now instead of the black that it had been all of those years ago. Her attire was different too, but in truth, her attire three decades ago was equally as unusual. He could not recall exactly how it had changed other than the colour. It was now all white instead of silver and blue.

She smiled at him.

"Mine thanks Merlin." He felt that he should have been more gracious under the circumstances but the situation that was happening to his body at this point in time filled his thoughts and emotions.

"Dear Lady, mine death awaits me when ye return me to mine body. I am powerless to battle the Minotaur and Hellekin." He listened to himself and was upset that he sounded like he was complaining. But he could not stop himself, he continued. "Keeping mine vow to ye will be easy enough as Morgan and mine candle of life will soon be extinguished." He dropped his head, ashamed.

To his amazement, the Lady of the Lake reached out and took both of his hands in hers. He slowly looked up at her.

"Come with me. Let us see the origins of the Minotaur."

***

Merlin and Matrona stood opposite a very handsome and muscular man. He was competing in the Greek games. The crowds were cheering. He had just completed the javelin throw of a lifetime. This felt like a vision. Merlin looked around him, knowing that nobody could see or hear him. He was in an amphitheatre; he recognised the architecture, definitely Grecian. Matrona pointed to the naked man.

"This is Alkaios. He was born a faerie, but secrets himself into the general population posing as a human. He uses his faerie powers to give himself a fine physique and mastery of all the games that entertain the crowd."

"A harmless enough pursuit surely," interjected Merlin.

Matrona held up a single finger. "He is a vain man that uses his beauty to seduce women. And this is the latest iteration of his identity. Prior to this he was known as Euthane; a successful athlete in the games that lived around fifty years ago. Again and again he reinvents himself as a rising star from a faraway corner of the empire, only to arrive in the capital and amaze everyone with his prowess in competition."

Merlin understood now. The faerie was living the life of a popular athlete over and over again.

"He hath done this now for over five hundred years and Alkaios is the tenth duplication of this hedonistic life. The number of virgins that he has desecrated over the centuries to satisfy his carnal lusts even I cannot count. He embodies everything that I now despise about the faerie people; fickle; vain; uncaring about the humans that surround them."

Now it was absolutely clear to Merlin, this was the ultimate self-indulgent vanity. He could feel the disgust in Matrona's voice. She finished off with four simple words that held the force of a bolder tumbling down a steep mountain side.

"He must be stopped."

Merlin put the pieces together. The build of the man was similar to that of the Minotaur. He guessed that Matrona must have had something to do with the fact that he turned into a bull one day, for some reason, and was never able to completely change back.

"Did ye inflict the Minotaur with his appearance?" asked Merlin.

***

They were back at the lake, both standing in the middle of its unbroken surface.

"It matters not," she said, dismissive of his question. "Gwenhwyvar was clever. She knew that wielding Excalibur she could drive the sword through the faerie's heart even though he had fortified himself from the sting of all other weapons. What the queen did not know is that the beast's head must be separated from its body in order to ensure death. He hath amassed a great deal of power over the centuries Merlin."

It was completely useless information. He did not have Excalibur with them on Skellig Mhor. Even if he did, he could not wield it as he is not a member of the Royal Family that carries the sword. Matrona was providing him with nothing that would help in the current situation. She smiled wryly; easily able to guess what he was thinking. Instead of addressing his concerns she changed the subject of conversation.

"Morgan hath developed a gift that I hath rarely seen throughout mine entire lifetime; the ability to take power from another magical being and make it her own. A unique gift anywhere Merlin, in any land."

She met his gaze. Merlin was confused. Matrona was speaking in riddles. It was not as if Morgan was in any better position to aid with her amazing ability. As long as they were beneath the cloud of magical suppression that the Minotaur had thrown over them, there was no hope.

"I can interrupt the Minotaur's spell that makes thine powers indolent. But it will take every bit of skill and energy from ye to perform the simplest feat of magic. So ye must choose something that will take the beast by surprise; something that ye would normally find very easy to invoke. Astonishment is the key to completely dissipating the spell that the beast has cast upon ye."

Chapter 48: Skellig Mhor

Merlin was back on Skellig Mhor, Morgan and Nimue were shouting at him.

"Merlin, wake up!" he shook his head. He was still ensnared by the force exuding from the Minotaur. He guessed that he must have been 'away' for a while because the creature was standing over him.

"Well!" he shouted at Merlin. The sorcerer guessed that he had missed the part of the diatribe that the Minotaur was now asking for a response to. He looked at the hideous bull face that was close to his. A thought struck him. The Lady of the Lake would be true to her word. He believed that completely. Therefore, the spell that cancelled out his magical abilities would soon be briefly interrupted.

"How long hath ye had this ugly face Minotaur?" asked Merlin in a tone so casual and mocking that it quelled everybody. There was shocked silence. Was Merlin completely crazy? This was sure to enrage the Minotaur; and it did. The beast lashed out with the back of his hand and struck Merlin across the face with such ferocity that Merlin briefly saw flashing lights before his eyes. The pain was immense. Were it not for the invisible chains that bound him to the spot the old man would have surely fallen over from the blow.

The captive crowd all drew in their breath simultaneously, shocked at Merlin's casual insult to the beast and the viciousness of the reprisal.

"Mock me at thine own peril, foolish old man!" screamed the Minotaur.

Merlin was not listening. He felt it; the magical suppression spell had dissipated around him. But it had only vanished around him. He was absolutely sure that an opening in it, or a protective aura around it, had appeared and now he was able to perform magic.

Merlin drew in his breath and faced the creature. He mumbled the words beneath his breath for the spell that he wanted to invoke. The Minotaur could hear some of the words even though they were spoken at a low volume.

"Stupid old man, what spell do ye think will work whilst I inhibit all magic on Skellig Mhor save for mine and Hellekin's. Perhaps ye are not the powerful magician that ye once were?" he laughed. "Maybe I will be doing ye a service by ending thine pathetic life."

Merlin could barely feel the effect of the spell that he was casting. By now it would have normally been done. But as Matrona had said, it was taking every bit of power that he could muster. A glowing silvery figure appeared between Merlin and the Minotaur. The beast took one step back in shock.

Hellekin called out."What is this. How can that worthless man be performing magic? Ye said that all magic except for ours would be rendered useless!?" He was unnerved by what he was seeing. This was not in the elaborate plan that he had set up. "Kill him now, quickly!" bellowed Hellekin at the Minotaur.

Merlin reached out toward the ghostly figure floating in front of him.

"Thine hands should be bound?" said the Minotaur, confused by what he was seeing. In that moment of doubt as to whether his spells had failed, or if he had seriously misjudged the actual power within the Sorcerer, Merlin had the chance to complete his conjuring.

He wrapped the beguilement figure around his own form and it closed around him enveloping him completely. Standing before the Minotaur was his faerie-self. Handsome, with a human head, his perfectly honed physique draped with classical Grecian clothing, the type worn by the winners of the athletic games that he participated in so many times thousands of years ago. Upon his head was a wreath that symbolised victory in the games. It was a vision of his unadulterated self.

The Minotaur's eyes widened so much that they looked as if they would fall from their sockets. He took one step backwards and then shook his head unable to believe what he saw. Without realising it, the intricate spells that he had cast to prevent magic and to bind the faeries dissipated in an instant.

Morgan was the first to realise what had happened. She could see the shimmering glow of the Minotaur's magical powers in a beautiful silver aura being cast from his head, shoulders and back.

Her powers must have been restored or she would not be able to see the beast's powers within him.

She turned to the group of faeries that were closest to Hellekin. "Bind him with faerie silk ropes, quickly," she insisted, pointing to Hellekin.

The group at first looked at her in disbelief. But one of the faeries tried to produce the rope by using his magic. It appeared. He reacted instantly and threw it around the stunned former faerie ruler.

Morgan knew exactly what she had to do in order to prevent the Minotaur from casting any more spells.

"If ye hath no power beast, then we need not fear ye!" she shouted as she ran forward and grabbed hold of the silver shadow with both of her hands.

It felt wonderful; she could feel the tingling of power through her palms. Pulling it backwards toward her she spun around and wrapped it over her body. It wasn't like before, this time she was able to take the power into her being without hesitation.

The beast felt the sudden drain and screamed in shock. He spun around and could see a stream of his power arcing from his body and into Morgan's.

"Not this time Sorceress!" he cried in rage. He drew his sword and made to strike Morgan down. But the faultless image of his former self positioned himself beside Morgan. The Minotaur was once again momentarily mesmerised by the unspoiled beauty that he once possessed. It was long enough for Morgan to steal a sizeable portion of the beast's powers.

Morgan could feel the energy that she had made her own. And she understood it. This time it was easy to see the various components of the power that she was assimilating. She concentrated on the area that was her own ability to see and draw-out powers from other magical beings. She willed this ability to be larger and more voracious; and immediately it was.

The Minotaur was desperate. He could feel the very powers that he had amassed over the centuries fall away and he had no idea how to stop it. A decision had to be made. To stop the Sorceress he had to strike her down, but the beautiful image of his former self would suffer the blow too. He cried out in agony.

"Nooo!"

It could not be helped he had to stop Morgan, even if it meant killing the one thing that he wanted more than anything else, his ideal-self. Once again, he raised the sword to deliver the killing blow. Morgan looked into the core of the Minotaur and saw the very spark that was the centre of the being's powers. She simply willed it to depart from the beast and enter her body and it did. A bright light coloured red and shaped like a rock with a hundred perfect angled faces seeped out of the Minotaur. He arched his back and bellowed in pain.

The light floated over to Morgan and entered her mid-section. She now had everything that the Minotaur once possessed. She had stripped him of even his most basic faerie powers along with every other power that he had learnt, stolen or discovered over the thousands of years that he had lived.

"Merlin," she said, her voice filled with gluttonous satisfaction. "I hath taken it all. The beast is powerless." She was drunk with magic.

Merlin reached over with his right arm and peeled away the image of the faerie from his body. The image shimmered. It broke up into countless small pieces and disappeared. Merlin was left standing beside Morgan. He looked at the now pathetic figure of the beast with sword raised above him. Lifting his arm, Merlin willed the Minotaur's sword to be in his own hand; and it was.

"Stay away from me!" screamed the beast. Merlin advanced menacingly upon the creature. The Minotaur stepped back to keep his distance from the Sorcerer. He stepped back again and again and bumped into Nimue.

The queen faerie held up her hands and made faerie-silk ropes appear above the creature, they descended and bound his arms tightly to his side. The beast cried out again.

"Mercy; it was Hellekin's desire to trap ye." He said trying to bargain his way out of the situation. Hellekin was infuriated at the immediate betrayal by the beast.

"Cowardly thing, I should hath left ye on the floor of thine labyrinth to rot!" he shouted at his former compatriot.

"Finish the job Merlin!"

The voice was Matrona's. He looked around in surprise. She was nowhere to be seen. Nimue and Morgan saw Merlin's reaction and queried it.

"What is wrong, what is it?" they asked.

It was then that Merlin knew that the bargain that he had made with Matrona encompassed more than just the faerie spell of fertility. She had told him exactly how the Minotaur could be slain for a reason. Even though he felt as if he was being used to perform an act that she would not, he relented. Morgan had confirmed that the beast no longer had any powers, he correctly assumed that included the former protection from weapons that the Minotaur had covered himself with.

He stepped forward and raised the sword. With one huge swing, he beheaded the Minotaur. The bull's head fell to the ground and rolled away for a short distance. The gathered crowd again let out a collective shocked gasp. The body stood there momentarily and then collapsed to the ground.

"It is done," said Merlin. Morgan and the faeries assumed he was addressing them and answering a question that none had asked. But he was in fact confirming to the Lady of the Lake that the Minotaur was now well and truly dead.

Hellekin looked at Merlin, then Nimue. "Now ye will murder me as ye hath callously executed the Minotaur!" he said his voice filled with panic. Merlin, Morgan and Nimue all advanced upon the former ruler. He was practically cowering before them now. Even as they approached he fell to his knees.

"Stand up, ye snivelling thing!" commanded Nimue.

He rose to a standing position, his legs visibly shivering.

"How is the spell of the Green Knight broken?" she demanded.

He pointed with his bound arms to his neck.

"Around mine neck is a talisman, break it and the spell will be similarly broken," he said, his voice filled with fear.

Nimue reached out and drew down his faerie silk robes. It was true, there was a small stone tied with silk around Hellekin's neck. Closer inspection revealed that it had a symbol of Gaelach upon it. It must have represented the full-moon by which the dead Knight would rise and begin his murderous pursuit of Arthur's knights. She tore it away from his neck and held it up before Merlin.

"The menace of the Green Knight may be stopped with this," she reiterated to him. Merlin pointed down at the ground with his sword; directing Nimue to place it on the ground in front of him. She did so. He raised the sword and brought it down on the small tablet and it broke into small pieces.

A great sense of relief filled Merlin. Arthur and his reign were secure once more. Nimue broke into Merlin's trail of thought.

"How shall we deal with this treacherous evil faerie?"

She was facing Hellekin but poignantly addressing the gathered crowd of faeries. The faerie attack force erupted in a chorus of "kill him" and "take off his head" and similar dour endings for the former king. Nimue seemed to be considering all of the ideas that were voiced by her subjects. Hellekin looked at her; the fear in his eyes was naked for all to see.

"Merlin, Morgan what shall we do with this would-be destroyer of Arthur's court?" She turned from one to the other.

Merlin scratched his beard. "He is one of thine subjects Nimue, whatever punishment ye see fit to bestow upon him will be enough for us."

He was being just a little diplomatic. Secretly he wanted Nimue to execute him just to be sure that he could cause no more harm. Morgan however did not offer support for Merlin's courteous solution. She stepped forward and in a voice that held so much self-assuredness that it would garner support no matter what she said.

"Hellekin hath proven himself to be dangerous in exile. Should that fate befall him again he would most surely find another magical spell to spite us with. The depth of his hatred is such that it would drive him to more and more desperate measures to punish those that he thinks have wronged him. Death seems the only option."

Everyone was mesmerised by Morgan's words. She looked around at all of them as if waiting for an answer to her rhetorical question. She looked at Nimue.

"But I can offer ye a solution Queen Nimue that will ensure that thine original punishment for this wretched creature will be fulfilled more completely than ye could have imagined…with thine permission Majesty?"

Morgan posed a question in such a forceful way that Nimue did not resist; even if she did not fully understand what she was allowing Morgan to do.

"Let it be done, sorceress," said Nimue.

Expectation filled the crowd. Merlin was taken aback at Morgan's assertion, and just as confused by it as everyone else. What did she mean? What was she going to do? Morgan stretched out both of her arms in a gesture that looked like she was about to embrace the quivering Hellekin. A stream of silver light flowed from Hellekin to Morgan. Hellekin convulsed and cried out. "What are ye doing to me?!" he demanded. "What is happening? I feel…I feel..." he trailed off. A wave of tiredness filled him. He felt like he could sleep for a week.

"Ye no longer possess any magical powers Hellekin," explained Morgan to the captive.

The news jolted him awake. He looked at her as if she was mad. Morgan dissolved the faerie-silk ropes that bound him with a flick of her fingers. The faeries that had been holding the ropes looked down at their empty hands in astonishment. Hellekin was free. He looked around him still acting like a caged animal. His first thought was to escape and he tried to transform into a falcon. But nothing happened.

"Nooooo!" he screamed when he realised that Morgan had spoken the truth. He could summon no magical powers. He tried a simple spell to start a fire in his hand; nothing.

"How is this possible? Ye wicked thing!" he spat at Morgan. "Restore mine powers immediately," he demanded.

"Ye are in a position to demand nothing Hellekin," Nimue corrected him brusquely. He looked almost mad with panic.

"What is to happen to me?" he said now visibly sobbing.

"Thine exile on this island would be too good a fate for ye," said Morgan. All eyes once more turned to her. "She closed her eyes and turned directly south. The expression upon her face made it look like she was seeing something; judging it or summing it up in some way. She opened her eyes. "I have the perfect place for ye to see out the exile that Queen Nimue bestowed upon ye. And without any powers there will only be thine wits to keep ye alive."

She raised her left arm and traced a circular pattern in the air. An instantaneous travel portal opened before her. Those that were not in a position to see through the portal moved and jostled their way into a better position to view the land beyond.

It was covered in ice and snow. There were strange birds that flocked together on the ground. They stood upwards, were coloured black and white and had wings that were so small as to not offer the hope of flight. Nobody had ever seen such peculiar creatures.

"This is where ye shall spend the rest of thine miserable life Hellekin. It is the southern-most land that I can find. It does not appear on any map that I have ever seen. But I know this. It is further away from Briton than ye could imagine and it is isolated by vast oceans. No more harm will ye be able to cause to anyone ever again." Her words felt like a condemnation of death.

Hellekin vainly looked around at the faeries that he once called his subjects. He begged some of them to have pity upon him. They turned their faces away in disgust. He turned in a complete circle but was unable to find a single friendly face. Then he began to shake his head.

"I will not go to that bleak land," he insisted.

Morgan levitated him through the portal to the other side. He screamed at the top of his voice

"No! Let me go!" but the circular doorway that led from the frozen land back to Skellig Mhor shrank and faded away. He was marooned in a land that he never knew existed with no magical powers and only the clothes on his body to protect him from the viciously cold winds that whipped over him. He said "no" in a small voice that was carried away by the fierce wind. The black and white flock of ground-walking birds seemed to take exception to him and the flock squawked and moved en-mass away from him. He was completely alone.

Chapter 49: The Spell of Fertility

There was silence at first, and then a great cheer arose from the faeries on Skellig Mhor. They had succeeded in their attack upon the Minotaur and Hellekin. It was for all intents and purposes the very first faerie battle campaign. And victory was theirs. It felt good. Nimue was smiling broadly.

"Morgan Merlin; we are victorious!" she embraced them.

Merlin felt like he should say something, but he was exhausted. The events had taken their toll on the old man. Morgan could sense the tiredness in Merlin.

"Merlin, I can use the travel spell to return us to Caerleon. There will be no need to be carried by our faerie friends."

It was an offer that was too good to refuse. He nodded gratefully.

"And thine people too Nimue. Allow me to open a window directly to the Queen's hollow that ye may return to Briton this very moment," Morgan said to Nimue.

"Mine thanks Morgan," said the faerie Queen, eager now to return to her home.

"But first there is a debt to fulfil," said Merlin; "the spell of fertility in return for victory against the Minotaur and Hellekin."

He looked a little coy. It was now incumbent upon him to recall the spell in all of its intricate detail and once more transcribe it onto parchment. He felt so tired that this was not something that he wanted to contemplate just at the moment; but a deal was a deal. He would honour it regardless of his disposition.

"I can aide ye with that Merlin" offered Morgan. Merlin looked at her.

She was still absolutely glowing with the assimilation of both the Minotaur's and Hellekin's magical powers. He gave her a look as if to ask her how?

She obliged by stretching out her arm toward a distant tree. It was one of the few in view. A section of the bark tore away and sailed through the air finding its way to Morgan's hand.

"Merlin, concentrate upon the spell. Think of the time that ye saw it first. It was during a vision eight years ago." Merlin thought back. Morgan's words somehow made it easy to recall the exact vision where he had first encountered the spell. It was a vision of the future that would never come to pass, thanks to Hellekin murdering Nimue's unborn magical child.

He remembered looking at the floating scroll and reading the contents. And then a flash of light snapped him out of his memory.

"There," proclaimed Morgan. Both Nimue and Merlin were amazed. The spell of fertility was now burned onto the flat, light-side of the bark. Morgan held it out for them to see. They leaned in and quickly digested the contents of the spell. The very thing that faerie rulers had searched for over the last five thousand years was resting in Morgan's hand.

"How?" asked Merlin.

"I took the image from ye mind and transcribed it onto this bark. We present it to the faerie people in gratitude for thine assistance to King Arthur and his court."

Morgan was the consummate ambassador from Caerleon, presenting a trophy to Queen Nimue in recognition of the service that she and her subjects had performed.

Nimue could scarcely believe her eyes. She gingerly took it from Morgan's hand. She had succeeded where all of the previous faerie leaders had failed. Now if she could just convince Merlin….no, Morgan, to enable the spell then her legacy to the faerie nation would be complete. It would mean her death of course, to provide the necessary elements for the spell, but it did not matter. What mattered to her was giving her subjects the ability to produce their own offspring.

However, now did not seem like the appropriate time to try and negotiate such a deal. It took a lot of effort from Nimue to simply accept the spell without asking Morgan to cast it for them.

"Mine thanks, and that of the faerie people of Briton, for returning to us something that hath been lost for an eon." Her words were genuine. She clutched the bark to her chest as though it were a treasured child.

"A portal to the Queen's hollow," declared Morgan.

She gave a dramatic swoop of her right arm and a large square opening formed over to the side of them. Inside the shimmering frame the tree holding the queen's hollow could be clearly seen. The sunset was casting shadows from the trees in the faerie forest.

Nimue signalled for her people to precede her through the opening. One by one they transformed into birds of all shapes and sizes and flew through the instantaneous travel portal. Nimue, Merlin and Morgan watched as the stream of mismatched birds trickled through. When the last of them had made the journey Nimue gave Morgan another grateful embrace.

"Morgan, this is a great day for us all," she said. "Merlin, somehow saying thank you once more did not seem to adequately describe what she was feeling.:

She kissed him on the cheek and without a further word walked regally through the opening. Morgan waved her hand and the portal disappeared.

"Now for us," said Merlin. He was very impressed, and a little intimidated by Morgan's new-found powers. He was already planning a series of questions and exercises to ascertain the extent of them. But for now, he just wanted to report the good news to everyone at Caerleon and to have a good meal and a full-night's sleep.

Morgan obliged. This time she conjured up a smaller doorway. It was rectangular. The main courtyard of Caerleon could be seen clearly beyond.

"Please," said Morgan.

"No, mine dear, after ye," countered Merlin. Morgan smiled and nodded at him and walked through the doorway. Merlin followed and looked back at where they had come from. Matrona was standing there looking at him. She gave him a small bow of her head and disappeared.

Morgan turned around to see why Merlin was not walking with her. She could see him looking at the image of Skellig Mhor through the portal. It faded away and he turned around to look at her. "Let us give the good news to the court," he said. They walked arm in arm toward the main entrance of the castle.

Chapter 50: Caerleon Castle

The celebratory feast that was spontaneously initiated upon hearing the news of the defeat at Skellig Mhor of both the Minotaur and Hellekin was amazing. Morgan had scarcely seen the like of it before. She and Merlin were the returning heroes from battle. They had to recount the battle in excruciating detail for everyone over and over again. Merlin deflected questions about how he managed to beguile the Minotaur as he was beneath the spell of magical suppression.

"I found the strength," was all that he would answer. Further probing about how he knew what the Minotaur looked like before he had the head of a bull were also deflected with,"a magician has his ways."

Morgan had her own set of uncomfortable questions that she did her best to answer in as little detail as possible. "How did ye steal the magic from the Minotaur and Hellekin?" and "What happened to the magic that was stolen, is it inside of ye?" None of these details were the kind of thing that a Sorceress should discuss in open company. But they persevered nevertheless and a raucous night was had by all.

***

It was well into the next day when Merlin awoke.

"Merlin are ye awake?"

It was Morgan's voice but she was nowhere to be seen in his chamber. Merlin looked around a little confused. "Awake? Aye!" he said gruffly. The incessant querying had actually awoken him otherwise he would have been happy to sleep into the afternoon. Realising that Morgan was not present he correctly assumed that she was using her powers to project her thoughts across the castle and to him. He briefly wondered how he was going to respond without either being inside a vision or a dream. That would be the normal course for conversing with Morgan across a distance.

"Good," she said. and appeared through an instantaneous travel doorway that appeared just in front of the door to his room. Morgan stepped through. Merlin tried his best to not look impressed, even though he was.

"No sleep-in after our battle?" asked Merlin. Morgan smiled and almost imperceptibly shook her head. "I was awake with first light Merlin, filled with the energy that hath come with assimilating the powers of Hellekin and the Minotaur. I am surprised that I managed to sleep at all."

Now seemed as good a time as any to the old Sorcerer to explore the depth and breadth of Morgan's new-found magical abilities; he asked his first question. "Tell me about the different kinds of magic that ye now possess? Are there powers that we hath not before encountered?" He leant forward waiting eagerly for the answer. Morgan was more sanguine with the answer that he had expected.

"No, not different powers, apart from the travel doorways; I find that I can transform into the shape of an animal with great ease now. There is no more pain associated with the transformation, and it is quick too Merlin, as quick as a flash of lightening."

She demonstrated by taking the form of a wolf-hound and just as quickly returning to her human shape.

"That could be useful," said Merlin not showing too much surprise. He was about to ask more probing questions about the amount of power that she now possessed when he noticed that she looked a little grim. He cocked his head slightly in wonderment. "What is it Morgan?" he asked softly. "Is there something wrong?" he followed-up hoping to elicit a response from her. She walked over to the stool that was closest to his bed and sat down. She looked soberly at him and said, "I feel that something is wrong, but I do not know what. I cannot say exactly what, but there is a growing uneasiness within mine heart." She stopped hoping that she had explained herself adequately.

She had not; Merlin squinted and frowned, "Uneasiness Morgan, how does this manifest itself; in a vision or just a vague feeling?" he sounded like he was trying to diagnose an illness. "Nothing as clear as a vision and more than just a feeling; something bad is going to happen." Once again Morgan seemed to stop short of completing her full trail of thought.

"But ye cannot say what?" he asked.

"No," she replied. This was quite a conundrum. Merlin felt that Morgan was not telling him everything, certainly not enough to formulate an opinion on why she felt this way. He tried to be comforting.

"Perhaps it is part of having access to such magnified powers. Maybe it will settle in the coming days or even weeks." He looked at her with an expression as if to ask for an affirmation of his hypothesis. "Perhaps that is all that is bothering me," she said.

Morgan was being just a bit coy. She did not indeed feel that it had anything to do with her newfound level of magical ability, but without anything more to describe why she felt this way; she felt that there was no need to push the point. "

Now that it's settled, tell me more about thine magic. What else do ye hath to show me?"

He was as excited as Morgan had ever seen him. And so, the questioning and demonstrating of her powers continued for a hefty part of the afternoon. But all of the time Morgan could not shake the feeling that something was terribly wrong.

***

It grew day after day. But there was still no adequately describing why she had this growing sense of doom. Courtly life had returned to normal. Merlin and Arthur were back in negotiations with the King of Humbor for his accession to Arthur's rule. Everywhere that Morgan looked, life was good, normal. And yet her uneasiness remained and developed. What could it all mean? It was the day before the full-moon that Morgan felt her ill feeling so strongly that she shut herself in her room claiming to be fatigued. She wished for the feeling to leave her in peace but it would not. Had Merlin not been so busy with negotiations with the King of Humbor he may have noticed Morgan's unusual behaviour. Tomorrow was the full moon. The first time that Gaelach would show her full-face since they had broken Hellekin's talisman that controlled the Green Knights. Alone in her room Morgan was shaking with fear.

On the day that the full moon was due to appear she did not eat the morning meal with the court, citing once again that she was fatigued and needed to rest. Morgan knew that she would not be able to eat until she was sure that the full-moon held no menace. But it did.

Chapter 51: The Fourth Apparition.

The tower guards were the first to raise the alarm. It was late afternoon and quite cold when Gaelach rose in the sky. Grey clouds tried unsuccessfully to hide her bright face. She managed to peer through the canopy that mostly covered the sky. Four horsemen were spotted riding through the village and up the hill toward Caerleon. When Morgan heard the cry of the guards, she jumped off her bed and ran out of her chamber flinging her door open with such force that it crashed against the stone wall with a resounding thud. Morgan scarcely remembered the journey through the halls and up the narrow winding stone staircase to the battlements. She ran along the outside of the battlements and to the point above the front gate to the main courtyard. Sir Guaen was there. She was unsure if he was just on duty managing the look-out for the day or if he had heard the cry and come to investigate.

Both of their hearts sank as they saw the riders approaching from the village. The shapes were unmistakable, they were human corpses riding similarly rotted bodies of deceased horses; but now there were four of them. Morgan wondered what poor peasants had been sacrificed to once again double the numbers of the Green Knights.

"What are we to do!" Guaen's panicked scream shook Morgan out of her wonderings. Morgan grabbed Sir Guaen's forearm in a futile attempt to try and quell his fears.

"We will find a way Sir Guaen, I promise it," said Morgan. Her words were dripping with conviction and force but it was all lost on the Knight he was so terrified at the sight the he beheld.

Guaen was shaking so much that he could barely stand. There were tears in his eyes that he was unable to hold back. If this was a repeat of all of the previous attacks then her magic would be quashed. She thought of a way to test it and get help at the same time. She concentrated and waved her left hand. A travel doorway opened. Arthur and Merlin looked up from Arthur's map desk in his study. They were amazed to see a rectangular doorway floating just and arm's length from them both.

"Quickly Merlin, Arthur come through!" Morgan's instruction was as unexpected as the sudden appearance of the travel portal.

Arthur hesitated but Merlin did not. He brazenly stepped through the doorway and found himself on the battlements above the main gate. Not wanting to be left behind Arthur summoned his bravery and followed. The jarring experience of suddenly being in a completely different part of the Castle was stupefying.

"What is..." began Merlin. But the sight of Guaen shaking stopped Merlin from completing his sentence. He followed Sir Guaen's gaze. So too did Arthur. The sight of four Green Knights rapidly approaching was horrifying.

"How?" asked Merlin hoping that somehow Morgan would have an answer. She shook her head in an exaggerated way and looked forlorn, raising her hands in surrender and exasperation.

"Merlin, are ye able to practice magic?" her question was pertinent. Obviously, she was able to do so, otherwise the doorway would not have been able to bring he and Arthur to be battlements. He held out his hand and tried to summon a small ball of fire in his palm. Nothing happened.

"No!" he said, looking even more alarmed.

"But we destroyed the talisman around Hellekin's neck, the spell should hath been broken?" he looked betrayed. And then almost slapped himself on the face for the feeling.

"How could we believe Hellekin would ever tell the truth about anything!" he shouted at no-one. "We were fools to think that he would surrender the spell so easily Morgan!"

Morgan had already thought of these things and was racing ahead trying to understand what was happening.

"But Hellekin no longer possesses any magical abilities, and the Minotaur is most certainly dead! Ye made sure of that!" said Morgan reminding Merlin that there was no way that either could be responsible for the approaching Green Knights.

The hideous apparitions were all but at the gate now. They rode two abreast.

"What does it mean Merlin that Morgan can practice magic and ye cannot?" Arthur's question seemed out of place in the current desperate situation. Merlin focused upon the inference of the question rather than the point of it.

"It means that this time we hath the advantage!" he said loudly in reply. The Green Knights were now at the Castle Gate. Someone had closed it in the interim. The quick-thinking guards stationed below or one of the king's Knights. They did not know which, but it put the deadly assassins outside of the castle and exactly where Merlin wanted them to be.

"Levitate them from the ground just enough that they cannot walk, their horses also," directed Merlin. Morgan did so with very little effort. The four of the Green Knights were raised off the ground only a small amount. Enough to get a fist between the horses-hooves and the dirt below. Immediately aware that something was amiss, the four horsemen dismounted only to find that they did not hit solid ground. Just like their mounts, they were unable to touch the ground and get any traction. They were helpless.

Sir Guaen let out a surprisingly loud holler of appreciation for the suddenly disempowered creatures. It took Merlin, Arthur and Morgan by surprise, they all turned to look at him. "Hideous vermin! Not so imposing now are ye?"

Merlin rolled his eyes slightly knowing that this was really only a temporary situation. They could not go on relying upon her to keep the Green Knights at a distance every moonrise of every month for the rest of their lives. A more permanent solution still needed to be found. This thought passed between Morgan and Merlin with a single look.

"Are ye able to open a travel doorway to the south land of ice and snow? The place where Hellekin hath been exiled?" asked Merlin. Morgan nodded. "Aye, of course." She answered. "Then do so, we depart immediately, and we are taking those things with us," he said summarising the instructions for his plan. Morgan could see the sense of it.

Until they could understand how the magic that was animating the corpses each full moon was still working, it would be best to have them as far away from Briton as possible.

Morgan opened a very large instantaneous travel doorway behind them and just above the battlements. It would be necessary to step up to the wall and then pass through it. The opening was completely circular and it was very large. The kind of power that it must have taken to do such a thing was not beyond Merlin's ability to estimate. He was very impressed with Morgan's abilities, yet again. The south-land was in a weird kind of twilight. The sun looked as though it had either just set or was just beginning to rise, it was impossible to tell which.

Arthur and Sir Guaen looked at with awe. They could feel the icy wind emanating from the floating doorway. Everything was covered with snow. There were no trees of any kind, just hills and valleys of snow covered ground. The odd looking black and white birds that were flocked together, the first-time Morgan opened up a travel portal to the land, were nowhere to be seen. Morgan waved her hand and suddenly Merlin was wearing his faerie silk robes, instead of the grey garment that he had been. He turned to look at Morgan with a gesture of 'why' on his face.

"The faerie silk robes will protect us from the bitterly cold conditions," replied Morgan to the unasked question.

Morgan too was suddenly wearing her faerie silk robes. Merlin was about to step up to the wall when he felt himself being levitated. He should have guessed. Why walk when it is easier to float. They drifted silently through the doorway to the amazement of the king and Knight watching them.

When they were safely through the floating doorway Morgan set Merlin and herself down upon the packed ice upon the ground. She turned to see the progress of the four Green Knights and their horses. They had at her beckoning floated up over the walls of Caerleon and were moving toward the circular opening. Merlin stepped to one side of the opening and Morgan to the other in order to allow the reluctant travellers through circle. They were growling and thrashing about, the horses too. The doorway that had transported them to this land blurred and disappeared.

Merlin's face dropped. Morgan saw the expression and asked him what it was in aide of.

"Why the long face Merlin, these wicked things are now farther away from Caerleon than we could ever hath hoped. If I left them here they would certainly not be able to travel back to Briton in any reasonable time."

He responded by pointing up to the sky.

"The full face of Gaelach is not in this sky. I had hoped that the Green Knights would...sleep or die…again…or at least stop moving; remember that it is the full moon that brings them to us every month."

Merlin's argument was sound. Now that he had mentioned it, Morgan too noticed that the weird twilight that filled the sky was devoid of the moon. Once more his insightfulness impressed her. It must have been part of his plan to see if bringing the Green Knights to a land without the moon would change the situation.

"Even if ye left them here Morgan, there is no guarantee that they would not somehow reappear the next time the moon is full." Merlin completed his thinking on the subject.

Morgan nodded in agreement.

"Best not to underestimate the evil that Hellekin and the Minotaur hath together unleashed upon us," she said sombrely.

"Can ye do something about that noise?" asked Merlin his nose wrinkled up in disapproval of the guttural whinging coming from the decayed corpses. Morgan frowned in concentration. Nothing happened. She looked a little perplexed and then a look of complete concentration took over her beautiful features. Moments passed, still no change. The Green Knights were as distempered as ever.

"Apparently not," said Morgan somewhat surprised that her newfound abilities did not stretch to stopping these things from growling.

"It matters not. Let us find Hellekin. Which way? Can ye sense him?" it was a guess on Merlin's part that Morgan would be able to sense where any faerie was now that she had amassed an old faeries powers. His assumption was correct. She looked not too far away and pointed at what appeared to be just more snow covered ground.

"He is there," she said. Merlin followed her pointing finger.

Not seeing anything, he did not immediately dismiss the direction as most people would. Instead he began to walk toward where she had indicated. He had absolute faith that if Morgan said that Hellekin was there, then that is exactly where they would find him.

With the four Green Knights and their horses floating behind them, they walked the short distance to a small mound. Merlin walked up to it and gave it a rather forceful kick. The mound jumped up in shock. The snow that had covered Hellekin as he tried to take shelter from the constant wind crumbled away from his faerie silk robes. He looked at Merlin then Morgan in horror and then at the Green Knights.

"Liar!" shouted Merlin at the faerie. "Destroying the talisman around thine neck did nothing to halt the appearance of these things!" Hellekin took a step back. He looked to his left and right. "No Hellekin, there is nowhere to run," assured Morgan. They could see in his eyes that he just wanted to get away from them. Morgan advanced menacingly upon him. He took another step back. Morgan levitated him forward so that they were face to face.

"Now before I throttle ye with mine bare hands, tell me how to stop the Green Knights from proliferating and attacking us every full-moon!" Merlin had purposely let Morgan take the lead in the interrogation. With her newly expanded powers he knew that she would be much more intimidating that anyone else could be. He was correct. Hellekin was clearly very afraid of Morgan and began to babble so much that it sounded like a child that had been caught doing something wrong and was now trying desperately to explain his way out of the situation.

"There is no way. Once the Minotaur and I combined our magic spells to resurrect the Green Knight it was set in motion. The fact that our powers still exist in ye gives the Green Knight all of the magical power it needs to keep coming back again and again." These were not the words that Morgan or Merlin wanted to hear. Morgan actually reached out and grabbed Hellekin by the throat.

"More lies!?" she threatened.

He vigorously tried to shake his head, still with throat held tightly by Morgan. "As long as our magic exists the Green Knight will exist."

"If I abandon the Green Knights here, will they appear in Briton again the next full moon?" asked Morgan her voice stern.

Hellekin did his best to nod. "Aye"

Morgan let go of his throat. She could sense in him that he was telling the truth. She looked to Merlin and indicated that she believed the snivelling coward. Morgan reached out and took hold of Merlin's hand. She wanted to have a private conversation with the old Sorcerer and did so by communicating directly with Merlin's thoughts.

"If I leave the Green Knights here they will not be able to return to Caerleon before the moon sets in Briton. All I can think of to do is then wait until the next full moon and do the same thing over and over again for the rest of Sir Guaen's life. But then what? What if he dies in a future battle? The spell said that they would stalk each one of Arthur's Knights in turn. The situation will be without end until all of Arthur's knights are either killed in battle or die of old age!"

Morgan's voice filled Merlin's head. He pondered her argument and replied in thought.

"And if ye are forced to do this every month year after year, how long will it be before thine newfound powers are depleted?"

Quite unexpectedly Morgan pulled her hand away from Merlin. He reacted. Had he offended her somehow?

"Merlin let us leave the Green Knights here and travel back to Briton with Hellekin. He owes something to Nimue that he hath yet to pay."

Her announcement caught both Hellekin and Merlin by surprise.

Morgan waved her hand and the growling Green Knights and their horses floated past them and then quite some distance away from the magicians before they were set down, none too gently, upon the slippery ice covered ground. Hellekin and Merlin were so busy watching the immediate fate of the Green Knights and their macabre horses that they did not see Morgan open a new portal.

"Come along!" she said summoning their attention. They looked to see Morgan striding through a rectangular doorway, beyond which seemed a familiar scene. She was already through by the time Merlin and Hellekin gathered their wits enough to follow; Hellekin first and then Merlin.

To their amazement, they found themselves in the Queen's Hollow. Nimue had practically jumped out of her throne; guards had glimmered to her side ready to defend their Queen from the sudden appearance of the three intruders. There were some elderly courtiers that were probably advisors gathered a short distance away. Merlin was astounded. Not only had they travelled from the southern ice-land back to Briton, but somehow in the transition they had become small faerie-sized versions of themselves. Merlin was yet again impressed by Morgan's magnificent powers.

Chapter 52: Nimue's Revenge

"Morgan, Merlin!" said Nimue as she rose from throne. Then she saw Hellekin and a look of disgust covered her face. She chose to ignore him and went on to query the magicians as to their sudden appearance.

"What brings ye to mine hollow?" She looked from one to the other in the hope of an answer. Morgan walked up to Nimue and offered her hand. Nimue took it. Her face altered expressions several times in the few moments that they held hands. When Nimue let go she looked directly into Morgan's eyes and said, "I understand."

It was clear to Merlin, if nobody else, that Morgan had communicated a great deal of information to Nimue although he did not know exactly what. He had assumed that their recent run-in with the Green Knights was a part of what was said.

Hellekin tried to bow stiffly to Nimue in a half-hearted attempt to be demure in the presence of the faerie queen. To his surprise, she walked toward him. He was about to blubber something of a greeting when she used her left arm to wrap around his shoulder in what looked to him like the beginnings of a warm embrace. He allowed Nimue to draw him close to her. Surreptitiously Nimue had drawn her dagger silently from its sheath concealed beneath her faerie-silken robes and with her right hand plunged the dagger deeply into his stomach.

Hellekin realised in a flash what had happened and he let out a girlish yelp of pain and anguish. Nimue cut upwards a good hand's-length severing vital organs in Hellekin's abdomen and surrounding area. He couldn't see anything anymore. She let go of the partial embrace in which she held him. His body fell backwards coming away from her dagger and dropped to the floor. Blood curdled up out of his mouth and he tried to cough it away, his body convulsing a few times as he gurgled on the red liquid. Then he was still; his lifeless eyes still looking at Nimue.

Merlin, the faerie guards and the other faeries in the room were all shocked at what had happened. Surely, he had deserved death but Nimue had twice spared his life and cast him into exile. Why she suddenly chose now to end his life was anybody's guess. Not one of the faeries present challenged her on the execution that she had just performed. All were silent waiting in anticipation of the queen's next words. Maybe there would be an explanation. They were disappointed.

"Mine thanks Lady Morgan. Ye are always welcome here in mine hollow."

There were no further platitudes exchanged. Morgan had already bowed to the Queen and opened a travel portal behind both her and Merlin. She turned gracefully and glided through it. Merlin could see that it led directly to the base of the great staircase in Caerleon. A couple of wide-eyed Caerleon servants were staring through it and into the Queen's hollow. Merlin was unsure exactly why the events had unfolded the way that they did. Keen to question

Morgan at greater length he gave Nimue an appropriate goodbye and followed Morgan back through the portal to Caerleon. The portal disappeared when he set foot on the flagstone floor of Caerleon Castle. Morgan had already begun to ascend the great staircase.

"Wait Morgan please?!" asserted Merlin.

She turned to look at him. He simply gestured with his shoulders and hands that he had no idea of the reasons behind their sudden departure from the icy-southern land, Hellekin's death at the hands of Nimue and what to do about future attacks from the Green Knights.

"Walk with me Merlin," she bade. Turning to the servants that were on the landing she directed them. "Inform King Arthur and Sir Guaen that the Green Knights will not return to Caerleon." They hurried to do as they were instructed.

Merlin joined Morgan ascending the staircase.

"Well?" he asked.

"The dried and powdered organs of a former faerie ruler will work just as effectively in the fertility spell as those from Nimue," she replied. "She need not sacrifice herself for the sake of her people." They continued to climb the stairs.

"Ye may hath forbidden me to enable the fertility spell for the faeries," she continued, "but they can at least prepare the spell for the day that they do find a worthy magician to help them." This was one third of the explanation that Merlin had requested without verbalising it.

"And?" he said hoping to illicit more information from the sorceress.

"I let Nimue know the situation when I held her hand. She understood and accepted that it was more fitting that Hellekin be sacrificed given the evil that he hath done over the years." Now Merlin felt that Morgan was dancing around the subject. "Why did we leave the southern land so suddenly?" he asked directly.

"Hellekin gave us the solution to the Green Knight problem Merlin, ye just did not hear it," Morgan spoke to him now as though he were the pupil and she was the teacher, trying to coax an answer to a puzzle from him. Merlin thought back to what Hellekin had babbled about. Then it did become clear, just as Morgan had hoped. "Whilst the Minotaur's powers and Hellekin's powers still exist, the Green Knights will continue to come every full moon until the spell is concluded. Ye need to rid thine person of ye newly acquired powers!" Merlin reached the same conclusion that Morgan had. Morgan smiled and nodded.

This was terrible news. And it raised even more questions.

"I had hoped that ye powers could be used to spread Arthur's rule throughout the entire land and finally rid us all of the Saxons, Angles, Jutes and Mercians. They had now reached the top of the stairs. Merlin was about to elaborate about how he had envisioned

Morgan's abilities to assist in the shared vision of a single land beneath one ruler but Morgan saw no sense in ruminating upon an idea that could now never be. Unless I sacrifice mine powers Merlin then the Green Knights will always be a threat. Four this time; eight next month; need I go on?" she said.

The very thought of sixteen, or thirty-two or sixty-four of those hideous Green Knights turned Merlin absolutely cold. Eventually they would win. Arthur and his Knights would be destroyed.

His head fell and he looked upon the floor. He could not look Morgan in the eyes.

"I understand Morgan…How will ye do it?" he asked.

Morgan evaded the question.

"I will sleep now. Good night, Merlin."

She leant forward and kissed him on his bearded cheek. She walked away leaving him alone at the top of the stairs.

Epilogue

Morgan did not sleep well the previous night. She had arisen early and readied herself then opened a doorway to Llyn Callyfyrth. She stood there admiring the serenity of the lake. It was ethereally beautiful. Morgan was aware of Matrona's presence as Matrona was aware of Morgan's. A disembodied voice filled the air around Morgan.

"Ye know what to do Lady Morgan." It had a note of finality about it. Clearly Matrona was unwilling to discuss alternatives to Morgan shedding her newfound powers. Morgan's heart sank. She had hoped that Matrona may have been able to offer her an alternative. But it seemed that would not be the case. Dejected, Morgan returned to Caerleon.

***

Morgan stepped through the doorway to the battlements of the castle. Sir Alynore was walking away from her when she set foot upon the stone walkway. Unless he turned around now he would not be in a position to see her instantaneous travel portal. Morgan made the doorway fade into nothingness. Holding up her arms as if trying to embrace the clouds, Morgan revelled in her magical powers one last time. She wanted to turn into a falcon and fly over the countryside. She wanted to become a flounder and explore the clear rivers. She wanted to take the shape of a horse and run as far and fast as her strong legs would take her. It was tempting to keep her powers just for the time between now and the next full-moon. But she knew that the longer that she held these unmatched magical abilities, the harder it would be to let go of them. Even now she could feel a kind of corruption creeping into the very core of her being. But it felt good.

"No more," she said aloud. Summoning all of her stolen abilities she bundled them into a single shape. It had many sides; it was a colour that she had never seen before. Gingerly disentangling herself from it she cast it into the sky and it tore out of her and rose into the cloud- filled void. With no receptacle for the incredible powers to take up residence within, they soon lost cohesion. Bits of the shape split away but all of it continued to rise into the sky. But the time Morgan's eyes were no longer able to see it, because it was so high, it had split into a countless number of slivers. Each shard continued to travel inexorably upwards and away from the ground dwelling population of Briton.

Morgan felt small. She felt the loss of something that perhaps no other human had ever possessed anywhere. But somehow, she also felt relief. And more importantly she felt like herself again. Unable to resist a wry smile even in the circumstances, she looked over the beautiful countryside that surrounded Caerleon. Arthur's reign was safe from the threat of the Green Knights. Without the combined magic of the Minotaur and Hellekin to give them life, they would no longer terrorise Sir Guaen.

Everything was well. There was still the hope that Arthur would succeed in his battle to form a single unified country beneath his reign. Morgan felt her sacrifice was worth it. Time to let Merlin know what had transpired; she turned to make her way towards his chamber.

The End

Connect with Aenghus Chisholme

Visit my website on www.aenghuschisholme.com

Works by Aenghus Chisholme

Merlin the Sorcerer AD491

King Arthur is facing a war with the murderous Saxon Lord Aelle over the artisan land of Anderidae. Unknown to him magical forces have conspired with Aelle to ensure Arthur's defeat.

Guinevere the Queen AD499

Queen Gwenhwyvar and Sorceress Morgan Le Fay pursue the stolen Excalibur to a magical labyrinth where it is guarded by powerful Minotaur.

Sir Gawain and the Green Knight AD499

An animated corpse has Sir Guaen in its sights. How can you kill something that is already dead?

Arthur the King AD517

Caught in an untenable situation King Arthur is manoeuvred into a battle he cannot possibly win.

Murder on the Mary Celeste

One by one, the passengers and crew aboard the merchant ship Mary Celeste are being picked-off by an unseen assassin.

Jack the Ripper: The murder of Madam Athalia

A clever young detective thinks that he can outwit the most cunning killer in the history of London.

The Best Things in Life Begin with the Letter B

Consumerism can lead to happiness, providing you know exactly what it is that will make you happy. Enjoy a tour of the material and immaterial world of the exclusive and the everyday.

Commissioned works

I am available to write something for you; fiction or non-fiction. Contact me through my website and tell me what you have in mind.

www.ingramcontent.com/pod-product-compliance
Lightning Source LLC
LaVergne TN
LVHW041111080826
845145LV00007B/1771

* 9 7 8 0 6 4 8 0 7 8 9 6 8 *